THE TRIANGLE TALES

ROY CHEESMAN "THE OLD MAN"

ISBN: 978-1-957351-44-5

Published by Nico 11 Publishing & Design
Mukwonago, Wisconsin
Michael Nicloy, Publisher
www.nico11publishing.com

Be well read.

Quantity order requests may be emailed to: mike@nico11publishing.com

The Triangle Tales
Author: Roy Cheesman
Editor: Marla McKenna
Proofreader: Lyda Rose Haerle
Interior and Cover Layout: Griffin Mill
Front Cover and Interior Illustrations: Kathleen Kaufman
Interior Sketches: Roy Cheesman, Abi Lynn Gordon

Printed in the United States of America

*"Give every day the chance to become
the most beautiful of your life."*

– Mark Twain

This collection of tales and capers is dedicated to my brother Ross and the memory of my sister Dolly. It is only because of them that there are any tales to share at all. I also dedicate this to my loving and supportive wife, Vicki.

I am also dedicating it to my family. I've not shared this with them and feel it is something they should hear about. I squandered many opportunities while my children were young, and they might have enjoyed these tales while being based on actual events. And now their children are of that age. Hopefully, they will find time between jam-packed sports schedules, school, and social media to enjoy and ask me questions.

I also would like to thank Ron McCord, a dear friend and Christian brother. His steadfast support, encouragement and sharp eyed editing skills were a blessing.

THE TRIANGLE TALES

PART ONE

PROLOGUE

THE OLD MAN'S
REMINISCENCE

REFLECTIONS

"As water reflects the face, so one's life reflects the heart."
– Proverbs 27.19 a. (Or so others reflect your heart back
to you) (NIV)

The Old Man was in the backyard, sitting on the ground under the grand Norway maple. He wondered if he could get back up again. "I guess I just don't give a damn. It'll be what it'll be," he would mutter as he leaned back against the trunk of the huge old maple tree. Even on a hot late summer day, in the tree's shade, there was a cool breeze. The tree is native to Eastern and Central Europe and Western Asia. It reminded The Old Man of the streets and boulevards he encountered on his journeys to those places.

He loved going into the backyard and sitting on the ground in the maple's shade when the weather allowed. The tree was at one end of the half-acre backyard. It was one of a multitude of trees (maples, cedars, spruce, junipers, and a few flowering species) that populated the backyard on three sides. The house and more trees flanked the fourth side. His wife, Vicki, had planted several flower gardens and a small vegetable garden in the yard. From the vantage point of where he sat, he could hear the sound of songbirds in the trees and see butterflies and the hummingbirds flitting from flower to flower.

It reminded him of what it was like being in the magical Glade where he and his brother spent so much of their youth.

He was in his early 80s. This wasn't that old; he had been told repeatedly by his family whenever he said he was tired. They did not realize that "biological age" is not based on the actual years. Biological age is like that of an automobile. We base it on miles driven, maintenance, conditions traveled, and speeds that are driven—not the model year alone. When those circumstances are taken into consideration, his biological age was in the mid-90s. His past lifestyle left him disabled.

Oh, to hell with political correctness, I am a cripple, he thought to himself. He needed a four-wheeled walker to get around. Getting up from the ground or the floor was iffy. He hoped he would not need to call for help when he was ready to get up. That help always came with an admonition about not sitting on the ground.

He did not have many facial wrinkles, and what little hair he had left he kept shaved off. A physical therapist had encouraged him to do so. She had said it would make him "look badass." The way she said it with her hands on her slim hips, tossing her long blonde hair off her forehead, left no doubt that it was what he should do. This may be what his ego needed to offset the crushing weight of suddenly losing all feeling in his left leg and being relegated to a wheelchair, along with 60 days in a rehab center. She was sweet enough to give him a thumbs up when he left the rehab center and mouthed the words "bad ass."

Five years ago, a disc in his lower back had "exploded" (according to the neurosurgeon). "I love it when they use those technical terms," the old man chuckled to himself. The debris from this "explosion," coupled with the vertebrae collapsing on one another, pinched all nerves to his left leg, severing some of them. It left his leg paralyzed. It is only with emergency surgery and ongoing therapy and exercising that he could be as mobile as he was. This limited mobility, coupled with a chronic lung disease, brought on by years of smoking; bone-on-bone knees; spinal stenosis; diabetes; and congestive heart failure completed the picture of a tired, worn-out old man—one who had lived a wide-open, reckless life.

Despite these maladies, and the fact that they meant he could no longer enjoy sugar or salt, he was at peace and thankful for who, what, and where God had divined him to be. He was reminded of the quote by Howard Gates Spafford, *"Whatever my lot, Thou Hast taught me to know. It is well. It is well with my soul."*

God has blessed him with a remarkable family, although it had taken him three marriages to accomplish it. There were three daughters and one son (the youngest), their ages spanned from the late 30s to the late 50s, along with seven grandchildren. The oldest grandchild was in her early 20s (from marriage number one). The next six grandchildren ranged from 14 years old to two years old (from marriage number three, which has lasted over 45 years). There were no children from marriage number two. (He had mucked that one up, as he usually did.) It was the young grandchildren of marriage number three that brought him joy—a sense of aliveness. They all lived close by, and Vicki was a fantastic grandmother. His close relationship with them has been rewarding, fulfilling, and challenging.

The time he has for the young grandchildren, he did not have for his first grandchild. He sorely missed the loss of what surely would have been an extraordinary time with her. The burden he had put on his daughter and her gorgeous daughter (who is about to make him a great-grandfather) sometimes brought him to a complete stop and made him loath what he had done with that sweet blessing. They live in Colorado, a far distance away and high up in the mountains.

This was the substance of the first 50 years of his life, a series of blessings that he ravaged and squandered with voracious greed and savage aggression. He used the blessings as his own personal possession and not gifts from the Lord that should be cherished and shared. It was his own personal *carpe diem*, his life of business and shadows. The Gospel according to him. This was a time he regretted, a time he could not get back. It was time that his family paid dearly for. He was away physically and emotionally invested in a faux life of international business ventures.

But under this tree, in the garden-like setting, he could lean back, close his eyes, focus on his breathing, and travel to any point in his life from childhood to the present as an unseen watcher of the events—aware not only of his own thoughts, reactions, and feelings but those of the other participants as well. He could affect nothing playing out before him and only experience what a detached observer would experience witnessing the events.

The Triangle Tales are about his young life in the southeastern Wisconsin—dairy country, specifically on the outskirts of an exceedingly small town named Ixonia. The total population during the 1950s equaled 100.

The Old Man smiled to himself and shook his head. These memories are from a long time ago. He hadn't appreciated how exciting, how dangerous, and what great fun those adventures were. That is what they were—adventures of the highest order. They are not told necessarily in chronological order but told as The Old Man recalled and dwelled on them. They are like a jar of buttons. In the jar, they are one body of matter but poured out they are different sizes, colors, and shapes. He recalled the details as best as an old, worn-down man can. He starts with "Tale Number Two." There is no "Tale Number One." Why is that? It's like his father told him, "There is always a faster gun or a better tale to tell. Expect the faster gun and leave room for a better tale." A life principle. A Life Principle is a standard or rule of personal conduct or way of life. So, he has left Tale Number One yet to be told.

In The Old Man's youth, many things occurred in his adventures with his brother that were unexplainable through normal earthbound, temporal occurrences. They, being young and exploring a new world on their own, allowed for magic, supernatural events, and beings to explain and inhabit their young worlds. The readers must accept these somewhat fantastical occurrences.

The Old Man recalled how he and his family were suddenly banished to the outskirts of this tiny town because of the Polio epidemic in the summer of 1952. As the weather warmed up each year, panic over polio intensified. They dubbed late summer "polio season." Parents were justifiably terrified of this unknown killer and crippler of children. There was no known cause or cure at the time for the merciless disease. It drove people to extremes, such as not filling deflated tires at service stations for fear of bringing home polluted air and spraying their children with DDT. Children were isolated and public facilities such as pools and movies were closed. They encouraged social distancing. Sound familiar? The young people, while seeing the fright in their parents, hearing the news, and being "locked down," really did not grasp what was happening and reacted mostly badly. They thought they were being punished for something that was not their fault. One must try to imagine life without the internet, social media, etc.

His parents had left the urban area and moved out to the country because of the epidemic. This happened fast, and the children, Roy (The Old Man), his brother Ross, and his much younger sister Dolly were not consulted and swooped up and dumped in a strange land, something like Dorothy in the *Wizard of Oz*. This was a story they were familiar with, and it affected their view of events that took place. The five-acre truck farm their parents had selected was indeed a strange land when compared to the city. "It wasn't Kansas for sure," Roy thought. The shape of the farm was a right triangle, so the boys dubbed it "The Triangle." They thought it was brilliant, so did their parents, probably just to make peace with the boys, which it did not.

The brothers bonded during this time of upheaval in their lives. They were always close, but now in this foreign environment, they grew even closer. They each gained strength to compensate for where the other had a weakness. Immigrants in a new land reacted the same way to this set of foreign circumstances. While this served them extremely well when together, it left a certain vulnerability when they inevitably separated later in life to go their own ways. Roy will always miss the companionship of Ross as well as having blind spots that Ross had watched out for. He never developed a close confidential friend to replace Ross's fellowship, and he remains what some refer to as an outlier.

It is during the time of *The Triangle Tales* that Roy's character and personality are taking shape, and he develops some basic life principles. They develop mainly through trial and error—mostly error. He either won or learned (Nelson Mandela famously said: "I never lose. I either win or learn"). Both brothers had plenty of parental mandates for behavior and plenty of sage advice from knowledgeable, caring people. They both had a solid awareness of right and wrong, but with the self-assuredness and strength arising from the unique bond generated by the displacement into an unknown and wide-open environment, they usually followed their own minds when decision time came. Roy relished climbing fences and exploring the unknown. He knew no inhibition to go "all in" throughout his life. This prime characteristic is nurtured and grew on The Triangle.

The "Tales" are presented in three parts:

Part One–The Beginning starts with the sudden wrenching from a comfortable and safe place and ends with Roy and his brother searching for and discovering a location that would provide the safe, comfortable place to settle in on.

Part Two–The Scholar and The Sage is about the boy's questions about the unique features of The Triangle and the answers provided by the Scholar (their dad) and the Sage (farmer John Franger of Hill Top farm). Roy and his brother will form their own conclusion after considering both the Scholar and the Sage.

Part Three–The Adventures these are the individual adventures of the boys. These are the stories, and I hope that Part One and Part Two add some backdrop to the tales. It is hoped that The Old Man's family and friends gain some insight into who The Old Man was and is.

So, let us start *The Triangle Tales*.

TALE NUMBER TWO

FEAR OF THE IRON LUNG

"Nature is that lovely lady to whom we owe polio, leprosy, smallpox, syphilis, tuberculosis, cancer."
– *Dr. Stanley Norman Cohen*

Roy kneeled in the back seat of his dad's car; his brother Ross was beside him. They watched as their neighborhood slowly retreated into the deepening evening shadows! He blinked back a tear in the corner of his eye and swallowed a lump of fear in his throat. They would never return to this street that had been home to them for more years than he could remember! Something terrible and deadly was causing them to run for their lives.

The villain is poliomyelitis, or polio, their dad told them. Roy wasn't sure what that meant exactly, other than it was a sickness that had parents in the neighborhood terrified for their children's safety. A kid who lived down the street had it, and he was going to be put in an "Iron Lung". His dad had shown the family a picture of one in a magazine. There was a room full of them in long rows with just the kids' heads sticking out and all they could see was whatever a mirror above their head reflected. Their dad said it would cripple many of these kids. Some would die.

What would I do if that was me? Roy thought. *How can this be happening?*

While this was scary, the whole thing seemed remote to the boys and their friends. He didn't feel threatened, but his folks sure acted like they were. The entire neighborhood did. There weren't any barbeques or card parties or anything. Everyone seemed to hide, and the parents made their kids hide as well. No one really explained to them what was happening until after it was done. Their sudden move to the country was a prime example: A moving truck just showed up this morning and loaded all the furniture and appliances and lots of boxes. Their dad came home from work, everyone piled in the car with suitcases and cardboard boxes, and it was over. No goodbyes because of the polio.

He was only ten years old at the time, and his brother was eight. The boys did not know their destination other than it was in the country and they would be safe from polio there. Fear of the unknown gripped Roy and his brother. The speed with which everything was changing unnerved them.

Roy could not shake the feeling he had done something terrible that caused them to run away. He didn't know what that could be, and his mom and dad assured him that wasn't the case. It was the polio's fault. Still, he worried about it.

I'll find out what it was and make it up to the family, he promised himself. This oath would be deep in the recesses of his mind and, even without realizing it, would drive much of what he did in the aftermath of their fateful move to the country.

Their dad was driving; the man always did. Their sister Dolly (her real name was Dorothy, but everyone called her Dolly, Roy didn't know why) was in front with Mom and Dad sitting in the middle. She was so tiny the boys couldn't even see her. But they could hear her asking "why" over and over.

I'm sure glad she is in front with them, Roy thought.

Their dog Bootsie sat at attention in the back seat between the boys, prepared to separate the boys if they got to squabbling at moment's notice. She did this by barking and licking, big slobbery licks.

As the neighborhood faded from view, Roy heard his brother sniffling and put his arm around him.

"Don't worry. Together we can handle anything. We will work this out. Just wait and see. I'll bet the new place will have plenty of grand adventures, and all we need is each other."

Bootsie sensed their distress and wiggled between them and woofed her support.

"Aw Bootsie, you're a funny old dog," Ross laughed.

That prompted her to go into a frenzy of licking and wag-wiggling. Both boys laughed and pet her. Their sadness and trepidation abated for a moment.

They had both been looking forward to a long, lazy summer of adventures in the alley and at the pond, getting together at the swimming pool and just hanging out with the gang, playing mumble-peg or marbles. Their dad was an engineer and would bring home ball bearings. These "steelies" would wreak havoc on the "ducks" (marbles in the middle) in the ring. Whether shooting or bombing, these steel monsters were devastating. The brothers always like playing "keepsy" but the other kids were not happy with that and wanted to play "friendsy". Roy always wanted the edge. Eventually, the brothers traded some steelies for some great marbles. The gang would surprise kids in the next alleys and spring the steelies on them until word got out.

Those games are a thing of the past, he thought. Can't play marbles in a cow pasture, a Life Principle.

They would also collect soda bottles and return them to Kaplinsky's corner store for their deposit. They would immediately cash the money in for cold pop or ice cream. Mr. Kaplinsky always rounded the amount up in their favor and always left the empties that were in his trash cans for them to collect and return. Mr. Kaplinsky was a great storyteller. Some were exciting and funny, others were sad and scary. He was from Europe and had been in a German work camp. He lost his family there. He always kept his wrist covered so the numbers stenciled there didn't show. Despite the terrors he had lived through, Mr. Kaplinsky always seemed to light up and smile when the boys showed up. He was a great friend. He said that sometimes one had to make do with what God put close to you, a principle of life he said. Roy was missing him already.

The houses thinned out, and before long, they were in the country. The street became a two-lane highway and Dad drove at an increased speed. That, coupled with the gathering darkness, made the surrounding landscape hard to make out. Dolly had fallen asleep, and Mom had told them to be quiet so as not to wake her. She and Dad were talking in low voices, so Roy could not hear what they were saying, but he was sure it was about the move. Mom was not happy about moving so far out in the country, nor was her family. Her mom and dad (Grandpa and Grandma Blackwood) also weren't happy with the move. They were unhappy with the marriage, according to Dad, and Roy had seen evidence of that. Mom and Dad weren't fighting, but they were close to it. There was a palpable air of tension and agitation between them he could sense and it just added to his uneasiness.

This is going to be a great summer, Roy thought sarcastically. His parents were squabbling, they were moving to the middle of nowhere in the night like criminals, and they were fleeing a deadly disease and its iron casket. *Yep, it was going to be a great summer.*

As it got dark, Ross fell asleep, and so did Bootsie. There was nothing to be seen out the side windows and from the back seat, he couldn't really see out the front where the headlights gave some visibility. Occasionally, a car would pass going the other way and he would get a glimpse of the countryside. There was lots of grass and trees, trees and grass.

Dad had his window down and Roy, who sat on that side of the car, had a steady breeze on him. The night air was pleasantly cool and had a new aroma. It was a sweet, earthy smell that Roy liked. Sometimes it smelled like newly mown grass, then like rich earth, like when Mom turned over her garden in the backyard every spring. Then every so often there was a fresh smell. It was a sharp odor that reminded him of some rotten eggs he had once smelled. This wasn't as putrid; it was distinctive though.

They passed a drive-up restaurant that was full of cars and loud music. Young people were milling about and revving their car engines. Many of the cars were convertible or customized. The cars made deep rumbles or loud roars when their engines raced.

"Hoodlums," Dad said, shaking his head.

"Bill, they're just young people having a good time," Mom said.

"They are loud, and their music is vulgar, as is their dancing," he said.

Mom huffed

Roy was gazing out the back window longingly. The activity and sound of the drive-in restaurant was cool. The sign on the drive-in named the place, "Kiltie".

Then they entered a city, and Roy welcomed streetlights and streets with houses on them. This differed from where they lived. *Correction had lived.* The street that they were on was crowded with gas stations, drive-up restaurants, ice cream shops and small stores. There were stop-and-go lights every few blocks. He heard his dad say that this was Oconomowoc, a lake town where wealthy people had lake houses on the several lakes in the area. Roy enjoyed the aroma of exhaust fumes mixed with the smell of fried food.

Then the city was gone, and the darkness resumed. As they were leaving the town, he could smell the lakes, the damp cool air that made him want to find the water and jump in. Roy loved to swim and dive under water to see the fish and weeds that they hid in. He couldn't see the water because of the darkness, but he knew it was there. He hoped they could come back here and swim sometime. He hoped it wasn't too far from where they would be living. He hoped for many things, but most of all that they could go back to their home, the home they just left, and go back to the way things were.

Then they went to something he had never seen before. His dad said that was a drive-in movie. It showed movies at night, and you stayed in your car to watch them. There were speakers you hung in your car to hear the movie. There was also a snack bar where you could get candy, popcorn, and sodas. All they could see was the back of the gigantic screen and a high fence around what must be the parking area as they drove by.

Ross, who had woken up, asked his dad if they could go to the drive-in sometime.

Dad said, "we'll see".

The boys looked at each other. They knew what that meant: No.

Mom looked at Dad and said, "Bill, I would really like to go to the outdoor movie." She turned to look at the boys. "If your father doesn't want to go, we'll go. It really sounds like fun."

It was Dad's turn to huff, and he focused on his driving.

Soon they were driving through another small town. The only light to be seen anywhere emanated from rooms above two-story businesses, of which there were only a few. Soon they reached the other side of the town. As they climbed a hill outside of the town, Roy spotted a strange looking small structure that had a cupola on top. There was also a railroad track on the other side of the road.

"This is their town, Ixonia," Dad announced from the driver's seat.

Roy couldn't believe it. *That wasn't a town, that was a crossroads. There was nothing there! he thought. And the name was like something that belonged in a foreign country. What is happening to them?*

Mom turned to his father and said, "Bill, where am I going to do my shopping, and how am I going to get around?"

Dad kept his eyes on the road and responded with his typical understated confidence. "It will work itself out." Dad was big on things working themselves out. It usually meant you were on your own. Work it out. He was busy.

Mom said "Bill" angrily, and then murmured something under her breath. That usually was a sign she was swearing. She turned to look out the passenger window and sat rigidly quiet.

Ross leaned over to whisper to him "uh oh".

Roy nodded his head in agreement.

Their sister slept through all of this, thankfully. There was enough tension in the car already.

Shortly, they turned left off the highway onto a packed gravel road. The road sign said Hilltop Road. They crossed the railroad tracks and drove a short distance to a smaller, less traveled gravel road that connected to Hilltop Road from the left. On the right Roy thought he saw farmland, although it was almost impossible to tell in the dark.

The air blowing in from their open windows smelled cool and sweet and fresh. Roy closed his eyes and just breathed the air in. There was nothing like this in the city, he admitted to himself. He opened his eyes and sat up when his mother exclaimed, and his father stopped the car.

"Bill, what is that?" His mother asked breathlessly.

Roy could not believe what he saw. Ross grabbed his arm and just stared out the window wordlessly. Even Bootsie was staring out the window. The night was filled with tiny blinking lights. It was beautiful yet frightening at the same time.

"Those are lightning bugs, or fireflies. People call them by either name. They are beetles and pollinate plants, like bees. They also keep pests down. They're good to have around. They only last like this a couple of weeks. This amount of them is something special. I've never seen such a congregation of them," Dad said.

Dolly had woken up at the commotion, and when she saw the mass of fireflies surrounding them, she exclaimed with glee. "Look at all the fairies! We are in fairyland. It's magic all around us. They are saying hello to us!"

Ross had questions. "What makes them light up, and why do they?"

Fortunately, Dad had answers. "It's a chemical reaction called bioluminescence. They do it to attract a mate. The brighter and longer they light up, the better their chance of attracting one is."

Roy never ceased to be amazed at Dad's knowledge of so many things. He wondered if his own thirst for knowledge and love of reading came from him.

They all sat there, transfixed by the sight. It was like being submerged in a sea of thousands and thousands of tiny glowing, glimmering lights in a flowing sea of darkness. The lights blinked on and off as the bugs flittered from spot to spot.

Dad finally broke the silence. "Well, we need to get going," he said, and he drove down the driveway.

They shortly stopped in front of a house on the left. There were two gigantic trees on either side of the road, and we parked between them next to a concrete sidewalk leading to the house. There were two steps up from the driveway. Everyone grabbed a suitcase or box and went up to the house, up the porch steps. They stood there waiting for Dad to unlock the door.

It was very dark, and they could not see very far. And it was quiet, so very quiet.

Once in the house, they set their suitcases and boxes down. Dad turned on the lights and said that this was the dining room. The dining room table was set up, and the movers had set the surrounding chairs. There were boxes everywhere. Dad had come out with the moving company and got some stuff set up, like the tables in the kitchen and the beds.

Dad told everyone to gather around. "It is late, so we won't bother with any unpacking. That can wait until tomorrow," he continued.

He'll be at work tomorrow, Roy smiled to himself. He would have to remember that trick.

"Your mom knows the house and can show you around tomorrow. We'll just get to our bedrooms and get ready for bed. Then we can have the treat I've got to celebrate our new home," he added.

Mom hadn't said a word, but just glared at Dad. She knew what he was trying to pull with this "tomorrow" stuff. There will be more said on that matter later tonight between them.

"Boys, your room is upstairs to the right. Dolly, you'll be sleeping in the downstairs bedroom next to the bathroom down that hallway. He motioned over his shoulder. "Your mom and I will sleep upstairs in the front bedroom."

Dolly found this plan terrifying. "I don't want to be downstairs all by myself!" she screamed.

Mom kneeled in front of Dolly and tried to reassure her. "We'll try it, and I will stay with you until you fall asleep."

She then looked back at Dad and smiled in such a way as to say, "see you in the morning."

Dad shrugged and headed upstairs. "Come on, boys," he said.

They followed him up the stairs; they were steep and narrow.

This is an old house, Roy thought. *I wonder if it is haunted.*

When they reached the top of the stairs, Dad said, "This is a sort of guest room. Your mom and I sleep here to the left and you guys are back on the other side of the guest room."

The layout upstairs was sort of an inverted "V". The so-called guest room was at the bottom of the "V", with Mom and Dad's room on one end and the boys' room on the other. The stairs were at the center.

The boys headed to their room. Dad told them about the pull chain to turn on the light as they walked in. The room was dark and boiling and stuffy. They could just make out the hanging light silhouetted by the low window at the far end of the room. Roy carefully went in and turned on the light by pulling on the chain that hung down from it.

Ross came in and they looked around the room in amazement. While the room itself was enormous, even with two full-sized beds in it, it was at the house's peak. The center and maybe five feet on each side were normal height, but the ceiling followed the peak downward to end up about four feet high at the edges of the room. It did not thrill the brothers, but they knew there was no use complaining about it. This was the way it was.

Roy had learned to deal with it when the circumstance was out of his control. He also knew that given time, circumstances could change, and he just had to wait and watch. His turn would come, and then he would change the situation. Nothing was forever.

Ross looked at him to see what the next move would be.

Roy knew dealing with the heat was priority one. "We'll make do. Let's go see if we can find a fan for the window."

They went downstairs and asked if there was a fan they could have for their room. Dad said he knew where they were and went to dig them out of the confusion of boxes stacked everywhere in the downstairs rooms.

Dad found several, some of them brand new. He had expected this issue and prepared for it.

"Come on upstairs and help me set these up. While they cool off the rooms, we can come down and have the treat I've got for us."

The boys went back upstairs with him. They had brought up four box fans to go into the windows. They were standing in the so-called guest room. It had two windows, one on each outside wall, at right angles to each other.

Dad gave the boys instructions as to placement of the fans. This is how he taught them lessons: hands on while he observed and directed when necessary. He usually explained why it was best to do it a certain way.

"Ok," he said, "pay attention. Put one in each window," he said, pointing outward. They will act as exhaust fans getting rid of the old, stale, hot air in the upstairs," he explained. "If there are not enough outlets, I have some outlet multi-plugs."

When they had done that and got them running, Dad told them to place one fan in each bedroom, blowing inward. When they had accomplished that and returned to the so-called guest room, Dad explained what they were trying to accomplish.

"It's just as important to remove the old hot air as it is to bring in fresh cooler air," he explained. "We've just set up a nice cross ventilation system here. The breeze is coming from the east, so we are running our ventilation from east to west. Fresh cool air in at the bedrooms, and old hot air out from the guest room here. Let's give it some time," he said, and led the boys back downstairs.

The treat was typical of Dad. It was a bag of dates. He was excited about it; Mom rolled her eyes and Ross and I just kept quiet and ate one. Dolly, with all the righteous indignation the boys were too timid to show, refused the dates and said those weren't a treat.

As we sat around the dining room table watching Dad chowing down dates, the quietness came creeping back in. This was going to take some time to get used to.

Dad stood up, rolled up the bag of dates, smacked his lips and announced it was time for bed and headed upstairs. The boys followed him. Mom and Dolly were sleeping downstairs.

Dad turned the lights out in the so-called guest room and went to bed. Roy and Ross stripped to their underpants, and Roy turned off the light. The fans had cooled it off a lot, but it was still very warm and muggy. The boys were pretty worn out from the stressful day and the hour was late, so the family fell asleep quickly.

Ross went to sleep first. It took Roy longer because of the deafening silence that was broken by a droning and chirping. Roy was excited about getting out and exploring this new realm he and his brother had landed in. Tomorrow was going to be great or terrible, maybe both somehow.

"Come on sunrise," he murmured to himself as he laid in bed gazing out the window into the dark! Then his eyes closed, and sleep came over him.

TALE NUMBER THREE

GLEANING THE TRIANGLE

*"It's a dangerous business, Frodo, going out your door.
You step onto the road, and if you don't keep your feet,
there's no knowing where you might be swept off to."*
– Bilbo Baggins

Daylight. It was the very first day in their new home!

Because they had arrived so late the night before, the boys really were not able to make out much of their surroundings on the drive in and were eager to get started exploring their new territory. Roy had awoken several times during the night because of the eerie silence of the country broken by unknown sounds of croaks, chitters, and chirps outside the single bedroom window. At least he hoped they were from outside. The boys had gotten up early, dressed quickly, and had gone downstairs to the kitchen.

The window in the east-facing wall of their room started one foot from the floor and was difficult to open and close. Roy had joked to Ross that perhaps it had been built for dwarfs—though he hoped not. It looked strange, but it gave them early morning sunshine. There had been no heat ducting installed, so the room was stuffy and either extremely hot and humid or frigid; the seasons dictated. In the winter water froze if left overnight in a glass.

What was it Uncle Ross always said, "A break for the weak side"?

"Yeah, a break for the weak side," Roy mused to himself.

"They may be the weak side for now but not forever," he promised.

Their dad did not like Uncle Ross, their mom's brother. Even though Dad did not like Uncle Ross, Roy's brother was named after him.

Parents and family were weird in naming children, he thought.

The brothers gulped down a quick breakfast of cold, sugar-loaded cereal and milk, while they constantly looked out the windows eager to get outside. They would need that energy.

They said hurried goodbyes to Dolly and their mom and rushed outside. Their dad had left for work before dawn back in the city, which was how it would be from now on. Roy felt that, as he was the oldest male present (11 years old), he had to look after the welfare of the family. He was deadly serious about this and failed to see the humor when other adults saw this as "cute" or "sweet." More than once, this would cause conflict as he exerted his perceived rank.

The brothers stood side by side on the front porch of the old farmhouse, when suddenly, before they could even take in their new surroundings, an extremely intense, dreadful shriek filled the air and scared them.

"WAAAAAAAAAAAAAAAAANK!!"

They crouched in an automatic reflex.

"What the hell is that?" Roy yelled.

WAAAAAAAAAAAAAAAAANK!! It shrieked again.

Roy looked at Ross, whose bright blue eyes were opened wide in fright. Roy, whose eyes were also wide opened, (a reflex, his Dad had taught them, expanded their field of vision to identify danger) gauged the distance back into the house and considered grabbing Ross and dragging him back to presumed safety. They were white lipped and in full fight-or-flight mode. Roy had already given up on the "fight" portion and was preparing to go wide open "flight," when the shriek came again.

WAAAAAAAAAAAAAAAAANK!!

Then it dawned on him what the noise was.

"Of course," he shouted to Ross.

There was a railroad track comprising the whole northern boundary of the farm. The tracks were raised up as much as 15 feet or more in certain areas along most of the property, forming a barrier from the outside world—a barrier that was patrolled by the behemoth train. In actuality, the farm property was low, and the embankment was the railroad's attempt at keeping the grade level. Roy later learned the reason: Trains are not known for their topographic adaptability, which is why they need tunnels, switchbacks, raised embankments, avoidance of mountains, and swamps. A 1 percent grade elevation is the North American standard (1 foot rise over 100 feet equals a gradient of 1 percent).

The front porch was on the opposite side of the house from the railroad tracks. The boys moved to the edge of the porch so they could see the tracks. A big diesel engine roared past, with the passenger cars rumbling along behind. There was an exotic looking "domed" car at the end, with the top completely covered in glass. The boys could see people sitting there as comfortably as you please, watching the world going by. This was the Milwaukee Road Hiawatha special passenger service between Chicago and Minneapolis.

What a way to travel, Roy thought. *One day I'll be sitting up there, watching the world going by.* Little did he know, that was exactly what he'd be doing but at between five to seven miles high in a first-class cabin of a commercial airliner.

"It's a train," Roy declared, as if he had known it all the time.

The boys settled down and felt a little foolish for their reaction, but they had never experienced the abrupt appearance of a train before. In the city, there always had been the clanging alarms and brightly painted guard rails being lowered—not some behemoth machine appearing suddenly out of nowhere and scaring the heck out of them. And the trains in the city moved much slower. Some of the older boys bragged about "hopping" a freight car for a ride across town. He believed it could be done, although he had never seen anyone do it.

"I don't think we'll ever get used to that," Ross said, "especially if it happens at night. "He shook his head back and forth to underscore the dire times ahead.

It would take very little time for the train noise to begin to fade into the background. In fact, when they were away from home, the lack of the train noise would cause some unease at first, and when they returned home, the train noise would be a welcome, comforting sound.

Roy would experience sleeping issues due to lack of "normal" sounds being absent and unfamiliar sounds being present as he traveled extensively and often in later years.

Roy had fiercely determined to himself never to let the train's sudden manifestation rattle him again. He clenched his jaw, and his pale blue eyes got that icy look about them as they did when he became unflinchingly resolute. Already at his early age, Roy was developing this feature of his countenance and character.

It was a bright sunny day in late May, an unseasonably warm one by southeastern Wisconsin standards, and even at this early hour, it was getting warm. The sky was a pale blue with wispy clouds lazily drifting by. The boys descended the front porch and walked down the sidewalk to the gravel driveway. The grass needed cutting badly and was full of dandelions. They knew immediately what one of their chores would be: lawn mowing. They hoped they would get to use a power mower.

As they stood there, while they could not see it, the sound of the train faded. They could still hear a faint click clack as the train wheels rolled over the gap and offset of the rails. The train horn blared again.

"It really is going fast. I guess it's warning people it's coming, so keep off the track," Ross said. "I don't think we'll ever get used to that noise," he said once more as the train again sounded its horn.

As the brothers looked all around, the openness of their surroundings struck them. They were used to the familiar, friendly confines of city living. The city blocks full of houses, the alley cutting the block in half lengthwise. Fences separated the backyards. Instead of being barriers, they were podiums on which one neighbor would lean on to kibitz his neighbor's current project, or Monday morning quarterbacking after the big game that weekend.

Houses were filled with families and a multitude of kids to play with or fight with, as the situation dictated. The school was within walking distance, as were the corner shops where many goods were available: groceries, candy, sodas, and ice cream. If you needed help somewhere in the neighborhood and your dad was not there, an adult who knew you was there and would help. Here on the farm, there was nothing but openness and aloneness. There was a sense of vulnerability. In time, the boys would build confidence and adventurousness, and lose this feeling of being vulnerable and out in the open—easy prey. They would, in time, become the hunters, not the hunted. Roy would take this to an extreme and the aftermath was often not pretty. But he kept forging ahead.

Then there was the resonance of the constant background of a city's noise, traffic, and voices of neighbors close next door. You could hear them laugh, cry, and yell. There were the sounds of the radios, phonographs, occasional TVs (it is the 1950s), and a distant (usually distant) siren. Then there were the kids, lots of kids making noises, shouting, and calling out the scores of games, the hide-and-seeker's countdown, and, at night screams of mock terror when startled by hiders of "kick the can." The level of sound varied with the season whether windows were open or closed.

This new openness was strangely unnerving. While it had the abrupt, intrusive noise of the occasional train, it was eerily quiet most of the time, yet not completely silent. If he listened intently, he could hear birds chirping and singing, a buzz of what he supposed as bugs, the croaking of frogs, a steady distant sound of a piece of farm equipment, and the desultory mooing of what he supposed were cows. This was dairy country after all.

Roy would eventually grow to crave the silence he grew to love that summer. It became a place where he could commune with his spirit and receive words of wisdom. He would become revitalized and strengthened. It would become a weapon, spiritual armor. Silence was to become a sought-after substance for him—the essence or core of his being. He found a spiritual grounding and an entity in the divined silence of his being. He would learn to shield the quietness of his soul and the invigorating refreshing and strength that came with it.

It was a tool, a weapon to be deployed at will, and many times made an opponent uncomfortable in the silence—a silence that could be palpable if done correctly.

Instead of the public street that ran past their house and sidewalks and another block of houses across from their house, there was the dandelion-infested, overgrown lawn, then a rutted loose gravel lane that was their private drive. On the other side of the lane was an expansive field. There were neat rows of barely distinguishable young plants. They didn't know then, but would soon, these were corn plants and, according to an old farming adage, the Fourth of July is an important benchmark for your corn crop. If all's going well, it should be "knee high by the Fourth of July."

The field width seemed a great distance but was actually one-eighth of a mile, bordered by a nasty looking, three-strand barbed wire fence. They knew about barbed wire from the cowboy movies they watched and read about in comic books.

Barbed wire usually meant trouble, nesters, Roy joked silently to himself.

Then there was the smell. The city had its own unique odor. Partly exhaust fumes, freshly mowed lawns, neighbor's dinner on the range, and freshly washed clothes on the clothes lines strung across backyards.

Here they were experiencing the earthy, clean aroma of unpolluted air, punctuated with the odor of occasional manure, a smell that isn't as totally off-putting as one would imagine. Then there would be the smell of freshly turned over soil, freshly mowed hay. The seasons would bring the various smells peculiar to the activity occurring on the farms and in the fields. They would welcome these signs of seasonal progression.

The boys walked on to the gravel driveway. They were standing in the shade of two gigantic trees, one on each side of the road like matched bookends. They were taller than the house and the boys could not touch their hands when they tried to put their arms around them. Their shade provided welcome coolness all summer long, and that was the coolest side of the house. Unfortunately, their room was on the other side of the house.

Ross looked around, his blue eyes alert. His blond hair, bleached white from the sun, hanging over his ears and forehead, almost in his eyes. The brothers had not had a haircut in weeks because of the isolation generated by the Polio Epidemic. His pale skin would soon tan to the color of ripened wheat and his freckles would show through, a darker brown dotting his cheeks and his nose.

Roy's hair would also bleach white. He had no freckles but would tan much darker than Ross. He loved the feel of the sun on his skin and seldom wore a shirt in the summer. Roy also had blue eyes, but they would change from a soft pale blue to a brittle icy color depending on his state of mind. This was his "tell." It would not only serve as a warning to others that he was getting really upset but was also a frustrating reflex he could not control.

Ross said, "Let's begin exploring where we entered the farm from the highway. It was dark last night, and we couldn't see much when we got here."

"Good idea," Roy agreed. "That is a great place to start. Let's take the driveway out to the highway."

"Come on Roy; let's get started," Ross said. "It's already getting hot."

While it was only late May, the weather was more like late June. The skies were a pale blue with wispy clouds scattered about. The sun was a bright golden ball approaching midpoint in its daily course across the sky. It was still in the northern portion of the sky but getting close to the midpoint, where it would take 10 to 12 hours to shower the land with its life-giving rays of warmth which would turn into hot, baking rays in late July and August. That's when the land would once again cycle down to fall and harvest time.

"Okay," said Roy, still glancing up toward a farm on the high hill.

The driveway was gravel with two hard-packed tracks where tires had packed it down and pushed loose gravel into the center and the sides, making walking difficult if one deviated from the packed tracks.

A barbed wire fence separated the driveway from the cornfield on their left. The field was flat by their property but ran up the massive hill to the farmhouse and the outbuildings atop of it. It was about two city blocks from the crossroad. The boys always referred to the distance between places in city block lengths which in the Midwest is approximately 660 feet.

"It must be a real pain to work on the side of that hill," Roy mused.

"This hill will be a killer to sled down in winter," Roy told Ross.

"Wow, it sure will be." Ross replied.

About halfway to the crossroad, the cornfield angled away from them, and a small piece of land appeared on their left.

"I think that's part of our land," Ross said.

"I bet you're right," agreed Roy.

On their right was a strange hump of land that merged with a small field overgrown with huge thistles, wildflowers, and sticker bushes. Bumble Bees were busy going from flower to flower. The field then butted up against an old orchard that looked sad and forlorn. As the boys walked past it, they wondered how in the world their dad was going to resurrect it. That is all he had talked about on the drive out here last night.

The property that the boys' father bought and moved the family was to serve multiple purposes. The primary goal was to move family out of the city and away from the polio epidemic that was scourging the neighborhoods and causing the lockdown of all children. There were cases in their old neighborhood, and the dreaded disease had confined the boys' friend to a science fiction horror machine called Iron Lung. Mom and Dad were beside themselves with worry.

That time was the 1950s, when the very real, utterly devastating effects of polio overshadowed everything. There was sheer terror just at the mention of polio. In 1952, the worst polio outbreak in American history infected 58,000 people, killing over 3,000 and paralyzing 21,000—most of them children. TIME reported, "The stories of children stricken suddenly by the telltale cramps and fever, haunted parents. They deserted public swimming pools for fear of contagion.

And year after year, polio delivered thousands of people into hospitals or into the nightmarish canisters called iron lungs."

Their parents and thousands like them felt betrayed. In their lifetime, they had survived two wars and the Great Depression. It was their turn to enjoy the fruits of a vibrant economy and peaceful world. The epidemic was unfair and, worst of all, it threatened their young family.

The supposed secondary reason for the move was to turn the property into a producing truck farm. Their dad longed to work the earth again. He grew up on a farm in Lafayette, Indiana. To be fair, it was hard to tell which was the first or second reason behind the move in his mind.

Roy thought, *the farm is number one to him.*

"I'm going to get that little farm up and producing!" He spoke. "The orchard and berry patch will have to be brought back to life, and I am going to start a big strawberry patch that I've researched at the university extension. They've sent me all kinds of information on growing different berries and vegetables, and they even might come out and look at the farm and give me some one-to-one advice!" he exclaimed.

Boy, is he excited about this, Roy had thought.

Dad continued, "There is even a small tractor and some equipment, like a plow and stuff, in the barn."

That got Roy's attention. "Can we help you out, Dad?" he asked.

His dad shook his head and said, "We'll talk about it later."

Both the boys knew what that meant. It meant "NO."

Roy blinked his eyes and got back to his morning of initial exploration on the farm.

They had reached the crossroads, and there was a street sign on the other side of the road. It said Hilltop Road.

Roy studied the sign and looked both ways and then spoke.

"At least there's a name for it. The farm is most likely named Hilltop Farm. What do you think?" he asked Ross. "Probably," his brother muttered and started toward the railroad tracks and the highway that brought them here last night. He wished his big brother would stay focused on the task at hand and not veer off whenever something else popped up.

"I bet we could have some grand adventures up at that farm," Roy said as he jogged to catch up to Ross.

The railroad tracks were about another two-city block lengths away. The gravel road was packed hard, and the going was easy.

As they walked along, side by side, they surveyed the property on the other side of Hilltop Road. Like the field across from their driveway, a barbwire fence protected it. But there was just what appeared to be grass in this field and not corn. It looked very uniform and there weren't any thistles or brambles in it. It looked like maybe it was a crop. It stretched away to what appeared to be a creek. Then another field with cows grazing in it ran all the way to a farmhouse and a group of outbuildings. While these farm buildings were on a hill, this hill was nothing compared to the size of the hill the Hilltop Farm was on. Hilltop Farm had the high ground.

"I wonder if the fence is to keep things out or to keep things in?" Roy mused.

Ross pondered it a moment and then replied, "Maybe both."

Roy laughed and clapped his brother on the shoulder.

"You're most likely right," and laughed again.

Ross studied the creek that divided the field.

"I wonder if that creek is any good for swimming or fishing?" Ross asked.

"We can check it out later. Right now, let's explore. We are stuck here, so we might as well get the lay of the land."

He didn't wait for an answer and started walking toward the tracks. Ross fell into step alongside Roy.

"That pisses me off when he answers and just takes off," Ross muttered to himself.

"Did you say something?" Roy asked?

"Yeah," Ross said. "Just talking to myself."

Roy didn't wait for an answer and just kept walking.

Ross kicked at the gravel and glared at Roy, who never even glanced at him but focused on the railroad crossing they were heading to.

Nerves still jangling from their earlier run-in with the passenger train, the boys cautiously looked both ways and listened carefully upon arriving at the tracks. The power and speed of the train stuck with them, and they made their way slowly and carefully around the tracks. They looked down the tracks toward their house. They could look all the way past the house to what they thought was the end of their land. The railroad right of way gave them an unobstructed view.

"Ross, you know what I think? I think our land is in the shape of a triangle. Hilltop Road is the bottom of The Triangle, the railroad tracks are straight on one side, and our property from where it butts up to the Hilltop Farm's property angles inward from Hilltop Road to a point way down past our house into what looks like a bunch of small trees and bushes and maybe another creek. The mound by our house looks like it is the center of The Triangle."

Ross considered this, and after a moment, he agreed with Roy. "You are right. It is a triangle, and 'Triangle' is the perfect name for it. From now on, our small farm will be called 'The Triangle,' Ross stated.

"That is perfect," Roy shouted! "The Triangle," it is. Good for you, Ross!"

And so, The Triangle Tale adventures start for the brothers.

Ties That Bind

TALE NUMBER FOUR

THE TIES THAT BIND

"The secret of getting ahead is getting started."
– Mark Twain.

Both boys were excited about observing and taking note that their property was triangle-shaped. It also confused them. What an odd shape for a piece of land, stuck here amid large dairy farms and bounded on one side by a railroad track. Did the construction of the track have something to do with the shape of Triangle Farm? Or did the shape of Triangle Farm dictate where the track was located? Maybe Dad could answer that tonight when he got home from work in the city.

The city was far away.

Roy recalled the long drive here last night. They had left their home in the city when the sun was just setting. They drove into the sunset until it became totally dark. That's why the boys were standing nervously on the railroad crossing of the road that led from the highway up the big hill to a farm. It had been dark when they arrived, so they could see little other than the fireflies. Their driveway branched off this road which was named Hilltop Road. They had walked out here this morning to begin an exploration of The Triangle Farm.

The sudden, unexpected appearance of a fast-moving passenger train had shocked the boys as they were leaving the house. Even though they now had an unobstructed view both ways down the tracks, they were anxious and uneasy standing there. They had never experienced a train moving that fast and appearing that suddenly, announcing itself with the loudest, blaring horn they had ever heard.

Roy bent down and put his hands on one of the railroad tracks and said, "I remember hearing that you can feel the railroad track vibrating long before you can hear or see the train." After a moment of grasping the rail and closing his eyes, intensely concentrating, he jumped up and proclaimed, "It is all clear. Let's walk the tracks to the end of the property. We can see it all from up here."

Ross shook his head, "No way. Where do we go if a train comes? They are so fast!" He shook his head again and set his mouth in a thin, straight line.

Ross was average height for a 9-year-old boy, with a slight in build, maybe even wiry. There was little resemblance between the boys. Both boys had hair that was light blond, and they both had blue eyes. But where Ross was slight, Roy was broad and solid, maybe even stocky. He was strong and tall for his age. The boys were blessed with the speed and agility which they had developed in the alleys and backyards of the city. Roy assumed they could always muscle their way out of any jam or use their speed to escape. Ross was more calculating and cautious. This divergence of personalities was healthy, although many times led to conflict.

"We could go down the embankment," Roy said as he smiled and shrugged. "What is the problem?"

"Have you looked at the embankment?" Roy's eyes followed Ross's outstretched arm as he pointed at the tangle of burrs, stickers, and brambles that completely covered the embankment from the track's edge down to the bottom. "How do you think we would get out of the way without getting torn to shreds in that mess?"

Roy snorted and jeered. "You are just too afraid of the train. We could get down the embankment with no problem at all."

Ross was getting angry, and when he did, his face went red. His pupils were getting bigger, his heart was beating faster. Blood vessels in your face are close to the surface, so your cheeks get red when you are upset—another Dad factoid. Ross clenched his fists and started toward the embankment.

"What are you doing?" Roy asked.

"I'll show you; I'm not afraid. I'm going to go down the embankment and show you just how bad you get torn up doing it," Ross yelled at Roy.

Roy grabbed his brother's arm. "Hold on, Ross," he said. "If anyone goes down that embankment, it is me. I'm the one that thinks there is no problem getting out of the way if a train comes. I also am the older brother and if there is any danger, I need to be first."

Ross stopped and looked at Roy. He took a deep breath and calmed down. He relaxed, and Roy let go of his arm.

"Okay," Ross allowed, "but be careful."

Roy nodded and started down the tracks a little way and stepped toward the edge and the embankment.

∿

The Old Man remembered how the boys had paced their steps to match where the railroad ties were. Sunken in a bed of gravel, connected to the rails by large spikes driven deep into the ties, pinching the rail securely to the tie. He thought about how the railroad ties bound the rails together so the train could travel the railway safely. That was how it was between the brothers and the family but especially the brothers. Their love for each other bound them tightly together. They looked out for each other and were ready to stand up and even fight for each other. The Old Man missed the camaraderie of his brother. They had drifted apart after they had gotten married. Roy had moved to Texas following an opportunity to start a business. A lot of the distancing was his fault. He had not been much of a brother (or someone a wife would want her husband to hang out with, for that matter). Roy had gone through a couple of marriages before he moved to Texas. What a shame he had forsaken his brother's love for life in the fast lane. Ross was the only one who had been honest and *had always been there for him.,*

The brothers' time together, alone a large share of time, thrust into a foreign, sometimes threatening, environment and totally reliant on one another, had strengthened the bond between them. Their relocation from the familiar confines of the neighborhood and their friends to this strange and sometimes frightening milieu, heightened the alliance between the boys making them inseparable.

~

It was settled: Roy would find out if the embankment was safe to go down, and Ross would vigilantly keep a hand on the rail. Roy stopped and faced toward the embankment, then stepped to the edge of it and turned to look back at his brother.

"Keep your hand on the rail so you can warn me to get back if you feel the rail vibrating. That way, I'll have time to get back to you," Roy called back to his brother.

"Okay," said Ross as he sat on a rail holding it with his hand. He was edgy and nervous. He hoped Roy would be okay.

Roy did not want Ross to know how scared he was. If the brambles that were comprised of Burdock Burrs (the basis for Velcro invention), Hawthorne (with thorns up to two inches), the cockleburs, blackberry bushes, huge thistles and stickers didn't get him, a speeding passenger train could. The embankment formed a formidable wall. He bet even Brer Rabbit himself could not jump around in there; it was so thick. He needed Uncle Remus of *Song of the South* to tell him about the secrets in navigating this dire situation that his big mouth had gotten himself into.

He looked for a place to start down. There did not seem to be any opening. The brambles formed a solid wall. He tried to force his way in and found he could with a fair amount of effort. He made it most of the way down the embankment before he turned around to start back up. This is where it got dicey. To start back up, he had to lean forward and grab onto bushes to climb back up the steep embankment. The brambles had thorns that scratched him, and there were little round balls of spines that stuck to his T-shirt. There was also one type that had two little horns that was aggressive and buried itself in the T's fabric and his Levi's.

By the time he got back to the top, his arms were scratched, even through his T-shirt. There were burrs and stickers all over his T-shirt and even on his jeans. He bit his lip to muffle any sounds that would give away the pain he was experiencing. But his face reflected it. He was pale, sweat-soaked, and wincing.

Ross stood up and studied his older brother.

"Man, you are a mess. Does it hurt much?" he asked and couldn't help but smirk at the mangled mess his brother was.

Roy could not help it. He looked at his arms and lifted his burr-covered T-shirt and winced at the scratches that were oozing blood and stinging as his sweat found its way into each crevice. He looked down at his jeans that had these little barbed stickers embedded in them that penetrated the jeans in some places and pricked him whenever he moved. He pulled off burrs and stickers and laughed out loud.

"Boy, were you ever right about the embankment. It is murder trying to get back up."

Ross walked over to him and pulled off burrs and stickers.

Roy said, "It's not too bad going down. I think we could get out of the way if we had to, but coming back up is too rough. I don't know what those little horned things are, but they are just plain murder."

It took a while to pick the burrs and stickers off Roy's clothes. He had a handkerchief that he wiped his brow with and cleaned up some of the blood. Some of it stained his T-shirt, but he didn't mind. It was sort of cool.

Ross looked down the tracks toward the house and noticed a rabbit sitting alongside the tracks looking at them. It just sat there as though studying them. He was a small cottontail rabbit—named for their white tail that they flashed as they ran. Dad strikes again.

Ross turned to his brother. "Do you see that rabbit down the tracks?"

"Yeah," said Roy, looking to where Ross was pointing.

"What is it doing?" Ross asked.

The rabbit was stomping its hind legs, making a thumping sound. Then it hopped over to the embankment and turned to look back at them and stomped its hind legs again as it sat and looked at them.

"Do you think it wants us to come over there?" Ross asked.

"That would be really weird and scary," Roy said in a drawn-out voice.

"Let's check it out," Ross said.

"You're okay with going down the tracks to where the rabbit is?" Roy asked.

"Yeah, but we need to pay close attention to what the tracks can tell us. We need to keep checking for vibration," Ross stated with firm determination.

So, they cautiously started toward the beckoning bunny. Their steps were measured to fall on the crossties. This made their walking easier, as the surface was smooth and the spacing was just right. The closer they got, the more agitated the small cottontail became. Then it hopped down the embankment and disappeared. When the boys reached the spot where it had disappeared, they saw a narrow path down the embankment.

Ross studied the path and announced that he knew what it was.

"It's a game trail. We can use it to get out of the way of trains," he stated. "It's so weird. It is like the rabbit wanted us to know about this."

"More than weird," Roy said, "it's spooky. And look, the crazy rabbit is sitting further down the tracks and doing his thumping thing." The rabbit had emerged from the tangle of the embankment about 20 yards farther down the tracks.

An excited Ross said, "Let's go!" as he hurried toward the rabbit, with no regard to the danger of a recklessly careening colossus of a speeding train, bent on their destruction.

Once again, when they got close, the rabbit ducked back down the embankment. And as before, there was a narrow trail down the embankment.

The boys both exclaimed, "Whoa, spooky!"

Movement down the track caught their attention. The rabbit came flying up the embankment and hurried toward them. Then a fox appeared in hot pursuit. The rabbit stopped between the boys and turned back to look at the fox, who had skidded to a stop when he saw the boys. The rabbit started thumping again as though taunting the fox, now that he had the boys beside him. The fox hung his head and slunk back down the embankment. He gave one parting glare, making it clear this wasn't over.

The rabbit looked up at them and wiggled his nose, turned and hopped back up the tracks, and disappeared down the first pathway.

"All right, what was that all about?" Ross declared. His voice was up a couple of octaves.

Roy laughed and looked back down the tracks. "It's clear to me that there is something incredibly special about The Triangle—something incredibly special indeed. And I bet it has something to do with that mound."

He was looking straight at the mound which was behind their house. It was about five feet high and round like an upside-down bowl, maybe 12 feet across. They were currently standing on the tracks directly across from it. Roy had read about the mounds built by the ancient ones as part of a school assignment. He was fascinated by the subject and had gotten books from the library and did more studying on his own. The idea of one of those mounds being on their property, right next to their house, was so cool!

Roy planned to rigorously explore the impact of such a mound on their property and what it meant. Who were the ancient ones, and why did they build it here?

Roy shook his head to clear the thought and bring himself back to the present. "Well, from here we can see everything. Let's survey the complete property. Okay?" He asked Ross.

Ross was still nervously looking up and down the tracks and kneeled so he could keep a hand on the tracks. "You check it out, and I'll keep on the lookout for more trains that may try to catch us off guard," he said. "Tell me what you see."

Roy chuckled to himself and agreed.

"Starting from Hilltop Road, there is this patch of overgrowth next to the tracks. It looks like someone excavated a chunk of land between the berry patch and railroad tracks all the way to about where the mound is. There is a cut bank along the excavation and the rest of land about four feet high. Most of the excavated ground has overgrown with grass and weeds, but some areas still have visible marks from the digging," he relayed to Ross.

Ross looked up at Roy and murmured, "That's ugly. I feel that the ground is hurting there."

Roy nodded in agreement and stood quietly, staring at what felt like looking at an open wound. "We can fix this somehow," he said. "I believe that's something that we are supposed to do."

"But how?" his brother responded.

"I don't know, but if we pay attention to it, it will show us," Roy said.

Ross shivered and said, "This is just too creepy."

"No," Roy flatly declared. "Not at all. This is an adventure. Our first one at The Triangle. Together we can do anything, brother. Together!"

Roy continued to survey the property from their vantage point. "The orchard is next to the berry patch. They both end at a little field that runs up to the mound and borders the excavation," he relayed.

"The berry patch, the small field and the orchard are in incredibly sad shape and overgrown with many weeds. They really show signs of neglect," Roy observed and shared with Ross. It's condition bothered Roy. It made him sad and angry at the same time.

Roy shared this with his brother, who was now standing next to him. Even though he still kept glancing nervously up and down the tracks, Ross was now taking an active interest in the survey of their new home.

Their driveway angled in from Hilltop Road, the wide end of The Triangle, all the way past the mound and house to the rickety, small barn. Except for a small piece of land that formed a mini triangle, it formed the other boundary of the property opposite the tracks. That mini triangle stopped opposite the mound. From the mound, the land sloped down to the house. There was a row of fruit trees and a small section of the lawn bordering the house. The house, barn, a dilapidated chicken coop, and driveway formed a small quad that was dominated by two huge apple trees with a sparse lawn.

On the other side of the barn, the property angled into the railroad tracks, to the point of The Triangle. This portion of the property was low and full of cattails and reeds. The trill of male red-winged blackbirds was a sweet sound, and their display of the blood-red epaulet was almost spectacular in contrast to their midnight dark black bodies that had a sheen that almost made one think they had been waxed and polished. The boys had never experienced something like this before. It enamored them. A gentle breeze blew an earthy scent by them that was clean and fresh. They both smiled.

Cornfields and pastures flanked the property. Where these all met, at the pointy end of The Triangle, there was a group of small trees and tall grasses forming a seemingly impregnable copse. The copse extended out from the railroad's tracks 20–25 yards with a trail of tall grasses hiding the surface of a creek that wound across the fields and disappeared in the distance. The area enclosed by the copse was intriguing, and Roy promised himself to examine it when he could.

The entire property was full of potential adventures. In addition, the big farm at the top of the big hill where Hilltop Road dead-ended was especially beckoning to him. There was a tall windmill in front of the farmhouse, and its vanes caught a light breeze, rotating slowly.

I wonder if that is an actual working windmill, Roy thought.

As Roy and Ross stood on the embankment carefully inspecting the peculiarly shaped property, Roy felt a powerful pull of attraction from the property coupled with a vague, yet real, sense of fear. A glance at his brother, who looked back at him, convinced him that Ross was feeling the same thing. Maybe leaving the city wasn't all bad, but Roy couldn't understand why he felt the way he did about their new home. Nevertheless, Roy promised himself that it would not deter him from inspecting all the ins and outs of The Triangle and its neighboring lands. He was going to take advantage of all the opportunities for adventures whenever and wherever he could.

We may not have the alley and the gang to play with, but we have each other and all this land to investigate, plus "magical bunnies" and Indian mounds, he thought to himself. *This is going to be a great summer!*

Roy looked closely at his brother and shared with him, "There are all kinds of stories here. I can feel it. The Triangle seems to have been waiting for us."

"What do you mean?" his brother asked.

Roy took a deep breath and responded as he turned to gaze around The Triangle, "There is a strong sense of welcoming that beckons to us from the property. There is also mystery and danger here. I've felt nothing like this before. It makes me uneasy and excited at the same time. I don't think we'll miss the alley."

"I think I feel something like that. I don't think I like it. What are we going to do?" Ross murmured.

"Nothing. We stay together and wait for The Triangle to show us what we are to do."

Ross blinked and swallowed hard. He was extremely nervous now. "This is all a bunch of crap, and I really don't like it." His use of that language was very out of character for him and a sign of how upset he was.

The two young boys sat down on the railroad track. Roy had his elbows on his knees and cupped his chin in his hands. Ross, sitting beside him, only used one hand to cup his chin and, with the other, he absently played with the stones on the railroad bed. They were gazing out over the property, trying to come to terms with what they had just experienced.

What was going to happen next? Was it going to be good, or bad, or both? What were they to do? How would they get ready? Ross mused.

They looked at each other and could see the fear hidden in each other's eyes.

Just then, they heard their mother calling to them. She was standing on the small porch in the kitchen at the back of the house. If they had gone out that way this morning, they may not have been startled by the train. The stoop faced parallel to the tracks, and they could have seen it coming.

Could've, should've, Roy thought.

"What are you two doing up there on the tracks?" their mother yelled. "Get back down here. Get down here now!"

Their sister, Dorothy, was standing on the porch rail; her nickname was Dolly. Dolly was much younger than the boys, and this gap in age led them not to include her in most of their activities. She was just as blond as the boys and had even more freckles and was average height and chunky. She always wore dresses which was the custom in those times. She could not keep up with them, but she didn't seem to care. The boys played board and card games with her occasionally, and she enjoyed that.

Their dog, Bootsie, was also on the porch and when she saw the boys, she bolted down the porch steps and ran toward them. She was a mixed collie breed with long hair and a tawny colored coat with four white feet. She usually followed the boys wherever they went in the city, but out here in the open country, their parents thought it was a good idea to keep Bootsie close until she settled in and would not run off.

"Bootsie, get back here! Come here, Bootsie," Mom yelled.

Bootsie did not heed their mother and ran headlong through the grass and up the embankment. When she reached the boys, all excited, she was covered with burrs and stickers.

The boys said, "Bootsie, look at you. You are a real mess."

The dog didn't seem to care. She wagged her tail and whined happily. Her wagging was so hard that the back half of her body was wagging Too. The boys laughed, kneeled, and hugged her, as they pulled burrs from her coat.

Their mom called them again, and she was getting angry. Even Dolly was yelling at them now. Her little squeaky voice hardly carried up to them.

Ross stood up and yelled back to them, "We're coming, Mom!"

He then walked to the edge of the railroad embankment and walked back and forth, looking for a path down like the one the bunny had shown them.

"Here is a path down. Let's try it," Ross said.

The boys worked their way down the embankment. The little game trail allowed them to avoid most of the burrs and thorns.

"We owe one to that rabbit," Ross said. "He sure helped us out."

"I think we're even with that bunny," Roy responded. "We stopped that fox from going after him, didn't we? Anyway, I don't think we've seen the last of that rabbit. He is a real Brer Rabbit."

They walked through the grass and weeds between the tracks and the house. The grass was so tall, Bootsie had to keep jumping up to see where they were. There was a dank aroma that was sweet and sour at the same time. The ground felt a little spongy under their feet.

"We are going to be busy getting the burrs out of her this afternoon," Ross said. "Maybe we can get Dolly to help. We will tell her it is a game. We will see who can get the most of them pulled off her."

"Great idea," Roy laughed. "You are sneaky. You know, she has got no one out here. We probably need to spend some time with her."

Ross nodded in agreement.

Roy said, "Let's not tell Mom about what is going on. Let's wait until Dad gets home and tell them together."

Ross nodded his assent and added, "After lunch, we can work out our story, so it makes as much sense as possible.

"Great idea," Roy exclaimed, putting his arm over Ross's shoulder as they bounded up the porch steps. "I'm starved."

Roy thinks about tonight when Dad returns home. *We must convince Dad that we had a special experience and enlist his help. That's going to be a tough chore. Just getting his attention is going to be tough.*

Dad was focused on his projects or ideas. He was obsessed with being successful and recognized as someone special. He was a great dad unless he felt overshadowed by someone or something. Then he could get mean and even vindictive. They learned to stay out of his way until the situation resolved itself, sometimes in an ugly manner.

There is also the matter of being on the tracks at all. It really upset Mom discovering them up there, and she would wait until Dad was home, probably at the dinner table after they had eaten. Dolly would be present, even though she had done nothing wrong as far as the boys knew, but she would chime in with, "That was naughty," or "Shame on you."

Tomorrow and the rest of their summer depended on getting Dad on board by letting them explore where they wanted to and helping them answer questions when the boys were stumped or needed something. Tonight, was going to make or break their summer which was already in shambles because of the move.

Lost In The Bog

TALE NUMBER FIVE

TO PUT A POINT ON IT

*"There will always be rocks in the road
ahead of us. They will be stumbling blocks
or steppingstones; it all depends on how
you use them."*
– Friedrich Nietzsche

Roy had spent all afternoon looking forward to Dad's arrival home with great trepidation. Mom had said nothing about the train tracks incident at all. Lunch had been quiet except for Dolly looking at them and wagging her finger every so often.

After lunch, they got busy cleaning up Bootsie. The burrs and stickers were all over her, and they seemed to be bothering her. Ross, true to his word, used his wily ways and convinced Dolly that pulling burrs from the dog was great fun, and she joined in enthusiastically. The three of them spent the early afternoon deburring Bootsie and talking about how much they missed their old home and their friends.

"You boys have each other out here, but I have no one to play with," Dolly said, looking down at the pile of burrs that had stuck to her after pulling them from the dog. They all had some on them. "Can you play with me sometimes?"

Roy, true to character as self-designated family protector, immediately agreed. "Of course, we will," he said.

Ross cringing at the "we" part of that statement because he knew he was going to have to babysit this pledge. Roy was always quick on the trigger to commit without thinking things through, and counted on his brother to follow up.

Dolly smiled and got up and hugged them both, leaving a present of burrs with the hug. "I'm so happy that we will play together. What are we going to do first?"

Roy smiled and looked at Ross.

"Let's finish the dog first," Ross declared angrily. So, they did.

When they finished, Bootsie ran around the yard and rolled on the grass, rubbing herself, rolling over and yelping happily.

"Boy, those burrs must have really been getting to her," Dolly said.

She has a great vocabulary for someone who is only four years old. All the kids did. A lot of that had to do with their parents' vocabulary. Dad has a master's degree in metallurgical engineering, and Mom had a couple years of college, an accent, and a more formal vocabulary reflecting her parents' origination in the British Isles.

"Look at her go!" Ross shouted, as Bootsie continued to roll, shake, and jump up on them for several minutes. All the time, she yelped with pleasure and glee. The kids joined in on her fun. They rolled on the ground, jumped up, ran around, and tried to yelp like Bootsie. The more they did it, the more she did until they all lay exhausted in the grass, side by side, a complete pack—all together as they should be, even though they seldom showed it. It was a solid bond that lay deep in their souls. Roy rolled over and saw Mom standing on the front porch smiling with pleasure at her children all getting along with each other for a change.

What can I do to make this common and not unusual, she mused to herself. *Maybe I won't tell Bill about the issue up on the tracks this morning. Maybe letting Bootsie get covered in burrs and need cleaning again is a good idea. I need to think about this and the safety issue with the trains.* She spends a great deal of time trying to accomplish this family harmony, with little success.

She turned and walked back into the house to prepare dinner and ponder how to handle this evening with the family discussion after dinner. She needed to get the fans going. It was getting to a boiling point in the house, and the stove was heating it up even more. At least there was a cool breeze coming through the house. It was good to have windows on all sides, so cross ventilation was natural. She turned on the radio and listened to the soap operas she liked and busied herself preparing dinner and unpacking.

The breeze carried the fresh smell of the grass and flowers around the house, and the steady drone of the fans was a comforting sound. She smiled again and thought, *this isn't so bad. I like this part, but the aloneness is going to be tough.* Then her thoughts drifted off too following the radio show.

Outdoors, Bootsie regained her energy and got up and, with her nose to the ground, went sniffing her way around the yard.

"What are we going to do now?" Dolly asked as she sat up.

Ross sat up and said, "Let's go to the pointy end of the property and see what that looks like. We already know about the front end of the property."

Roy agreed, but Dolly complained she didn't know about the front end of the property. They had left her home this morning. Ross just shrugged his shoulders, and Roy got up and started off toward the unexplored end of The Triangle, without a word as usual. Ross and Bootsie followed him. Dolly didn't hesitate very long and ran to catch up.

Wow, she thought, *she was going on an adventure with her brothers.* She looked up at them like they were some sort of heroes.

They walked down the driveway past the little old barn. It was dilapidated and the red paint was peeling in many areas. The main door was open and as they walked past, the front end of the little Cub International tractor peeked out. The boys stopped and gazed at it. It beckoned them, and they ran to it. They walked around it, touched it fondly, and studied it lovingly. They had never seen one up close. It was love at first sight. One could almost hear the sweet strains of a love song in the background.

The tractor was old and beat up, but to the boys, it was marvelous. It virtually shimmered. They oohed and aahed as they fawned over it.

Dolly shook her blond curls and thought, *what a couple of dopes they can be sometimes.*

"Let's sit in the seat," they said almost simultaneously. And climbed up on it.

Dolly scolded the boys in her small, high-pitched voice, which to Roy sounded like fingernails on a blackboard. "Better not! Dad will be really upset about this!"

"How will he know?" Roy asked.

Dolly just stood there, staring at them with her hands on her hips.

Roy looked at her with narrowed eyes. "You still want to go with us exploring the pointy end of The Triangle," he growled?

"Oh," she murmured and backed down.

"Good girl," Roy said. "Just do as we say."

Ross looked at him and said "Roy!"

Roy turned and stared at him with a hard set, narrowed eyes and then went back to climbing up on the small tractor.

Ross is taken aback by the harsh, unyielding posture Roy had adopted immediately when challenged by his sister.

Roy turned the steering wheel back and forth, moved the hand throttle forward and back, pushed brake pedals, and moved the gear shifter around. He was in a daydream world, plowing and cultivating.

"Your turn," he said, climbing down. The tractor was the perfect size for them.

"No thanks," Ross said. He had lost the desire after Roy's flash of dominance. The cold gray cast to his eyes was unsettling. He hadn't experienced it before. He could tell Dolly was still unnerved by it.

As they left the barn, Roy stepped between them and put an arm over each of their shoulders and gave them a big warm smile with his eyes twinkling with big brotherly love. Things were back to normal as far as he was concerned—subject closed.

"You know the tractor is really dirty," Dolly said. "It really could use a good cleaning, as could the barn floor."

Roy's eyes lit up.

"Great idea, sister. We should tell Dad we want to do this for him. That will make all we want to talk about and ask for go down easier!" Roy exclaimed.

"Yeah," his brother agreed, "and we can say Dolly will help us. That will make Mom happy too!"

"Okay, let's explore the pointy end of The Triangle."

"What triangle?" Dolly asked.

"The Triangle, our triangle," Ross stated. "The shape of this farm is like a triangle, so we named it The Triangle."

"That's really cool," she said and repeated it twice. "The Triangle, The Triangle, I like it," Dolly exclaimed!

Roy thought to himself, *that will get Mom onboard*, and smiled.

Bootsie led the way. Her long, silky haired tail arched up over her back like a banner and, her nose to the ground, she disappeared into the tall grasses.

They walked single file -- Roy leading, then Dolly and Ross bringing up the rear. They kept Dolly in the center, so she wouldn't get lost or wander off. As soon as they got past the barn into the tall grass, things changed. Under the bright, hot June sun, the air smelled different. The ground felt different, and the various grasses were different.

The air had a heavy, damp musky smell, something like wet leaves in the fall, strong but pleasant. The ground felt spongy, the more so the further they went. They stayed close to the fence on the property border because the grasses were much taller toward the center of the property. They got shorter again on the other side of the property next to the railroad embankment. There were cattails and what appeared to be an open area in the center. A black bird with red and yellow patches on its shoulders trilled a strange call and flexed its wings. There were several of them sitting on cattails and other tall scrub brushes, just like the ones the boys had seen this morning. Before today, the children had never seen or heard anything like them before and were transfixed by them. Besides the cattails, there were several grasses and bushes new to them as well.

Their father would explain to them the birds were male Redwing Blackbirds. They lived in marshy areas, and their bright feathers showed off to the females.

Ross wanted to go on to the end of the property, the pointy end and said so. Roy agreed, so on they trudged. They had lost sight of Bootsie and would have lost sight of Dolly also if they hadn't kept her in the middle. The grasses and bushes stretched higher than the boys' heads in the center of the bog, and there were stunted trees scattered, each about 10–12 feet tall.

The day was hot, and the children were sweating profusely. The mosquitoes were coming out and were very pleased that their dinner had come to them. Dolly was complaining about the heat and bites. Ross cautiously informed her to button up and keep moving when he saw the look in Roy's eyes. He wondered if Roy would leave her in the bog if he wasn't here.

"We are going to keep going to the end of the line, the pointy end of The Triangle. I am breaking the trail so it should be easier for you guys to follow," Roy said over his shoulder. He had to finish the trek and so did they. *What could he do to help?* The soil was getting spongier, and water seeped up around his shoes as he walked.

Dolly just stopped and sobbed. Ross called to Roy, who was still forging ahead. Roy came back with an angry look on his face, but when he got up to Dolly, his face softened.

"Help her up on my back, and I'll piggyback her the rest of the way," he said to Ross.

"Maybe we should turn back," Ross countered.

"No! Help her up, we're finishing!" Roy insisted.

Ross wished he hadn't said that. He knew better.

Dolly looked up at Roy like he was a superhero when it was Ross who had been her champion. Ross just shook his head and boosted Dolly up on Roy's back. She wrapped her arms around his neck and legs around his waist, almost. Her chubby little legs couldn't reach around his thick waist, so she sort of pinched his waist with her legs.

"Too tight, you're strangling me!" Roy gasped. And she loosened up. "Perfect," he said and laughed. "This is a fine situation I got us in," trying to imitate Hardy of Laurel and Hardy (a slapstick comedy duo of the 1950s). Then they all laughed. Again, Roy believed he put everything back to normal.

They marched on through very tall grasses, sometimes over their heads. Roy's thick muscular body was made for this type of work. He could lean into the grasses and plow through like a bulldozer. The added weight of Dolly caused his shoes to sink in the soil even farther, and water almost covered his shoes.

The situation alarmed Ross. They could not see where they were because of all the grasses and stunted trees. They were sinking into the ground. The air smelled foul, there were all kinds of bugs and frogs chirping and croaking, and they were being eaten alive by swarms of mosquitoes and other tiny bugs that descended on them.

What if they were doomed to wander in this swamp forever, he worried.

"Roy, can you see the end?"

"No, but it must be just ahead."

The grasses seemed to have gotten taller and thicker. They tugged at Roy's arms and wrapped around his shoes, as if to pull him down to the spongy, wet ground. Roy struggled and had to stop to catch his breath. He set Dolly down. She was content and began searching the ground to see what she could find.

"We can always go back," Ross said and turned around. The grasses had all sprung back up, and there was no trail to follow back to the farmhouse. Now Ross was really agitated and panicking.

Roy wasn't the least bit concerned. He just took a few deep breaths and looked around and said, "This is really cool. Anything could be right next to you, and you wouldn't know it!"

Ross just looked at him.

Just then Dolly stepped between them and exclaimed, "Look at what I found!" holding her hand out. In her hand was a little snake. It was dark green and yellow, striped, and climbed from hand to hand with its forked tongue flicking in and out. "Isn't it cute?"

Both boys took a step back. They were afraid of snakes and opened their eyes up wide. Ross stammered, "That's a snake, Dolly. Put it down, and we'll kill it before it bites you!"

"We'll kill nothing," Roy exclaimed. "There are probably more of them around. Besides it's just a baby. Please put it down."

Dolly looked at it fondly and set it off in the grasses where the boys couldn't find it and hurt it. "Goodbye little snake, goodbye. I like snakes," she said.

Ross was dumbstruck. "Are you serious?"

"Yes," she simply replied, as she scrambled to climb onto Roy's back.

"Give her a boost, Ross."

Ross stepped over to give her a boost up on Roy's back, looking around carefully for more snakes or any creepy crawlers. Just then they heard it: a train.

"Just great," Ross blurted out. "Here we are, stuck in a swamp with weeds over our head, so we can't see the way out, surrounded by snakes, with a little girl who loves them, and now we have a train bearing down on us. Just peachy fine Roy, good job!"

Roy laughed and clapped Ross on the shoulder. "I got us into this, and I'll get us out."

The train came rumbling by sounding like rolling thunder. The boys could just see the tops of the cars. There were two engines, and they were pulling box cars, gondolas, and flat cars with many things tied down. The noise was so loud they couldn't hear each other talk.

Roy got Dolly up on his back and started out with fresh energy. It wasn't long, and they were out of the bog and at the end of their property—the pointy end. They sat down in the grass, too tired to worry about mosquitoes and such.

"Man, that is a really long freight train," Ross shouted over the cacophony of the train. "I'll bet that's why there are two engines."

Roy nodded in agreement. Dolly busied herself looking for snakes and creepy crawlers. The boys kept a wary eye on her.

Finally, the caboose went by, and the brakeman returned their wave.

"How did you know which way to go?" Ross asked Roy.

"It was the train. When it showed up, I knew where we were and which way to go," Roy explained.

"Of course," Ross said.

Dolly said, "Why are we stopping? We can move so much easier in this shorter grass."

"Because we are here; we are at the pointy end," Ross told her.

"This is it?" she asked incredulously, looking around. "This is what we went through all that for?"

"Yep," he answered.

"Why? There is nothing special here."

"We did it because it needed to be done," he replied.

She looked at him questionably.

Roy stood and helped her up. "There are some things that are walls and bar you from entering, or you can make doorways through them. It just needs doing if you are to know what they are all about. We just put a doorway in that wall. We now own that marsh," he told her. Ross nodded in agreement.

"We also have some specific questions that need answering," he added.

"What are they?" she asked.

Ross replied, "We need to know what that marsh is comprised of that is so spongy? What those black birds were? What is in the center of the marsh? It was too thick and soupy to get there on foot and see for ourselves."

"And why is this property shaped like a triangle?" Roy added. "I'd also like to know about the mound at the back of the house and the excavating done between the orchard and the tracks."

"I didn't see those," Dolly said plaintively.

"We were on the tracks, and that is too dangerous for you," Roy said. "This was actually too much for you."

Dolly looked crestfallen.

"You made it though, and it was an adventure," Ross said, ever the protector.

That perked her up.

Roy had already started moving. "Let's cross this fence and head back through the pasture. It is easier."

The trio crossed the fence, being careful not to get caught on the barbs. This fence met the fence that ran past their house. Then it turned ninety degrees and separated the cornfield from the cow pasture. The cows were at the other end of the field, and a couple looked up when they crossed into the pasture. The kids kept a wary eye on them, ready to bolt if these large bovines attacked. They had no experience with cows before and did not know if they were dangerous.

Later that evening, when they told Dad about how cautious they had been; he had roared with laughter.

"They are more afraid of you than you are of them. But if there is a bull with them, stay clear."

"How can you tell them apart?" Roy had asked.

Dad had looked at him like he thought Roy was a moron. "The one without the udders! Are you kidding me?"

"Let's go home," Roy said. "I've had enough marsh adventures."

"No argument here," Ross said. "But I have got one question I need to ask."

"What is it?"

"Promise you won't laugh."

"Of course," Roy said.

"When we were in the swamp did you feel there was someone or something watching us?" Ross asked haltingly.

Before Roy could answer, Dolly piped up. "Of course there was. All kinds of things," she said and then returned to her search.

Both boys gaped at her in surprise.

Roy agreed. "Yes, I felt we were being watched, but that was to be expected. This place is special and strange. There are all kinds of things in that marsh."

Roy looked down at the pasture running along the embankment. It ran up to a copse of thick trees and bushes. It tapered into a line of tall grasses that formed the edge of the pasture. They probably bordered a creek that ran under the railroad tracks and meandered across the countryside. He could not see where it ended. The creek running under the track through the embankment was intriguing. He made a mental note to come back here with Ross and inspect that copse.

Suddenly there was a loud rustling in the reeds behind them, and something sprang out of the marsh! The boys yelped and sprang backward as Bootsie jumped out at them with tongue lolling out, feet covered with mud, and stinking to high heaven!

Dolly laughed so hard she fell down, pointing at them. "Bootsie scared you!"

Bootsie was all over the boys, licking and woofing and wiggling all over.

"She's all covered with burrs again and stinks like the marsh," Ross lamented.

The boys moaned.

"We'll have to deburr her again and wash her all over."

The boys stood up and called for Bootsie and Dolly to head home. They walked back home in the short grass of the pasture, keeping a vigilant eye on the cows at the far end of the field. Dolly, in the middle again, kept looking around at the ground for snakes and such. Bootsie busied herself chasing moths and grasshoppers.

Roy walked right out until he stepped into an enormous pile of cow poop. "Damn it!" he swore, hopping on one foot. "Look out for cow poop!" (They later learned to call them "cow pies").

He sat down and tried to clean his shoe by wiping it on the grass. He got the big chunks off and put it back on, then he diligently tried to clean his hands. He looked up at his brother and sister, who were unsuccessfully trying to suppress grins.

"Hilarious, just hilarious," he snapped at them and then laughed, and they joined in.

They continued home in the mid-afternoon heat, with the sun in their faces and the stink of swamp on them and the odor of cow poop Roy brought to the group. They would have to leave their shoes outside and keep Bootsie tied up outside too until they cleaned and deburred her. She would not like that.

The boys planned what they were going to talk to their dad and mom about this evening. How this discussion went was going to have a big bearing on how their summer went.

There was a lot more at stake than they could imagine! The Triangle had many surprises in store for them!

Watching
Fireflies

TALE NUMBER SIX

POINT OF VIEW

"What I See Depends Which Way I Am Facing."

– The Old Man
(when explaining his diverse points of view on life)

Bill Cheesman turned off State Highway 16 onto Hilltop Road. It was the gravel road leading to the driveway of the truck-farm he had just moved his family to, hoping to escape the polio epidemic. It was terrorizing the cities, especially in the summer months.

It was late afternoon, but the sun was still bright in the sky. He loved the long days of the summer. He was looking forward to getting familiar with the property. He stopped at the railroad crossing and got out to look over the land. The unusual shape of the property intrigued him.

It was a triangle, how peculiar. I wonder why?

It seemed the best place to view the property was up here on the railroad track embankment. He was sure the boys would be up here soon enough. He knew better than to ban them from it. They would only sneak up here, especially his oldest, and that would be dangerous. He would have to teach them how to do it safely. He would also instruct Jean on the safety measures so she could enforce them. Luckily, most of the tracks bordering their property were visible from the house.

He had to admit to himself that he wanted to get back to a farm. Work on the earth, plant, cultivate, grow, and harvest. He had grown up on a farm. His little five-acre plot was a sad excuse for a farm, run down and overgrown, but he would fix that. He was going to keep working in the city at Rex Chain Belt and commute daily. Unfortunately, he would have the sun in his eyes both ways. It was over 40 miles each way, and it took over an hour if everything cooperated. During the shorter days of winter, he would leave and return in the dark.

Another big factor for this relatively remote location was that he would have more control over his family, like his father had. His folks still don't have electricity on the farm. That's the way his father wanted it, and he didn't have neighbors right next door to hassle him. Their farm was located outside of Lafayette, Indiana, on the Wabash River.

He looked out over the neat fields of neighboring farms spread out before him and sighed. Then he got back into his car and drove down the road to his driveway. Turning into his driveway, he stopped in the same spot he had last night when all the lightning bugs filled the night sky. That had been a remarkable sight. He had seen nothing like that before, even when he had been a kid on the farm. He continued down the driveway, noting the sad condition of the orchard and the overgrown little fields. Lots of stuff to do. The tractor in the barn needed a good cleaning, as did the barn itself. He would get the boys to do this cleaning, whether or not they wanted to.

He parked the car at the end of the driveway by the barn. He looked down toward the end of the property beyond the barn. He hadn't really checked out the property before purchasing it and was now surprised that a portion of the property consisted mainly of a marsh. That was disturbing. He would check that all out later. Now he was hungry, and he hoped Jean had supper ready.

He headed across the backyard to the back porch. He noticed the kids had tied up Bootsie outside. She strained at the rope as she barked at him.

"Well, girl, what have you done to deserve this?"

When he got close to her, the smell and state of her coat made it clear why she was not in the house.

"I'll get someone out here to take care of you, girl."

He went up the backstairs to the porch and went in the door. He was in an enclosed porch-like area. This is where one took off muddy shoes and outerwear such as coats. He noted the three pairs of shoes sitting there and the potent smell of marsh mud and cow manure.

This would not do, not do at all!

He took off his shoes that had oil and grit on their soles from the shop floor that he frequented and put on his slippers that he had left there this morning. He walked into the kitchen and Jean turned to him and smiled.

"Dinner is almost ready," she said.

"It may have to wait," he snapped. "Where are the kids?"

Jean was taken aback. "Don't you snap at me," she snapped back.

The evening was off to a great start; she thought.

Bill went into the dining room and yelled out.

"Kids, where are you? Come here at once!"

The boys came down from upstairs and Dolly came from her bedroom down the hall. The boys looked at each other, knowing they were in for it. Dolly smiled brightly and ran to her dad.

"Hi Daddy," she exclaimed excitedly as she hugged him. Dad's scowl melted away as he bent down to hug her back.

"Hi, sweetie."

He stood up and looked at the boys, and his scowl returned.

She may be little, but she knew how to work with Dad and Mom, Roy thought.

"You boys care to explain why Bootsie is tied up outside and is full of burrs and stinks? And why are there three pairs of shoes that are muddy and stink on the back porch?" he irritably demanded.

Roy was instantly angered. He did not like it when Dad just went off on them before hearing what happened. He looked at Ross, who appeared ready to calm things down.

"Dad, we were checking out the land behind the barn and got lost in the tall grasses and reeds. We got muddy before Roy led us out of the marsh." He then laughed. "Roy stepped in cow poop on the way home."

Dolly laughed too and chimed in, "Roy carried me out of the swamp. Bootsie jumped out of the marsh and scared the boys so much they yelled. I also found a snake, but the boys wouldn't let me keep it."

Dad's mood had mellowed, and he looked at Roy, who was quieting down and smiled at Dad.

"We did a lot of exploring this afternoon and this morning, Dad. And we have a lot of questions for you."

"They will have to wait," Dad said, "as will dinner."

"Bootsie needs to be cleaned and deburred, and the shoes need to be cleaned before anything else," he ordered. "Get cracking!"

"That will be too long. Dinner will be ruined," their mom complained.

"I'll help them, and speed it up. Give us 20 minutes, okay?" Dad offered.

"Okay," she said, "and if I can, I'll help too."

Dad changed clothes, and then he and the kids went out the back door and grabbed the shoes on the way outside. Roy ran over to get Bootsie, who ruffed at him in chastisement.

Dad took Bootsie and began crooning softly to her and told Dolly to help get Bootsie cleaned up. He instructed the boys to clean the shoes.

"We're all hungry, so let's get cracking on this." That was one of his favorite sayings -- "get cracking."

Dolly started getting the burrs out, and Dad got a hose and started washing the dog off at the same time. As expected, that combination resulted in both people as wet as the dog and the resulting laughing and barking got Mom out on the stoop. There she stood with hands on hips and a smile that she could not suppress. The boys got into the act when they borrowed the hose to clean the shoes.

"Do I have to come down there?" she warned.

"Oh yes, come down and help." Dad challenged with hose in hand.

"Oh, no you don't," she laughed and went back inside, yelling over her shoulder "You're going to have a cold dinner."

Just like that, the mood lightened.

They finished the cleaning, dried Bootsie and the shoes, and headed inside. They all scurried to change into dry clothing—the boys into T-shirts and shorts, and Dolly into a dress, Dad slacks and a long sleeve shirt. Dad seldom wore anything more casual than that.

Mom had been keeping the dinner warm and now hurried to serve it in the dining room.

They all dug into the meal. Mom had made their first meal in the new home special. Her special meatloaf, mashed potatoes with lots of butter, green snap beans, and pan gravy. There were also Bisquick biscuits that they all loved. Dad told them about his day at work. He was in quality control and hoping to get into the Tech Center they were going to establish. He had been with Rex Chain Belt as a government inspector since 1941. During the war he volunteered for the Army and was directed to the government inspection corps, the Inspector General's office. He had an equivalent rank of lieutenant. His future father-in-law was his superior and equivalent to a captain.

His engineering degree in metallurgy made him perfect to serve as quality control for all the materials being employed in the manufacture of arms. Specifically, cannons. He was assigned to Rex Chain Belt and given responsibility for the calibration of gauges and tooling to produce the 105-millimeter howitzers.

The boys grew up with talk about the material chemistry, hardness, malleability, and application around the dinner table. Using Brinell and Rockwell classifications, reviewing blueprints and failure analysis were commonplace. The boys developed a very early familiarity with these items. When they entered the job market, they had a tremendous advantage over their peers.

The boys couldn't bring up the things they wanted to speak about until Dad was through. No one could complain. If the evening ran out, so be it. So, after the dinner was through and plates, pots, and pans cleared away, the boys hoped to talk about the things they were excited about. But Dad had several items he wanted to get cleared up, and they would have to wait. Roy's limited patience was wearing very thin, and he was having to bite his lip to maintain silence. His Dad could see that and seemed to take a perverted pleasure in drawing things out. If Roy lost his patience, he would be in trouble.

Dad began with a loud belch, "Good dinner Jean, very good." He got comfortable and began, "There are a few things that need to be done, boys. These are important to me, and I will not take any backtalk."

Nice way to start, Dad, Roy thought. *Get everybody on your side.*

Bill felt good about his situation. He was in control, and no one was next door to interfere.

"I am planning to use the tractor to get this land back into shape. It's a real mess, dirty, and needs lubrication. I want you guys to get the cleaning done tomorrow. I'll set out the soap and rags and brushes for you tonight. I'll also move the tractor out so you can get to it tomorrow. Understood?"

He continued, "While the tractor is out, it is a great time to clean up the barn stall. You should be able to get that done along with the tractor."

Dolly said, "I'll help too."

Roy saw Ross getting ready to chime up to say they had already thought about doing that. He jumped in before Ross could speak up. "You want to have us spend the whole day doing chores and no time for ourselves?"

"That is correct, son."

"What about helping us on a couple of issues then, Dad?"

"What are they?"

Now Roy looked at his brother, giving him the floor.

Ross took the cue.

"We found out they shaped the property like a triangle, and want to name the place The Triangle, Okay? We also were wondering why it's shaped like a triangle."

Bill and Jean looked at each other and shrugged.

"Okay boys," he said, "The Triangle it is. I'll get a sign made for the end of the driveway. There is also a numinous quality to The Triangle. I am curious about the shape as well. "

Everyone looked at him questionably.

"A mysterious, supernatural, or spiritual quality, that's what numinous means," he explained. "I'll look up the property history. What else, boys?"

Ross looked at his brother and got an Okay nod to proceed.

"We were up on the railroad tracks this morning and ..."

"You were where?!" Dad roared and glared at his wife. "Did you know about this, Jean?"

Jean glared back and said "Yes."

"And you didn't tell me?" he snapped at her.

"No," she snapped right back.

Roy knew this exchange had to stop before it deteriorated into a screaming argument that would go on all night like it had on prior occasions. Only this time there would not be the built-in restraint that neighbors right next door with open windows—a benefit the city offered that this open country location did not. He was afraid of just how far they could go. Dolly was quaking, and Ross was looking down and fidgeting; he was ready to bolt. The entire plan was going to crash and burn if Roy didn't do something.

"Dad, please listen to me. We didn't just rush up to the tracks," Roy blurted out and interrupted his parents, risking severe punishment. "We used the way you told us about how to be safe on railroad tracks." Roy looked directly into his dad's eyes. "Remember?"

Their dad looked perplexed. "You told us to feel the railroad tracks for vibration. We can feel a train coming long before we would hear it or see it."

Their father started to calm down and said, "I'm glad you followed my advice, but the embankment is high and covered in brambles. Getting out of the way is tough."

"We also made sure we had a safe way down if we had to get down in a hurry, Dad. There are some small game trails up the side that allow us to get down without getting chewed up." He decided not to share the part about the rabbit in the adventure, in the interest of simplicity.

Bill looked at his wife and said, "You should have told me about their venturing up on the tracks." He said this calmly, not snapping like he had before.

Roy held his breath and hoped his mom would calm down and not snap in response.

"I didn't have time to, Bill. I would have when I had an opportunity," she said calmly.

Catastrophe avoided, Roy thought, and breathed a sigh of relief.

Their father turned to the boys and sternly, "You know you should not have ventured up there without me saying 'okay,' even after I taught you about how to be safe when on the tracks."

Both boys piped in, "We are sorry, Dad."

"We just sort of wound up there as we explored The Triangle. We're sorry Dad. Mom yelled at us when she saw us up there, and we came right down." Ross further added.

Bill sighed, his flash of anger gone, and he felt his control solidly in place.

"Okay, don't go back up there until I show you the proper safety conduct, alright?"

Both boys nodded their agreement.

"Jean, from now on I'll ask you if there is anything I should know when I get home first thing." He smiled and nodded, satisfied with himself.

Ross said, "Dad, there are a couple of other things we need your help with."

Dad nodded his okay, "What are they?"

Ross looked at his brother and Roy stepped up. "There is a mound behind the house that looks man-made. Can you check it out for us?"

Dad nodded his agreement.

Ross added, "We need to know about the marsh area at the end of the property. It's weird."

Their father made notes on his little notepad he always carried.

"Anything else?" he was warming up to this. They impressed him with their keen interest and observation skills.

Dolly piped up, "Don't forget about the snakes."

Dad smiled gently at his pretty little girl. "What did it look like, sweetheart?"

"It was green and pretty. I liked it and wanted to keep it, but the boys wouldn't let me."

"It was dark green and yellow striped," Ross added.

"Hmm, sounds like a garter snake. They are harmless," Dad said.

"But they are snakes!" Mom exclaimed.

Dad chuckled, "They are okay, they keep after the rodents and other pests."

"Yippee," Dolly exclaimed.

Mom just shook her head, "Not in the house, young lady."

Dolly's excitement would not be dampened.

Dad stood up. "I want to walk around the property before it gets dark. Jean, you want to join me?"

Jean got up to go with him. "You children behave while we are gone."

This started a routine that was one of the few times Mom and Dad showed any kind of closeness between them.

After they had left, Dolly went back to her room. Roy turned to Ross and said, "That worked out slick. I just learned that it is smart to stay silent until you learn what Dad wants and make it work for you if you can. You can always throw a fit if nothing works. We already had planned on cleaning the tractor and garage before Dad ordered us to. Now he thinks he got us to obey against our will, and we got him to help us in exchange for something we were already going to do."

"Yeah," Ross agreed.

Later that evening, after dark, Dad and Mom came in and told the kids to come out and see the fireflies. They all went out the front. Dad turned off the porch lights, and they walked around back by the mound and gazed and the wondrous sight of what seemed to be a sea of tiny flashing lights in the dark night. Dolly ran out amongst them with her arms outstretched and head thrown back.

"Look at all the fairies," she exclaimed.

Dad corrected her, "Those are small flying beetles."

"Not all of them. Watch the ones that don't flash. They are the fairies, and they are singing softly," she laughed. "As long as they are here, we are safe."

Roy studied the lights. It was difficult to focus and any one of them when all were flashing, but some of them appeared to be a steady light, darting around the night. And if he really listened closely, he thought he could just make out a soft humming sound.

Ross could hear them, too. "I see them and hear what could be singing. It is beautiful. You must stand very quiet."

Dad and Mom scoffed a bit and said, "That's nice sweetheart."

Roy thought about that. *It seems the older you get, the harder it is to be quiet enough to see the fairies and hear them sing. That's too bad. Maybe if you practice enough and hung out with young kids, you can be able to see and hear them again. I wonder …*

TALE NUMBER SEVEN
— EPISODE ONE OF TWO —

FINDING SHECHEM,
A REFUGE IN THE GLADE.

"In order to make a man or boy covet a thing, it is only necessary to make the thing difficult to attain."
– Mark Twain.

"… my God, my rock, in whom I take refuge."
– Psalms 18:2 (ESV)

As they gazed down the tracks, Roy and Ross stood on the railroad crossing, shielding their eyes from the bright morning sun. There wasn't a cloud in the azure blue summer sky. Roy looked down at his wet jeans and shoes. Instead of taking the driveway and Hilltop Road, they had cut across the field and through the sad little orchard. Even though the tall grass had been cut in the field and orchard, the loose-cut grass still laid there waiting to dry out and to be gathered up. The dew was on it, and it had soaked the lower legs of their jeans and sneakers. Their sneakers were not only wet but covered with seeds and chafe.

Mom is going to be upset if she sees the new Keds high-tops like this. She said she spent a lot of money on them, Roy thought.

They had gotten to see the actual fit of the shoes through the X-Ray machine; and watched their skeleton toes wiggle. (The Old

Man remembered these machines being removed after the 1960s because of the exposure to radiation emissions.)

Ross was looking down as well.

"I think they'll dry, and we can brush the seeds and stuff off," he said.

"I sure hope so," Roy said.

The boys looked back up and surveyed the landscape from the raised vantage point of the railroad crossing. Dad had cleared them to be on the tracks, and he had charged Mom with seeing that they followed their rules of safety. They had to get her permission to be on the tracks.

Big deal, Roy thought.

He looked back at the grass they had walked through. He and Ross had cut it with a scythe and a sickle. Once they had gotten the hang of the proper swinging motion and how to keep the tool sharp, it went smoothly, and it was even fun. He had learned how to keep an edge on the device from his dad. Now his pocketknife was sharp as a razor.

Bootsie was with them, and they were concerned she might frighten the little cottontail rabbit that usually joined them when they were up here. They had tried to sneak off without her noticing them, but Bootsie, ever ready for an adventure, spotted them sneaking off and bounded over to join them, and as usual, her long coat was becoming loaded with burrs and stickers. Hopefully, they could get Dolly to help remove them —if they could get her away from her growing collection of snakes. Roy shivered every time he visioned her affinity for reptiles.

Something out there haunted Roy with the feeling of vulnerability and exposure to evil things. He could sense something that could consume him and dominate his life and those around him. He had felt this the night they fled the city and on the first day on The Triangle. It was not the virus that drove them to the farm that he feared; it was something else. Something that had possibly created the virus.

The boys' goal for this morning was to walk the tracks to where they would be across from the peat bog area. Roy was driven to get to the center of this peat bog that made up the back portion of their truck farm. He sensed it might be a place of safety, of strength, of power to stand against whatever it was out there that he sensed and dreaded.

From the ground level, he could hear the frogs croaking, birds chirping, and something splashing. The sweet yet fetid odor of the decaying vegetation was strangely pleasant. Sometimes accompanied by Bootsie and Dolly, Roy and Ross had repeatedly attempted to reach the center of the peat bog. They tried approaching it from different angles, only to be stymied over and over.

Roy led them on a straight course using a compass. He needed a compass because the reeds were so high, he could not reference any landmarks. In addition, these reeds sprang back up after they passed over them, so they could not reference a way back out. This was very unsettling, even scary. They got the feeling of being swallowed up and never getting out of the peat bog. That's when the odor became putrid, and the mosquitoes and gnats swarmed over them. It became so stifling hot that they became drenched in sweat, and breathing was hard. The insect noise, frogs croaking, and birds squawking became deafening. He was sure he could hear voices whispering, beckoning him closer.

No matter how much they walked, they could not reach the center. It seemed the bog was never-ending and wanted to possess them. It was a seductive feeling but frightening at the same time. Roy knew that Ross and Dolly would panic if they were left alone out here, and it took all the courage he could muster to maintain some sense of order and not to go stumbling off in different directions trying to get out of the nightmare.

Roy would gather everyone up, hold hands and go silent, squeezing the others' hands while huddling close together for a while, and the deafening crescendo of squawks and croaks would quiet down, and their breathing would become more manageable. The sweating and swarms of bugs continued, but the kids steadied. Roy would turn his back on the beckoning center and slowly, methodically, walk away from it. In a short matter of time, they would emerge from the peat bog at the barbed wire fence and cross it into the neighbor's pasture. Everything returned to normal, and they sat and looked at each other with large questioning eyes until Bootsie leaped out from the reeds and startled them. They laughed and rolled around, wrestling with the dog and each other, acting as if nothing had happened, but they were uneasy deep inside for several hours until the memory faded.

Roy needed to find a place of refuge, a sanctuary where he could feel safe and free. He would return to the peat bog again.

He was going to map a route to the center of the peat bog using the vantage point of the height of the railroad embankment. He planned to walk down the tracks until he was across from the peat bog. The height of the embankment should allow him to see the center and reference it to compass settings.

They looked down at the tracks, and, sure enough, the small rabbit appeared from the brambles and sat alongside the tracks. It thumped its foot as usual. Bootsie spied it right away and went trotting off towards it. Ross called her back, but she would pay no attention to him and headed straight toward the rabbit. They were sure the rabbit would dash away down the embankment, and that would be the last they would see of their companion when the dog was with them. But it did not bolt, and when the dog got up to the rabbit, they touched their noses and then sat next to each other, looking at the boys.

The boys looked at each other in wonderment.

"This isn't natural," Ross stammered, his eyes big with amazement. "It can't be happening."

"It is happening, and maybe it is natural," his brother responded, staring at the odd pair sitting together. "Maybe everything is supposed to get along. Maybe rabbits and dogs and people are supposed to get along. Maybe it is only here on The Triangle, or it is just a weird dog and rabbit. I don't know, but it is cool, ultra-cool. Come on, let's get going." He started down the tracks toward the peat bog.

Ross followed, shaking his head in disbelief. *I don't know whether to laugh or scream,* he said to himself.

As the boys approached the odd pair, they turned and led down the tracks, one hopping and the other ambling alongside it.

The boys stopped when they were approximately across from the center of the peat bog. Their peculiar pair of escorts also stopped and faced the peat bog, gazing at it. Ross noted they lay their ears back and their noses twitching. It was clear they were ill at ease here.

Roy looked over at the peat bog. From up here, it was not very imposing. The peat bog made up the lower end of the farm, equal to one city block. It made little sense that he could not get to the center, no sense at all. Then he had an idea.

He turned to Ross and instructed him to stay up on the train tracks while he went down the embankment and walked to the center of the peat bog. It was strange that from up here, he could not see any pond in the middle, but down below, he heard all kinds of splashing. He knew Ross didn't hear it.

"If you stay up here and I go down to the bog, you can see me from up here and give directions if I go off course."

Ross nodded agreement, apparently happy not to be the one going down into the slimy, stinky, scary peat bog.

The sun was getting higher in the morning sky and getting hot on the skin, and the humidity was rising. A typical summer day in southeastern Wisconsin, hot and humid, and yet clear and bright—overall, pleasant.

"You are going to get chewed up in those brambles going down the embankment, big brother," Ross warned.

"I know, Roy agreed, "but I've got to figure out why I can't get to the center of this stupid little peat bog. It is driving me crazy."

With that, Roy started down one of the small animal trails that proliferated the railroad embankment.

He went slowly, trying not to get hung up on any of the nasty two-inch-long thorns. He twisted and turned, grabbing onto bushes where he could. The embankment was very steep, and he crabbed slowly down it. He yelped when a thorn pierced his skin like a nail.

Neither animal had followed him. Bootsie sat with her head cocked to one side, as if trying to figure out what one of her young masters was trying to do. The rabbit was nervously twitching as though ready to run for it.

Ross looked at and thought, *either of them is more intelligent than he is.*

He yelled down to Roy, "Maybe there isn't a center."

"What?" came the reply.

Ross cupped his hands around his mouth and yelled again, "I said, maybe there isn't a center."

Bootsie barked in agreement, and the rabbit thumped its foot.

Roy was at the bottom and yelled back up, "Don't be silly. That can't be."

"Just saying," Ross yelled back and shrugged his shoulders.

Roy just shook his head in dismissal.

"Ready?" he yelled up at Ross.

Ross gave him a thumbs up.

Roy readied himself to enter the peat bog. He took a reading on his compass, looked back at Ross, and started in, immediately smelling the sweet, fetid smell of the decomposing vegetation, and the insects swarmed up to swirl around and bite him. Roy had planned ahead and wore long sleeves to protect his arms, but his face and neck were vulnerable. Once again, he was struck by the chirping, croaking, buzzing, and inexplicable splashing of an unseen pond.

Roy heard rather than saw the Red-winged blackbirds take flight as he roused them. They cried out in anger at him as they flew away from their nests. He was careful not to disturb any more nests, pushing his way through the reeds and bushes that towered over his head. It was only by keeping a watchful eye on the compass that he was confident he was going in a straight line. It was getting hotter, and the smell was going from cloyingly sweet to nauseating.

Once again, he thought he could hear unintelligible whispers.

When he stopped and listened intently, he felt he could make out laughter, then screams of terror. When he moved forward, the sounds would get slightly louder. Roy made his way further into the bog, clinging to the thought that if he could get to the center, he would be able to understand the voices, and it would be cooler and pleasant by the pond with all the frogs and whatever splashing in it, if he could only get there!

Then he heard Ross yelling at him, so he stopped and turned around to listen to him better.

"Stop walking in circles," was yelled at him. "What do you think you are doing?"

Roy yelled back, "I am not. I'm walking in a straight line."

"No, you are not." Ross did not use the consonant for emphasis.

Ross could not see Roy, but from the vantage point of the railroad embankment he knew where Roy was and where he was going by the waving and shaking of the reeds and bushes as Roy brushed them aside. Roy had been going in circles for the last few minutes. Ross could not understand why. The peat bog area was not that big. It formed a right triangle with its base starting a little way from the barn and continued to the pointy end of the property, a little less than a city block. That made it about as big as one half a city block, not that big. Certainly not big enough to get lost and turned around in, especially with a compass.

Ross yelled down, "Try again."

He kept a lookout for trains and mad birds that Roy had unintentionally scattered. The sun was burning down, and he wasn't comfortable with the dog and bunny sitting side by side looking at him when he yelled to Roy, then turning their attention back to the peat bog and the jostled reeds and bushes. It just wasn't natural. Dogs were supposed to chase rabbits, and he had seen Bootsie do it before with other rabbits in the yard. He knew this wasn't the same rabbit because it had one ear that sort of flopped to one side.

Roy was getting upset, but he wouldn't let this little peat bog scare him. His shoes were covered in slimy goop and would need significant cleaning, as would he. He yelled back up to his brother that he was ready to start again.

Roy got himself squared away with the compass and began stumbling through the jungle of reeds and bushes again. Biting insects swarmed over him anew, and he was soaked with sweat from the heat and immersed in the disgusting smell that had to be more than decomposing vegetation. But the splashing and sounds of frogs and birds and faint whispers compelled him to keep trying. The whispers promised he would find a sanctuary at the center. He could share a haven with his family, and that they would always respect and defer to him. He had to get to the center!

Was that Ross yelling at him? He wasn't sure; there were so many other sounds, it was confusing. Roy didn't want to stop. But then he heard Bootsie barking also, so he stopped and turned around.

"What in the heck do you want now? I must almost be there," Roy yelled up and Ross.

"You're going in circles again."

"I can't be," Roy screamed back in anger, looking down at his compass.

"You sure are," Ross yelled back. "You're not even near one half of the way in."

"I'll show him," Roy muttered angrily to himself.

He took off his cap and pulled down one of the tallest reeds near him. He put his cap on the reed and slowly released it. The hat waved on the reed like a banner.

"Can you see that?" he yelled up to his brother.

"Yes," he heard.

"Okay, I'm coming back up to see for myself," he yelled and started back the way he had come, referring to his compass.

He stepped out of the reeds way too quickly to have been as far into the peat bog as the time struggling forward dictated. He scrambled up the embankment, paying little regard to the thorns and briars. In his anger, this disregard of the thorns and brambles left him scratched and bloodied. These wounds, coupled with the bites incurred while straining in the peat bog, would make him miserable that night.

"Now show me how I didn't head straight into the peat bog. Show me, dammit," he lashed out.

He was sweating profusely, and blood ran down his arms and soaked his torn shirt. Even his face was bleeding in several places. Ross didn't say a word; he just pointed to the peat bog.

There, not over 30 feet into the peat bog, was his hat bobbing up and down on the branch.

"How c-c-c-can that be," he stammered. "I-I-I-I used the compass. You got to b-b-b-believe me," he stuttered. Roy was shaken that he only had gotten that far. He watched in disbelief as a male Red-winged blackbird dove in and snatched his hat with its sharp bill and disappeared into the reeds.

Roy swore, and Ross laughed so hard he had to sit down. Bootsie came running over to join in the excitement, woofing and jumping upon them. The rabbit observed them from a distance with what one could call a dubious look, if that were possible, for a rabbit.

[*The Old Man fondly remembered the little rabbit who had been his companion while on the adventures on the embankment. He never saw it elsewhere, although there were many rabbits in the area. None of them had that cast to their ear as it did. He often wondered why it never showed up anywhere else.*]

Ross had sat on a railroad track and now got quiet and put his hand up for silence.

"Train coming," he jumped up and started back towards the crossing at a fast trot. Roy and Bootsie followed without hesitation. The rabbit shot down the embankment. He had no problem navigating the brambles. They protected him from predators like hawks, owls, coyotes, and foxes, just like Br'er Rabbit in the old movie *Song of the South*.

The brothers also would have to dive down the embankment if the train got close. They hoped they wouldn't have to; the briars and brambles would tear them up. Roy already had a dose of the pain the embankment could dish out and didn't want another. Just then, they heard the train horn behind them, and they ran. Roy looked over his shoulder and saw the train's light way back in the distance.

"We have plenty of time, "he gasped between breaths.

Just then, having taken his eyes off where he was going, he stumbled and fell on the railroad ties. He tumbled and bounced between them, only to jump up to his feet and keep running. He now had splinters and bruises added to his wounds. Mom was going to throw a fit when she saw him, and with good reason.

They made it to the crossing in plenty of time. The train wouldn't rumble through the crossing until the boys were already down Hilltop Road and starting along their driveway. As they walked along, Roy, with an increasing limp, recalled the misadventure in the peat bog. That ordeal still rattled him. The rancid smell of the peat bog, mixed with the odor of sweat, clung to him. Roy could not smell the sweet aroma of fresh-cut hay blown along by a soft breeze because of it. The sweat continued to run down his arms, legs, and into his eyes. The sun was high, and the temperature had risen with it. The humidity was soaring.

"I can't figure it out," he lamented. "I know I was following the compass and going straight. I just know it." He shook his head back and forth and looked over at his brother.

Ross's eyes were looking straight ahead, deep in thought. He turned to look at the railroad embankment and the train going by. It was visible over the field, and he watched the double engines pulling a long string of cars. Roy and Bootsie also stopped. The train's rhythmic clickety-clack sound as it rolled over the joint in the rails could be heard way over here, and it was so quiet otherwise.

"I wonder where all those cars come from and where they are going?" Ross mused.

"Don't know, but it sure would be a grand adventure to hitch a ride on one and watch the country go by," Roy answered.

They watched until the caboose came by and waved at the caboose man. He waved back.

"That has got to be the best job in the world. I want to do that when I grow up," Ross said wistfully.

"No, the best job would be the owner of the train company because you could go anywhere you wanted to, whenever you wanted."

"No, I don't believe so. Too much work. I want to sit back there and watch the world roll by," Ross retorted.

The boys resumed their walk home. Their bellies were rumbling with hunger. That and the straight-up sun told them it was lunchtime. Bootsie had given up on them and taken off home as they watched the train.

When they walked up onto the front porch, their mom was waiting for them. She had grown used to them coming home full of burrs, caked in dirt, and smelling to high heaven. She didn't like it, but she accepted it.

"Take off those stinky clothes, and put on these fresh ones," and passed them the clothes she had gotten down in anticipation of this. "Your dog will need cleaning before lunch and look at your shoes. You better hope they clean up!"

"Aw, come on, Mom, we're hungry," they moaned.

"Nope, clean bodies, clean clothes, clean dog, then eat," was the firm answer.

"I'll help," said Dolly. "Then, after lunch, I can show you the new snake I caught in the barn."

The two boys winced as Dolly led Bootsie away. The boys washed up and changed clothes. Their little sister's fondness for snakes was eerie, but she certainly helped the boys out when they needed her. They loved her, but the large difference in ages (she was five years younger than Roy) made it difficult to have common interests.

The hose water was cold and refreshing, especially for Roy after his trying experience in the peat bog and the thorny trips up and down the embankment. Mom made them clean and changed them outside after their adventures. They stacked the dirty clothes on the porch and went to help Dolly with Bootsie.

Tomorrow would be a fresh start at finding the sanctuary in the peat bog, if that is what is enticing him. Yes, tomorrow ...

The Glade = culvert
under Railroad Track

TALE NUMBER SEVEN
— EPISODE TWO OF TWO —

A REFUGE IN THE GLADE

"Don't let yesterday use up too much of today."
– Will Rogers

The mid-morning sun finds the brothers sitting side by side on the railroad track. They were staring at the peat bog. Bootsie and the rabbit were a little further down the tracks, mimicking the boys' posture. The odor from the peat bog's composting vegetation drifted upward on a warm summer breeze. Ross turned up his nose at the smell while Roy found the potent smell strangely seductive. This attraction bothered him. It wasn't natural. Bootsie sneezed, and the rabbit shook its head. Roy stood up and pointed to the bog.

"I should at least get my hat back. What do you think?"

He turned and looked down at Ross. Ross looked up at him and shook his head and laughed.

"It's gone for good, dear brother. Lost in the bog's tangle, gone forever. You're lucky your head wasn't in it at the time the attack blackbird assaulted your hat." He guffawed, holding his belly.

Bootsie barked, and the rabbit thumped its hind leg.

"Ok, okay," Roy said, holding his hands out, palms up in surrender. He was laughing as well. He walked over and sat down beside his brother.

"All kidding aside, Ross, I feel responsible for the family having to run away and hide. It is my fault."

"I know you do," Ross said quietly, "but it is not your fault. You had nothing to do with the polio virus. You didn't make it happen."

"Yeah, but I am the one who wouldn't stay in the backyard. I kept sneaking out and going down the alley to visit friends. That was stupid. It was all about me, and now look at us."

"Okay, but what has that got to do with the bog and this magical center that only you can hear or smell?" Ross asked while scratching a mosquito bite. "These bugs are starting awful early today," he added.

"Yeah, you're right," Roy agreed, also scratching a bite. "They are early, and it is boiling hot for this time of day."

"I imagine there is a cool place at the bog's center," he continued, "without bugs and only fish and frogs, no snakes, that I could discover for us. To make up for my screw-up that got us stuck out here. We could swim and fish and catch frogs. Only you and me would know about it. It would be our hideout."

Ross was silent and just looked at Roy.

"Hey, you're my brother, my big brother." Ross replied softly. "I always know you are leading and looking out for me, and I have your back, always." He put his hand on Roy's shoulder and Roy just stared at the bog and shook his head.

"I can't understand why I couldn't get to the center. I did everything right. How could I possibly end up walking in circles?"

"That's because there is no center like you imagine it. You'll always go in circles trying to get to a place that doesn't exist," Ross adamantly stated. "This place is weird," he added.

"Weird or special," Roy mused, a distant look in his eyes. "This place is special, maybe even magical," Roy exclaimed.

Ross rolled his eyes. "Here we go again."

Then they both laughed and stood up. Roy looked over at their animal companions and said, "Look at them. If that isn't special, I don't know what is."

(The Old Man smiled as he recalled the bond of love and trust he and his brother once had. They were spiritually inseparable, looking out

for each other. So close that most of the time they didn't need to speak. They knew what was required and did it. Two boys, then young men, could have been unstoppable.)

The dog and rabbit got up, and they looked ready for an adventure. Bootsie shook her coat and woofed her agreement. The rabbit sort of hippity hopped a little dance.

Ross put his hands on his head and moaned, "This is not right, it is really weird," and chuckled.

Roy, with hands on hips, looked around and said, "We've looked at everything but that small bunch of trees there at the end of The Triangle, the pointy end. Let's check that out. We've wasted enough time looking back. Let's move ahead."

He started down the tracks toward the copse of trees.

Ross hesitated. "It's not even our property," he exclaimed, "this is going too far."

"Nothing is too far, brother. Watch our back," Roy said over his shoulder. "Come on, let's go!"

Ross gave up. Roy had completely erased the issues of the bog, turned the page, and began the creation of another adventure.

As they walked, Ross recalled last night's activities.

Their dad had been very late for dinner, something to do with a "tempering" process done incorrectly and a bunch of parts ruined. They hadn't finished eating until dark, so there was no time for family talk. Mom and Dad went for their traditional stroll around the property. He and Roy, along with Dolly and Bootsie, went out to sit on the mound and wait for the fireflies to appear. Fewer and fewer of them showed up each night as their season waned. Dolly claimed there were still fairies in amongst the lightning bugs, and she could hear them.

Ross had thanked Dolly for helping deburr Bootsie, and Roy told her that her new snake was especially pretty. It was a bright red and white banded and about 12 inches long. She had told them it was an eastern milk snake—harmless.

Their dad had gotten her a reference book on Wisconsin snakes for her to identify the different snakes she came across. She would also go on about all the habits of the snake in question, and on and on.

"What are you feeding them?" Roy had asked.

"I give them ants and grasshoppers, but they don't seem to want them."

"Why don't you let the oldest ones go free and replace them with new ones? They are wild things, after all," Ross had suggested.

Dolly cocked her head and considered this.

"Okay, if you'll help me."

"We'll do that," Ross said, and Roy nodded his head in agreement.

Roy's loud exclamation snapped Ross back to the present.

They were standing above the copse, and what lay before them was indeed special. The normal railroad embankment was covered in briars and bramble, impenetrable except for small game trails. The portion that was in front of them was clearly different. The briars and brambles gave way to lush flowering bushes and grasses. It was festooned with what looked like small sunflowers that were yellow and purple, and red and white blooms resembling roses, all were soft and lush. This patch of flora was about one hundred feet wide at the bottom of the embankment and came to a point at their feet on top of the embankment.

Ross was stunned and realized he was looking at another triangle. They were at the top of it, and it spread out equally from there, like a pyramid. Beautiful trees hid the bottom with a white bark that was sort of peeling. He could hear running water, birds chirping, insects buzzing, and frogs croaking. Was he going crazy and hearing imaginary things like Roy was?

"Do you hear that?" Roy cried out. "Do you hear that, brother? Come on, let's get down there and check it out. I think we found our hideout."

With that exclamation, he started down the embankment, which was easy without all the briars and brambles. Bootsie was right behind him and the rabbit, while keeping its distance, had started down as well.

Ross shook his head. Roy was just like Dad said: "When he feels froggy he jumps." He never thinks it through, like what may be at the bottom of this part of the embankment. Roy knew he always had Ross bringing up the rear and keeping the escape options open. So down he went, following the trail Roy had made.

When he got to the bottom, he stood alongside Roy, and looked around in awe. It was like a fairytale place. The air was cool and sweet smelling. The clear water journeyed under the railroad tracks through a large steel pipe, a continuation of the creek from the other side. When it left the pipe, it tumbled down some rocks and made a trickling, bubbling sound. The water had formed a small pond, about 10 feet across, then it exited the pond about 20 feet further on and continued its path through the fields to wherever creeks end. The tall grasses that formed a tunnel-like facade along its waterway almost hid from view the continuation of the creek. The boys dubbed it "The Hidden Creek." During the high-water runoffs in the spring, the fast-flowing water had carried rocks through the pipe, adding to the small waterfall and carving out the pond.

The trees grew up around the pond and down the creek for a short distance. They grew close together and along with the grasses and bushes; they enclosed the area around the pond, creating a small private glade concealed from the outside world. They formed a canopy overtop that allowed dabbled patches of sunlight through but would deflect most of the rain when it came. It was like a small woodland chapel, complete with a choir of bird songs accompanied by the drone of insects and the bass of croaking frogs.

Ross's mouth was open. "Oh my," he uttered.

Roy smiled broadly and clapped his hands together. This was indeed the sanctuary Roy had been desperately searching for. He dubbed it the "Glade." And it was enchanting, almost haunting in its simple, clean beauty. Grown wild, free of destruction or shaping by humans or large animals. Its unfettered growth is dense with greenery and quiet. This barrier of trees and tall grasses absorbed outside sounds, leaving this place so silent one could hear what was being said on the inside of one's spirit. Mystical tales and folklore were about places like this. Storied supernatural and enchanting creatures would dwell in a place like this if they existed. Dolly's fairies would live in the pipe tunnel or the crevices created by the askew rocks.

"Brother, this is the sanctuary. When we are here, we can be anyone, anywhere, at any time," Roy said emphatically. His blue-gray eyes, instead of their normal hard appearance, were dreamy- looking.

"This is what I was looking for. Here we are finally safe."

Bootsie began barking, and the rabbit started hopping all around.

"Apparently not safe for dragonflies," Ross said as he stared across the pond.

He started down along the pond to where it exited and jumped over the four-foot width. Roy followed, not yet sure what was going on, but his "pack" was upset.

"Look," Ross said, pointing to a very large black and yellow spider. "Man, that thing is big —big and ugly."

Bootsie was going nuts, and the little rabbit about had a meltdown. The spider was showy and big enough to be threatening to most people. There was a large, beautiful dragonfly with an iridescent blue body and shiny black wings tangled in the web. The web differed from other spider webs that the boys were familiar with. There was a large spring-like structure down the middle of the web. While the spider was heading toward the captured dragonfly, the dragonfly did not seem to be scared. It was not struggling, but it was alive. Roy could see it breathing. It seemed to wait calmly to be rescued.

Roy grabbed a rock and made ready to bash the spider. Now the dragonfly was upset. It thrashed around. The spider stopped and scuttled back up the web.

"Wait!" Ross shouted.

He grabbed Roy's arm to stop him. Then the spider scuttled back to the dragonfly and released it from the web.

Roy was amazed.

"How did you know to do that?" Roy asked.

"I don't know," Ross answered. "But I remembered Dad telling us, "A man who wants to live and thrive must let the little spiders run alive.""

"I remember that." Roy looked at the spider hiding in a corner of its web. "This place is a place of peace, and there is to be no killing here," Roy said firmly. "Thanks for stopping me, Ross." He put his arm on Ross's shoulder.

Just then, the dragonfly came back and landed on Roy's finger when he extended it to the dragonfly.

Roy brought the insect close to his eyes and studied it intently. It was beautiful. Its long, blue iridescent body shone and reflected the light. Its wings were a solid dark black. Roy had never seen any dragonfly like it before. After a few moments, he passed it to Ross.

Ross also studied it up close. The insect didn't seem to mind the closeness at all, and in fact, seemed to study them at the same time.

The dragonfly finally lifted off and flew over by the rest of the pack, Bootsie, and the rabbit.

Roy, with his hands on his hips, chuckled and said, "Most guys have dragons and wolves as their mystical sidekicks. We have one old dog, a tiny, floppy-eared rabbit, and a dragonfly."

Ross then reminded him, "Remember what you said: 'In here, we can be anyone, anywhere, at any time.'"

"That's right, we can," Roy agreed. "Let's sit by the pond for a while. We're going to have to go home pretty soon for lunch."

The boys jumped back to the other side of the pond and sat in the grass by its edge. The animal contingent of the pack lined up opposite them on the other side of the pond. The life in The Glade and the pond returned to its normal rhythm. The clear pond water allowed them to see small minnows swimming around and the occasional crayfish darting furtively here and there. The crayfish were funny because they scuttled backwards, keeping their pinchers at the ready. There were tiny snails, frogs and water bugs all living is this pond.

Grasshoppers and crickets went about their own business. Flies and other flying bugs buzzed around The Glade.

The boys laid back and rested. There was a special silence here. A soothing silence that allowed them, especially Roy, to hear the voices inside of them. The voices that he had not heard before and wasn't sure he wanted to hear them now.

"Right now, a loud internal voice is saying, 'I'm hungry,'" Ross declared.

"I hear the same voice," said his brother.

"Let's go get lunch." Ross got up and stretched.

Roy jumped up and said, "Let's go back through the pastures so we don't leave a trail down the embankment. We can go out down here and not leave a trail."

They carefully wended their way out of The Glade and started home through the pasture alongside of the bog. Bootsie trotted after them, but their other two companions stayed behind.

"We have to keep this to ourselves," Roy said. "I don't want anyone to know, or I'll lose it as a sanctuary."

Ross noted Roy's sudden singular possession of The Glade using "I" instead of "us." He had let it slide and would see how it played out.

"Ok, I agree with you. It's our secret,"

They walked on home for lunch in silence, side by side with their dog.

Roy, for the time being, felt safe with a place of refuge. He now felt settled and at home here on The Triangle Farm. He felt in control again. He was ready to live his life in Ixonia and start looking for the next adventure with Ross and Bootsie. He wondered what it would be.

"Bring it on," he whispered.

And "bring it on," life did.

∽

The Old Man watched the boys and dog slowly fade from his thoughts and the backyard come into focus. The sun was starting to set, and the sounds were beginning to change from active chirping and chittering to a more subdued peeping and the katydids quiet and the cricket begin their chorus. The coming evening promised to begin with a glorious sunset with an outpouring of red, yellow, and purple, framed with wispy cirrus clouds reflecting the sunset colors.

These would be shared with Vicki on the deck, holding hands and imbibing the evening cocktail. His is an outstanding old bourbon and hers a gin and tonic. That is if he can get up. He stretched and rolled to his hands and knees. Using the rollator as a brace, he finally managed to stand after several tries.

"That was close," he muttered.

As he started toward the house, he saw Vicki standing on the deck smiling and shaking her head.

"I love you, old man," and blew him a kiss.

"Love you also honey," he responded, and started toward the house. "It's going to be a spectacular sunset."

EPILOGUE
— PART ONE —

TRIANGLE TALES,
THE BEGINNING

"He who chooses the beginning of the
road chooses the place it leads to. It is the
means that determines the end."
– Harry Emerson Fosdick

The Old Man gazed inward as he recalled that moment when they discovered The Glade. There was a constant stream of life there, and now the boys were part of it. It felt safe there, and the boys knew their role was to take care of it, and it would take care of them.

How special it was to Roy at that time; how total. In that instance, Roy was settled and safe. He now could have a sense of direction and control. He would visit The Glade many times alone or with Ross and Bootsie. There were times of imaginary high adventure that ran the gamut from "cowboys and Indians" to battles with invading aliens. There were deep discussions of family issues, friendships, silly young crushes, profound wonderings of developing maturity, and sad, painful times of loss, misery and distress. All these issues Roy brought to and shared with The Glade—as close to The Church he experienced in his youth.

Unfortunately, the safety and security Roy identified in The Glade was misplaced. He was putting his faith in a temporal thing, a thing in this world. The Glade, as with all worldly things, is decaying and subject to man's erratic whims. It would fail him and leave Roy adrift, searching for another place to call Shechem. This would repeatedly happen as he searched for a place where his soul would be still. Somewhere or someplace else where a persistent sense of guilt and a vague fear of impending judgment would be relieved, a place where all was in harmony, and seeking peace and love was his life's mission. Roy knew that such a place existed and where he was now was a place of debate and death.

Roy searched for a long time. A time filled with adventures and misadventures as he and Ross grew up and finally grew apart. A lifetime would transpire until Roy eventually found a true spiritual Shechem, a place of peace and safety as described in the Bible. Journeys that would take him from The Glade to around the entire world, finally to discover that it was within him all the time. It is all a matter of perspective and wisdom. It is not a matter of individual strength, cunning, wealth, or power. It is, in fact, just the opposite. It is a matter of genuine humility, a declared weakness and deeply felt repentance.

When one is a self-professed outlier, this is his lot.

THE END OF PART ONE – THE BEGINNING

THE TRIANGLE TALES

PART TWO

The Scholar & The Sage

PROLOGUE

FACTS, MYTHS, AND LEGENDS

*"When you have eliminated all which
is impossible, then whatever remains,
however improbable, must be the truth."*
– *Arthur Conan Doyle*
The Casebook of Sherlock Holmes

*"There is a universal self-disclosure of God addressed to
all people at all times in all places—those footprints of
God visible in the world in which we live.
However, humankind's ability to read God in His
natural revelation has been impaired by sin.
As a result, humankind misreads it."*
– *A. W. Tozer*

The brothers had many questions about the strange and beautiful features of The Triangle and the surrounding countryside features like the Mound, the Glade, and all the other questions regarding the unique, almost mystical atmosphere that exists on The Triangle and the Hilltop Farm. Then there is the very name of the town–Ixonia. Strangest of all was the shape of the farm itself, triangular—a very odd shape for a piece of property indeed.

They were learning about the land and its spiritual connection to its inhabitants. The boys took full advantage of the night and its peculiar time of peace and high adventure, roaming the farmlands with their dog, Bootsie. Everything was different at night. The smells, the sounds, the creatures, and the atmosphere itself was different.

There were several resources for the answers they were looking for. They had, foremost, their unflagging inquisitive nature. They also had the Scholar (their father) and the Sage (John Franger, the farmer on Hilltop Farm). Dad had introduced the family to John Franger soon after their move to The Triangle.

The boys also had the resources of the Encyclopedia Britannica, dictionaries, Time-Life books on nature, and the local libraries of neighboring towns, if the city was big enough for one. Ixonia wasn't big enough for a library. They also had their mother as a source. While she was college-educated, her education was more in the liberal arts, which gave her a much more open life perspective than Dad. Mom's mother and father were immigrants from Wales and Scotland, respectively, making for a significant source of stories about fairies, leprechauns, and other mystical beings. Given the opportunity, Mom could spin a wonderful tale, as could her father and mother. They had the accents to heighten the effect.

Their father would take time while at work in the city to go to the library or call their Ready-Reference service to get answers to the many questions the boys would have. He would often bring copies of the information home and go over what he found openly, enthusiastically discussing them. He was in frequent contact with the state agricultural service for his own purposes but would include some of the boy's queries in his communication with them. He handwrote and mailed most of the inquiries; there was no internet, and long-distance phone calls were costly and challenging on a four-household party line.

Dad had grown up on a farm on the Wabash River in Lafayette, Indiana. He and his twin brother, Willard, worked hard on the farm. While well-versed in the nuances of crop farming, it was not the same as dairy farming which was prevalent here. He was as interested as the boys and would actively pursue answers with them. His interest though was for a different reason than the boys.

Dad's father still operated the family farm. He had kept the farm very rudimentary. Their great-grandfather had immigrated from England and their great-grandmother immigrated from Germany. Even when Roy and Ross visited them, the farm still did not have electricity or running water in the house. Roy vaguely remembered a steel-wheeled tractor still in use. Staying there was a truly excellent adventure for the boys; it was like traveling back in time.

Their grandfather and the boys spent many nights on the front porch of the farm listening to him spin tales with the background sound of June bugs at the window screens, crickets, and the hiss of kerosene lamps, which cast a golden glow from the windows. His pipe's aroma mixed with the smell from the oil lamps was very soothing. His tales were exciting, scary, and funny. He reminded the Old Man of photos of Samuel Clemens, aka. Mark Twain, with his big droopy mustache stained by tobacco juice. The rhythmic creaking of his old wooden rocker kept a cadence with his speech. The Old Man hopes to write some of those tales down before it's too late, and he forgets everything.

The boy's father went to Purdue University and graduated with a degree in engineering, majoring in metallurgy. Willard, his twin brother, graduated from Michigan State University and worked for a large pharmaceutical company in patent law. They weren't identical twins but looked very similar. Both were average height and wiry in build. Dad seldom smiled but often had a crooked grin that most people thought was about some private joke. Roy believed gas was the cause.

Their father worked as a quality control officer at Rex Chain Belt Company in West Milwaukee during World War II. It was manufacturing the 105 MM Howitzers. His education in metallurgy was the exact fit for the application. After the war, he stayed with Rex Chain Belt and worked in the QC/QA departments, then their Tech Center, before retiring. He held several patents. He always carried a deep desire to be back on some land. It was in his blood, and he loved his time at The Triangle and Hilltop Farm.

His worldview was through an engineer's lens, everything ordered and logical, and in it we would recognize him as a leader, a creator. One of his biggest fears was to become irrelevant or useless. He needed to be correct and would go to great lengths to prove he was right. While he loved his family, his priorities were business success and acclaim. He had no time to "waste" on the supernatural or mystical things. There is nonsense in his worldview.

The second source is John Franger, owner, and occupant of Hilltop Farm. When introduced to the Cheesman family, he brought a large smoked ham as a welcoming gift. Roy can still smell that distinctive aroma of a home-cured ham. John had immigrated to the USA from Prussia, now Germany, after the First World War. The maiden Lloyd sisters (Nellie and Catherine) who owned Hilltop Farm and several other farms had sponsored him. Catherine was the only one alive when the boys were there. She was very fragile but enjoyed visits from the boys before she passed. John was her only caregiver while she was alive. He was initially to assist the farm manager Herman Zacharias. John eventually became the farm manager himself and then inherited the Hilltop Farm. The rest of the holdings of the Lloyd sisters went to Lloyd family members.

John Franger was tall and rawboned; he had that weathered look from outdoors working the land. The corners of his mouth were stained brown from Red Man chewing tobacco, and he seemed to always have a two-day stubble without ever being cleanly shaven. Roy often wondered how he did that. He invariably wore a gray and white striped railroad engineer's cap unless going to church or some other more formal type of get-togethers, then he wore a fedora. His uniform of the day was Oshkosh bib overalls and a denim shirt with wellington rubber boots. When reading or doing close-up work he wore a pair of rimless spectacles. He permeated an earthy barn smell, slightly overwhelming at first but pleasant after a while. Like many farmers, his body suffered injuries working the farm. Safety standards weren't as comprehensive as now. He walked with a limp, the result of his pants leg getting caught in an unguarded power take-off unit. A couple of fingertips are missing because of getting too close to the blades of an oat elevator. Even his dog "Stumpy" had lost the lower portion of his front legs when he impeded a hay mowing machine. (Working on a farm is a serious, potentially deadly business.) He spoke slowly and clearly in a deep and pleasant manner. He inherited not only the farm but also the legends and myths the Lloyd sisters had been keepers of. The Lloyd sisters and their clan had many firsthand experiences beyond the normal.

The Lloyd ancestry was part of a colony of Welshmen that settled on the land between Watertown and Ixonia, close to the Rock River, in the early 1800s. The family had been influential. They were rumored to have inadvertently brought a contingent of supernatural beings with them. They never really denied it but also never admitted it. Wales is a land full of tales of fairies and mystical beings. The boys had a direct connection to Wales, their maternal grandmother was from Wales.

The Lloyd family achieved national notoriety. They claimed Abraham Lloyd to be the shortest man alive. Born in 1856, he was 27 inches tall and weighed 20 pounds fully-grown. Called the Emperor because the style of dress he wore was reminiscent of the plumage of the Emperor Penguin as were his sharp tongue and quick temper. He never chafed at the nickname; indeed, he viewed it as if it were a title bestowed on him. The little man would strut all over town. He claimed to communicate with supernatural beings and to prophesy for the future. He died in 1881 and had accumulated a large amount of money.

John's input was mainly local history, legend, and myth which made a sharp counterpoint to the Scholar's version. He was a bachelor and welcomed the company of the brothers. Along with teaching them the ins and outs of running a dairy farm, he would spend hours sharing the legends and myths handed down to him by the Lloyd sisters and his viewpoint and personal experiences. John was a mentor to the boys during their time in Ixonia. They listened to him with apt attention and showed respect for a man they viewed as their counselor and advocate.

The third source of information is the boy's mother, Jean. Her maiden name was Blackwood, her father Robert having immigrated from Scotland to Canada. Her mother's maiden name was Beacroft. She immigrated to Canada from Wales. His Grandmother claimed she was "black Irish" because of her dark features, hair, and eyes as opposed to red hair and green eyes. Jean was born in Canada and was a USA naturalized citizen. She would speak of her ancestors' legends and myths when she had time. Her folks, the kid's grandparents, would also tell of legends and myths. Their versions were much more entertaining because of their Irish and Scottish accents.

Encyclopedia Britannica's resources gave the boys a lot of additional factual data and pictures to employ in their investigations, as did the Time-Life books. This inquisitive nature and drive to get answers carried through to other aspects of their lives, such as academics and vocations, standing them in good stead throughout their lives. They developed a natural sense of deductive and inductive reasoning, a powerful tool.

Roy had a strong bent toward the supernatural and its occurrences in everyday life. Often, most people dismiss the supernatural as an anomaly or outright deny or ignore it. Not so with Roy and sometimes Ross, every unexplained item or occurrence demanded an answer, no matter how outrageous or other-worldly, in Roy's manner of thinking, anyway.

There were plenty of outrageous items and even other worldly experiences that made life very interesting and even scary sometimes on The Triangle. Some life-threatening issues are life-invigorating when faced head-on. With the academic guidance of The Scholar and the accumulated lore of The Sage, the boys learned how to observe logically, collect facts (data), analyze, and draw conclusions, always keeping an open mind to the possibility that the answer lay in a time, or place beyond, and not found in books or laboratories, yet. Roy was also a great fan of Sherlock Holmes stories by Sir Arthur Conan Doyle. The brilliant detective's ability to identify the slightest clue was his challenge.

What follows is a compilation of some tales about the unique places or items investigated and explored on Triangle Farm, Hilltop Farm, and the surrounding countryside.

The determinations with consideration of The Scholar's input followed by The Sage's, and any other information (Mom or Literature); will be infused by the boys into a conclusion.

It's time to explore, study, probe, and glean the weird items/places the boys investigated. "The Game's Afoot" (Sir Arthur Conan Doyle, Sherlock Holmes).

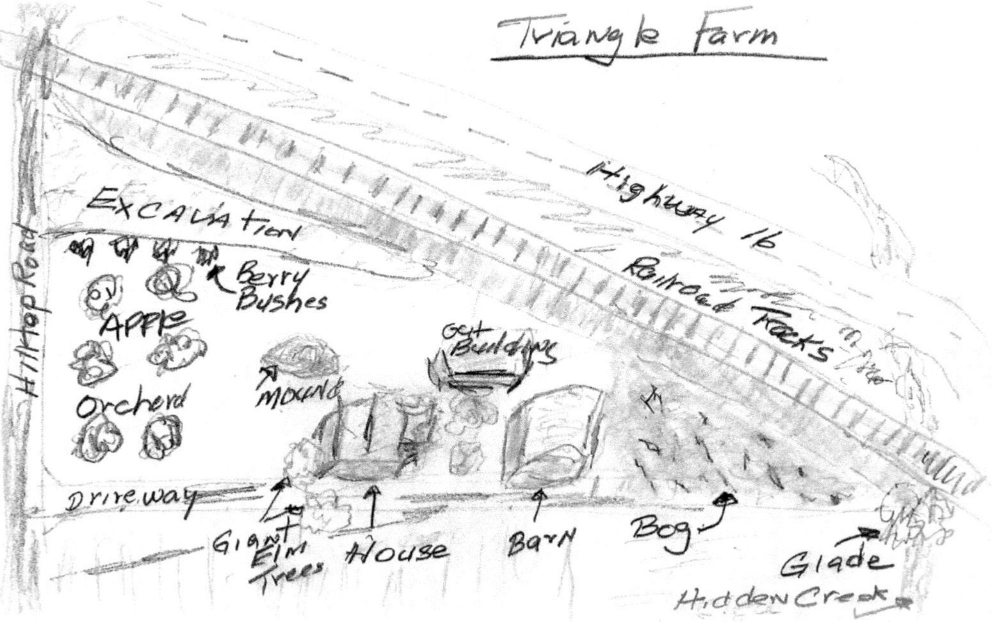

Triangle Farm

Highway 16

Railroad Tracks

EXCAVATION

Berry Bushes

APPLE

Orchard

Mound

Get Building

Driveway

Giant Elm Trees

House

Barn

Bog

Glade

Hidden Creek

Hilltop Road

TALE NUMBER EIGHT

THE TRIANGLE

"To exist, The Triangle demands three complementary elements: love, power and danger. Mixed incautiously, these elements, like those in physics, are volatile and potentially explosive."
– *Ruth Harris,* Decades

"So now faith, hope, and love abide, these three; but the greatest of these is love,"
– *1 Corinthians 13:13 (ESV)*

O n the first day on the farm, the boys discovered that the farm is shaped like a right triangle and dubbed it The Triangle. Like all other triangles, a right triangle's interior angles add up to 180°, with one of its angles equaling 90°. This is a very unusual shape for a piece of property, let alone a farm, no matter how small. A right triangle has one side named the hypotenuse, which is the longest side. That is the side where the railroad track is on The Triangle Farm. Hilltop Road is the base of The Triangle, the shortest side. The perpendicular side of The Triangle is where The Hilltop Farm abutted The Triangle farm. See the diagram.

This is a very inefficient layout for a farm especially when about one-third of it is given over to a peat bog. The boys asked their father and John Franger to help in determining how the farm's shape came about.

Their dad contacted the county registrar of deeds, the realtor, and talked to the local officials in Ixonia and Watertown. He discovered that the railroad line created an odd-shaped piece of property when it was built in the 1800s. The railroad always did what it could to keep its tracks in a straight line, thus it created two pieces of land shaped into triangles when it diagonally split the piece of property. There's another triangle facing the opposite way on the other side of the tracks. Both pieces are considered untillable, so they laid fallow. Their dad said while the trajectory was straight, it is surprising that they went through the bog because of the lack of firm soil to build on. They must have dug down quite a way and had to bring fill material in. The railroad had to do a lot of filling to get the roadbed stable for the tracks. It caused the excavation of part of The Triangle when the railroad construction company needed fill to build up the portion of the roadbed going through the swampy land. That answered the question about the excavated part of the property the boys noted on their first day on The Triangle.

John Franger agreed with what Dad had found out. He added that the property on the other side of the railroad tracks was further divided when U.S. Highway 16 was built. He said both these actions happened over the Lloyd's objection, there was some sort of law that made it possible. That created a triangle on the other side of the railroad tracks. There was a lot of disturbance of the adjacent lands, particularly to The Triangle farm as the railroad and highway were constructed. His success as a farmer completely depended on the vagrant characteristics of weather and nature so he observed what was happening on the land. As such he would know anything suspicious or negative occurring on The Triangle from his high perch on his hilltop.

"Eminent Domain," Dad said. "That's the right of the state to take private lands for public use if they pay for them."

"That's the one," John agreed with a nod of the head and a spit into a plastic cup he used when chewing in the house. If he was outside or in the barn, he would eject a glob of tobacco juice and spittle with amazing force and deadly accuracy.

Mom cringed every time he did this, and the boys couldn't wait until they were old enough to carry a pouch of Red Man or a plug of tobacco.

Dad brought up, to the boys, the supposed supernatural qualities of the triangular shape. He shared some information he found.

In the 6th century, BCE Greek philosopher and mathematician Pythagoras believed that geometry was the rational understanding of God, man, and nature: it commonly ascribed various meanings to these shapes, particularly when used in religious or magical contexts. Many of the shape meanings in western philosophies arise from his writings.

Pythagoras associated the number three with triangles which is meaningful to many groups. Triangles and other three-part symbols may present such concepts as past, present, and future or spirit, mind, and body. The shape is also supposed to symbolize leadership and the desire to be right in all things, difficulty to admit their mistakes, and excessive self-absorption.

Roy thought, *That's Dad to a T, and possibly me as well.*

Dad dismissed the supernatural and magical context as rubbish but gave pause when he did. The triangular shape has many modern-day applications in architecture, mathematics, and science. It is part of our everyday life from the structural designs (one of the strongest shapes) to the Egyptian Pyramids and traffic road signs.

John told them tradition had it that the Emperor (Abraham Lloyd) claimed that a large piece of land, that The Triangles were part of, was to be left fallow for the fairy folk that had accompanied the Lloyds when they immigrated to this area from Wales. So much of the surrounding land was being cultivated causing conflicts between the humans and the mystical beings. On the reserved land, the mystical creatures were free to live. The unusually large congregation of fireflies was evidence of the presence of the beings. The fairies sometimes mingled with the fireflies at night and sang sad songs. This, of course, was all myth and legend, but The Triangle had an inordinate number of fireflies on it. Catherine Lloyd had told the boys the same tale. Roy recalled his sister's claim that she could see fairies among the fireflies, and she said they were singing.

John did not share any personal experiences with the mystical beings, that legend had it, populated The Triangle and pieces of land on the other side of the railroad tracks. He did not offer any position pro or con on the subject but reiterated the Lloyd sisters absolutely believed in the myth. That was all he shared on the subject.

The boy's mother added to the discussion saying her mother would tell her stories when she was a little girl. Her mother was from Wales. The stories she would tell her were probably the same as what the Emperor heard. She further added that their grandmother is convinced the tales were true and would be excited to visit The Triangle and maybe experience the fairies again. Mom recited bits of a poem her mother used to tell her about the "pwca and sylph" at night when putting her to bed.

Their mother explained that pwca (pronounced pookah) were impish fairies. They often mirror and amplify the treatment they receive. Treat a pwca well, and they will amply reward you. Mistreat a pwca or abuse their gifts and you may end up thrown in a bog and left to drown.

The sylph were beings inhabiting the air, holding a place between the material and immaterial. Sylphs are depicted as guardians who protect secret knowledge, beautiful women, or the environment, but it's not out of the question for a sylph to cause mischief among men. Perhaps the most impressive aspect of sylph intelligence is its supernatural foresight. The future holds few mysteries for a sylph.

Their father's brow furrowed, and he shook his head side to side.

"Come on Jean," he snapped at her. "That's just rubbish. You're going to give the children crazy ideas. Roy has enough silly ideas as it is."

Jean just smiled.

John looked at her with newfound respect. He was well aware of Bill's no-nonsense, closed-minded attitude and short temper about the supernatural. He believed all things were answerable in the natural world, and if the answer wasn't readily apparent, it would be soon enough. Pursuing the issues that were erroneously classified as not natural is a waste of time and talents, not to be tolerated. Now John knew Jean's mindset was much more open, and he noted that.

Roy ignored his father's ire and was excited about the possibility of talking to his grandmother and getting access to eyewitness experience. He also planned to spend time alone with John and enquire of him what the Lloyd sisters knew about the mystical activities of The Triangle.

His brother would consult the encyclopedia and the papers their dad had given them. He would compile information in the form of notes and sit down with Roy who would have made notes of his discussion with John. They did not have the opportunity to talk to their Grandmother Blackwood. He had instead asked their mom to recount some stories. This all had to be done without their father's knowledge. They would go over their findings with Dad after they had finished.

They went to the Glade to merge their information and arrive at a conclusion about the shape of the farm and what it meant to them. It was a sunny afternoon with the sunlight dabbling on the ground of the Glade. As they settled down by the pond's edge, they watched the bunny come down from the railroad embankment to join them. It sat on the other side of the pond. The damselfly glided out from the culvert and settled down on the edge of the big black and yellow spider's web. The spider came over beside the damselfly. They were friends and had been all along. When the boys first met them, they had mistakenly thought the spider was going to attack the damselfly. Roy almost crushed the spider and would have if Ross hadn't stopped him. He believed it was a test to check out their true nature. The spider kept several of its eyes on Roy. Bootsie went over to their side of the pond.

The Glade was a strange and magical place that welcomed the boys and all who visited her in peace. On the hottest days, the overarching trees kept it cool. The trees and the thick tall grasses surrounding the Glade acted as an acoustical barrier, so the outside noises did not encroach on its seclusion. Even passing trains were muted to some extent. They seemed very distant. Glade had its own music, melodious and quiet in the background. It comprised the soft buzzing of flying insects, chirping of crickets, the occasional chitter of a small creature in the grasses, and the trilled love song of a red wing blackbird. There was a soft breeze and the wildflowers on the railroad embankment provided a fragrance of freshness and sweetness. The water leaving the culvert under the tracks tumbled down stones and made a burbling sound as it entered the pond. Frogs jumped into the pond with a splash as the boys neared it. Sometimes the boys would spend an afternoon capturing and hypnotizing them by holding them upside down in the palm of their hand and slowly rubbing their bellies until they went to sleep. When turned over and put down they woke up and jumped away. They wouldn't have time for that this afternoon.

The Glade's atmosphere always calmed the boys. Roy especially experienced a sense of serenity and well-being when he was in the Glade. Not only an environment of peace and safety there was also a spirituality about the Glade that beckoned to him. It was an attraction he didn't completely understand yet, but he felt assured he would, given time. His brother didn't share his feelings, yet still felt the Glade was a special place, although the actions of the animal companions were unnerving for him.

"It's just not right." he would repeat whenever he saw them hanging together. John had told them that fairies would often disguise themselves as damselflies, dragonflies, or other things during daylight hours certainly didn't make him any more comfortable. Roy had noted that there were a lot of gorgeous damselflies and dragonflies on The Triangle, especially around the bog. Ross agreed and studied them from afar, not afraid but cautious. Roy tried to get them to land on his hand as their damselfly companion does, but they wouldn't.

Roy stretched his arms over his head and twisted his torso right and left.

"I'm stiff and sore from carrying those milk cans from the barn and lifting them into the water chill tank last night," he said, "John told me they weigh over 100 pounds."

Roy helped John with the milking chores in the evenings. Ross raised his eyebrows in acknowledgment of the feat.

"How many of them?" he asked Roy.

"Eight."

Ross thought a minute and then said, "Wow that's 800 pounds!"

"I feel it," Roy said and leaned back on the grass, stretching out.

Ross laid back also, and the damselfly came over and lit on his bent knee.

"We should name our Triangle companions. Bootsie has got a name." Ross said.

Roy agreed but added, "Let's do it later. I want to finish our Triangle investigation."

"OK," Ross agreed.

They both sat up and the damselfly returned to the other side of the pond with the other animals.

Roy started the discussion.

"John is firmly committed to what the Lloyd sisters believed in the supernatural and magical features of the land."

Roy consulted his notes and shared them with Ross. The Triangle was part of a much larger tract of land. The railroad and state took the land for the railway and highway under the power of Eminent Domain. While the Lloyds were reimbursed for the land, they had no say in the selling of it. Based on what The Emperor claimed, this land was supposed to be totally fallow, unused by man, reserved for the fairies and such. The construction, traffic, litter, and now people living on it have gotten the fairy folk upset and angry. John recounted what the sisters said about the fairies. Most people think that fairies are small beings, but they can assume any size or shape they want. They can be malicious when angered. Two of the common forms are naturally tall, lovely beings with wings, or short and wizened trolls. They seldom show themselves as what they are. This is why The Triangle does not produce crops and the orchard is in such sad shape and always probably will be.

"We should be careful here, especially at night according to John."

Ross laughed until he saw the solemn set on Roy's face.

Ross asked, "Are you taking this seriously?"

Roy responded in a quiet voice, "I'm not sure; let's finish this and then decide."

He took a deep breath and pushed the hair back off his forehead. His and his brother's hair was white, bleached from all the time in the sun. They also had slimmed down some with all the walking and running they did while prowling the countryside. Ross was much slimmer than Roy who still was chunky although he was very solid. Working with John on Hilltop farm was filling his physique out, replacing fat with muscle. Ross was normal height and build for a boy of 8-9 years old. Roy was much bigger than a typical 10–11-year-old. The summer sun had turned them both very brown. Ross's face was loaded with freckles.

"What do you have, Ross?"

"Ok," Ross replied and looked over his notes.

Bootsie lost interest in what they were doing and wandered away, sniffing for animal scents to follow. The Damselfly and spider stayed and paid close attention to what they were doing. The rabbit even crossed to their side of the pond but didn't get too close, just close enough to clearly hear them.

The obvious interest the damselfly, spider, and particularly the rabbit had in what they were doing was unnerving to Ross, especially with the rabbit inching in behind them.

Ross turned around and back again trying to monitor the creatures.

"I don't like it," he complained. "I feel like we're surrounded, like Custer's Last Stand.

Roy chuckled "Yeah, we're going to be scalped by a little rabbit, spider, and damselfly. Come on Ross let's get started. What do you have?"

Ross took a deep sigh and began. "OK, Dad determined that the railroad track construction caused the shape, further added to by the highway's construction. Nothing supernatural there. The land was owned by the Lloyd sisters. They hadn't wanted to sell, but forced them to. The land was not being used for anything, so they didn't have much of an argument to prevent the sale.

Dad gave us information about the mystical nature of triangles and the use of triangles in signage and architecture. "When you think about it, The Triangle is everywhere. It's pretty cool, but I don't see anything supernatural in how it was formed. It was cut out of a piece of land that wasn't used for anything and was swampy." He spoke.

Ross leaned back as if to say, and that is that.

Roy nodded in agreement.

"Now we need to consider what John and Mom related about the property and the supernatural. While John hasn't come right out and said it, he believes this property and what is on the other side is haunted by mystical beings, and they are angry about the ancient agreement being violated."

The damselfly flew over to hover near them, and the rabbit moved closer. Ross's head was on a swivel trying to keep track of them.

"Come on Ross," Roy said with growing irritation. "Settle down, they will not bite. Even if they did, it wouldn't be fatal. They just want to hear what we have to say."

"They're not supposed to care what we say," he whispered.

"Then why are you whispering brother?" Roy whispered back.

Ross was getting angry.

"Ross we both knew from day one that this place is different. It is special. So, let's get on with it. OK?"

"OK," Ross said and took a deep breath.

Roy started from his notes.

"John said that the Lloyd sisters believe in what was supposed to be the Emperor's declaration that the land here and on the other side of the tracks and road was to be left fallow. I think we can count on John giving us the straight story from the Lloyd sisters, he was devoted to them. You can actually see the complete property from the Hilltop Farm. It's an enormous piece of land in total and obviously unworked. A sizeable chunk of it is swampy so that might be why.

Too bad we don't have Catherine Lloyd around anymore. Also, the amount of property The Triangle uses is not very significant."

"We both felt that this property had been ravaged. We both agreed that we should, no, we would do something, to fix it. Agreed?"

"Agreed," Ross said looking down at the grass.

"We both noticed the strange behavior of the little rabbit right away. In fact, it was you who noticed it. Right?"

Ross agreed grudgingly.

"Then there was the incident in the Glade, first thing, with the spider and the damselfly. You stopped me from crushing the spider. Correct?"

The spider began clacking its jaws together.

"Stop it," Ross yelled.

"And you're talking to the spider?"

"I'm not talking to it, I'm yelling at it," Ross retorted.

Roy laughed.

"Ok, you're yelling at it. Remember the nights out back on the mound with Dolly? She would say there were fairies in amongst the fireflies and they were singing. You even thought you could see and hear them if you were quiet enough."

Ross sort of rolled his eyes and nodded.

Roy said quietly, "You know, I can't see or hear them no matter how hard I try to be quiet. I believe that as you get older and have more things going on in your life, you can't be still like a small child. At least not without a great deal of practice. I'm talking about inner stillness, a quieting of the soul."

"Now you're getting crazy. You're sounding like one of the science fiction movies or comic books," Ross said skeptically. "Time travelers, people from other dimensions, monsters—have you flipped your lid? You're supposed to be the smart one."

"You like those TV series, movies, and comic books as much as I do Ross. Can you agree that there is a lot of unanswered questions, mysteries about this place?"

Ross agreed.

Roy said, "Let's see what we can deduct from the evidence we have."

So, they did. They were using the process that their dad had taught them, and they had seen him use it frequently.

1. The Given.

   a. The property is shaped like a triangle.

   b. The Triangle Farm was originally part of a much larger piece of property.

   c. The construction of the railroad tracks formed The Triangle. The tracks formed the long side of The Triangle—the hypotenuse.

   d. The construction of U.S. Highway 16 formed another triangle between the railroad tracks and the highway.

2. Initial Conclusion:

   a. There was nothing supernatural that caused these triangles to be formed. They were generated by the growth of industries, agriculture, and society.

   b. The unusual, inefficient shape of The Triangle is just the byproduct of the railroad right away. The Triangle on the other side of the railroad is the byproduct of that right of way and the highway's right away.

"OK," Ross said, "that's it then."

"Not quite," Roy says. "While The Triangles weren't formed from any supernatural force, the property that they were taken from is said to be populated by mystical beings to whom the land would always be theirs."

"Come on Roy, are you serious?"

"Yes, I am. We can't discount the legends that John was told of by the sisters. The excessive amount of fireflies that are present here, and Dolly's claim to see and hear fairies among them.

Before Ross could belittle her value as a witness he added, "and you said that you could see what she saw and maybe hear as well."

Ross clamped his mouth closed tightly and snorted his chagrin.

"The personal experiences we have had here, the little rabbit on the first day and now the damselfly and the spider, added to that is the special feeling of the property, like it whispers to me sometimes, and this place, The Glade."

Ross looked at him and sighed. "What do you want to do about it?"

"The shape is a closed item that we can share with the family. The legend and mystical stuff we'll take on as a separate investigation."

Ross thought on this for a while "OK", he said without a great deal of enthusiasm.

Roy laid back and the damselfly and rabbit seemed excited; the spider clicked away.

"I wish they would stop that," Ross said.

Roy smiled and was sure this was going to be a splendid adventure. Even better than when they peaked into the window at old Mrs. Peabody's dead body. She had lived across the street in the city.

Yes, this was going to be a glorious adventure into the world of mystical beings and legends. He was sure that this not only was going to be exciting, it was also going to be dangerous.

TALE NUMBER NINE

THE MOUND(S)

"Don't Make a Mountain Out of a Mound."
– Roy's Father

T he morning had begun sunny and warm, but now there was a very dark cloud bank moving in from the west. It completely covered the horizon. Dark, almost black roiling clouds started at the horizon and rose almost to the top of the sky. Occasionally, you could see the flash of brilliant light deep inside the bank. And after several seconds, the thunder would rumble slowly and ominously. The air was getting cooler, and a strong westerly breeze was making the fields of oats across Hilltop Road look like waves on a lake during a storm. The corn in a neighboring field was rustling, and Roy thought it was like a secret language that only the corn knew.

Dad grumbled, "I don't have a lot of time for this silliness."

Roy and his family were outside, standing by the mound. Everybody, except Dolly and Bootsie, who were playing on the mound. Roy wondered if that was sacrilegious or something and they would all be cursed. He chuckled to himself. Tonight, Indian zombies would climb out of the mound, dirt falling from their twisted, gnarly, mummified forms, moaning and wandering across the fields blindly. Looking for victims to envelop and return to the living to seek revenge for something or other. *I need to save that for a night we sleep outside,* he thought with a quiet chuckle. Ross noticed the chuckle and looked at him. Eyebrows furrowed in question; Roy waved him off.

The reason they all gathered there was to consider how they were going to proceed with investigating the who, what, when, and where of the mound.

"Come on Bill," Mom said. "You encourage the children to be inquisitive and discover things."

"I'm trying to get this farm in shape. It's all I can do to keep up with it. I need their help, not their questions."

Mom was concerned this was going to deteriorate into an angry shouting match and Roy and his dad would go at each other's throats. This was an increasing problem. Bill's impatience with Roy and his sense of being challenged by him. Roy was as bad with his almost constant defiance of his father. It was as if Roy was vying for the leadership of the family. She didn't think he could be thinking that. Hopefully, he wasn't. That would almost certainly end up badly.

"Why don't I stay here with the children and develop a plan of action and then, over lunch, we can discuss it?"

"Ok," he said sullenly.

As he walked away, he turned and added, "Then the boys can help me clean up the berry patch on the ridge."

Roy scuffed the toe of his Keds in the grass, getting green stains on the toes.

"Roy, stop that. Those are still fairly new. And start showing more respect for your father. He deserves it; driving all that distance to work in town and then home again. He works so hard for us."

"He works hard to be away from us and to keep us isolated and have his farm," Roy retorted.

"Roy!" Jean snapped.

Ross and Dolly wandered over to the far side of the mound, getting away from the tense situation between Roy and their mother. Bootsie stood between Roy and his mother, licking his hand and wagging her banner-like tail.

He patted her head, smiled at her and said, "Thank you Bootsy."

She replied with a "woof."

He hugged his mom and said, "I'm sorry Mom. I should not have said that."

But it is true, he thought.

"Ok," Jean said. "Where do we start?"

Dolly and Ross returned and joined them.

Ross started, "Well, we believe this is a ceremonial mound built a long time ago by ancient Indians. Roy did a study on them in school this year and has some information from the class. There is also information in the encyclopedias and maybe some in the Time-Life books."

Roy added, "Dad could check at the library when he is at work."

If he is not too tired from all that driving, he thought ruefully.

Jean said, "I'll speak to him about that; let's get an idea of this mound's size."

"How are we going to do that?" Ross asked. "We don't have any measuring thing this big,"

She turned to Dolly, "Do you want to help dear?"

Dolly, who had been poking around the mound looking for serpents, as usual, jumped for joy. The thought of being involved with them in an investigation thrilled her. The boys looked at each other and groaned at the prospect of their young sister being actively involved.

Their mother laughed and said, "Come on boys, we'll all have fun doing this together."

She turned to Dolly and said, "Honey, please run and get that new clothesline I bought the other day, also bring a clothes pole."

Dolly was off to the house like a flash. Bootsy was hot behind her.

"What are you going to use that for?" Ross asked. "Going to hang clothes out here?

Both the boys laughed at that.

"You'll see, you smarty pants boys."

Dolly and Bootsie came charging back. Dolly held the major portion of the clothesline while Bootsie had a loose trailing end in her mouth. The other hand tightly clasped the clothes pole and dragged it behind her.

"Okay," Jean said as she peeled out some clothesline. "Roy, honey, please take one end of this clothesline and go stand on the top of the mound, about in the center. Ross, you stand on the side of the mound about halfway around and let Roy know if he is in the center from where you stand. Dolly, take him one end of the clothesline, please."

The children did as they were instructed.

"Ross, is he centered from where you are?" Jean asked.

"No, he has to move back a little."

Roy took small steps backward.

"Stop."

Roy stopped immediately.

Jean then said, "Roy, take one small step to the right."

"Ok."

"Get down and put the end of the line where you were just standing. That is close to the center of the mound."

Roy followed her instructions.

"Good," she said. "Ross, come here, please."

Ross walked over to his mother and looked at Roy, who shrugged his shoulders.

"Ross, stand back and tell me if the pole is straight up and down."

Ross did as instructed. He stepped back a few steps, then walked around the pole looking at it from different sides. He then told his mother which way to move the pole, and when it was straight up and down, she reached up with the clothesline and asked Ross to tell her when it was straight and had Roy keep a tight hold of his end on the ground. When the line was straight, as far as Ross could tell, she grabbed the pole there.

"Ross, come here, please," Jean said.

When he was there, his mother lowered the line, holding it where it had met the pole when Ross said it was straight, and handed it to him.

"Don't let go of that place. It is very important."

She then took the pole and marked it with a pencil she kept in her apron. Housewives of that era, especially in the country, always wore aprons. They kept the dress clean from the many things one got into in the country, and it was also a good repository for essential items such as pencils, scissors, and so on.

She then asked Ross to come to her so she could cut it in the spot he had been told to hold on to.

"Wonderful," she exclaimed.

The boys looked at her as though she had gone crazy. Dolly and Bootsie had returned to wrestling up and down the mound.

"You boys don't understand what we just did, do you?"

They both shook their heads. Roy cast sideways glances at Dolly and Bootsie, rolling all over what could be a sacred mound used for sacrifices and all other kinds of grisly things. The zombie Indians were sure to rise now. He knew that if he said something to Dolly, his mom would tell him to stop making things up to scare them.

Their mother took a deep breath and shook her head.

"Ok, first, Roy, stop looking at Dolly and thinking of ghosts and zombies to frighten us."

Roy thought *that wasn't fair. I didn't even have time to do it and I'm blamed.*

"Second, you should know what we just did. I'm glad your father wasn't here. He would have been upset."

The boys hung their heads.

"What we did was to measure the diameter and the height of the mound. All we have to do is measure the clothesline I cut and the clothes pole where I marked it. We can easily do that at the house using the measuring tape I use for making clothes and curtains."

Roy grabbed his head with both hands and shouted, "Of course!"

Ross stomped onto the ground and shook his head.

Dolly and Bootsie stopped horsing around as if they had been yelled at.

Roy said, "Now we can figure the diameter."

Bootsie had gotten serious and went to the top of the mound and stood with her nose uplifted, smelling the wind.

The breeze had grown to a wind that smelled of rain and was getting colder. It wouldn't be long before cold drops would fall and based on what the storm looked like; it was going to be a veritable torrent. The thunder was heard only a few seconds after the lightning struck. They could see John leaving the field he'd been cultivating, and the cows were instinctively heading up the hill to the safety of the barn.

Bill came up from wherever he had been working and yelled at them to come to the house and get into the cellar. They all hurried to the house.

They practiced a safety drill when bad weather threatened. This was another little bonus from Mother Nature. The Rock River Basin, which they were part of, was prone to tornados during the summer.

It just keeps getting better, Roy thought.

The cellar is aptly named. It wasn't a basement. The basement had a concrete floor and cement block walls. Their cellar had a hard-packed clay floor and small stone boulder walls. There was a coal-burning furnace and a coal bin for storing large chunks of coal. There was a dank odor permeating everything like a cave's smell.

Dad had one kerosene lantern and Mom had another. The boys had jugs of water, blankets, and some snacks. There was a transistor radio already down there. There was no electricity in the cellar, as was with most cellars. It didn't matter during storms as the electricity went out most of the time, anyway. They kept the storm materials upstairs as the cellar was home to house mice. Besides mice furtively scurrying around in the dark corners, the exterior cellar door was blocked by jars of snakes lining the steps, preventing access to the double doors.

The floor was crumbly in the corners and allowed for earthworms and night crawlers to invade the cellar when it got wet, like when it rained a lot. Just like what it was going to do in a few minutes. The thunder was getting closer and soon would shake the house.

Roy grumbled to no one in particular, "Do we have to keep the snakes down here? Can't they be kept in the barn or shed?"

Dolly wailed. The dog barked. The storm descended on them with all its frightful power. Thunder shook the house. The wind rattled the cellar doors so violently that they would have flown up if not prevented from doing so by the crossbar binding them together.

"Tornado a-comin," Ross yelled.

Roy picked up and chanted with him, Dolly screamed and ran to Mom. Throwing herself into her arms, almost knocking her over. Bootsie started running back and forth, barking and howling.

The chaotic environment was out of control.

"Everyone shut up now!" Dad yelled at the top of his lungs.

Everything but the storm stopped, even the mice and Bootsie. All was quiet.

Dad was staring wide-eyed with an almost maniacal glower on his face. His body was rigid with rage. He then turns on the transistor radio. The late 1950s were before minute-by-minute meteorological updates, with storm alerts, sirens, etc. As he gets it tuned in, his body relaxes as he can hear what is going on outside.

There was no danger of a tornado, besides high winds and heavy rains, the storm would blow past in about an hour.

"Let's pass the time inspecting your sister's reptile collection. I'll go up and get the reptile books," Dad went without waiting for a response.

That was a command, not a request. The time was spent sitting in a circle, passing around and inspecting each snake and frog Dolly had collected. Roy was assigned the Time-Life book covering the animals and Ross the encyclopedia about the species. It was fun, and Roy enjoyed watching his sister's delight at being the center of attention with everyone enjoying her pastime. Dad also taught everyone how to put a frog to sleep by laying it on its back and stroking its belly. It didn't work on the snakes, as the boys discovered. Everyone had to help in snake wrangling.

After the storm passed, everyone gathered in the kitchen for a cold lunch and discussion of the mound investigation. Mom told Dad about the data they collected, and the following assignments were made: Dad would check the Ready-Reference at the Milwaukee Library and see if there were any associations that existed addressing ancient mounds. The boys would visit John and see what he knew about the mounds, and Mom would calculate the dimensions of the mound. All information would be collected by the boys and presented to the family in two weeks, if possible. The meeting adjourned. Dolly helped Mom clear and wash dishes from lunch, and the boys went with Dad to help him with clearing the berry patch. They discovered not only currants, but red and black raspberries. There were wild blueberries along the bottom of the railroad embankment. It was going to be great snacking out here when they all ripened.

The boys went up to see John the next afternoon. He was busy clearing branches from the yard that had been blown down by the storm. The boys helped him gather them into a burn pile. When they were done, they went to the windmill in the front yard and got some icy cold sweet water to drink. The water came from an artesian aquifer over one thousand feet deep, John told them.

They sat on a berm under an enormous elm tree next to the windmill. There was always a light, cool breeze in the shade of the old tree. The sweet smell of fresh cut hay was carried up to them from the field below. John pulled out his pouch of Red Man chewing tobacco and offered it to the boys. They declined, and he took a big pinch and put it in the side of his mouth.

"Now, young Cheesman's, thanks for the help and what can I do for you?" he drawled.

He propped himself back on his elbows and looked out over the land with a look of pure contentment. He was part of this land.

The boys followed suit, leaning back on either side of him. They were chewing on big stalks of reed grass that stuck out of their mouths.

"We want to know about the mound behind our house. Is it an Indian mound?" Roy asked.

"Is it a burial mound?" Ross chimed in after Roy.

John eased himself up and sat looking down on The Triangle Farm. He leaned forward and spit a stream of tobacco at an anthill and hit it dead center, sending the insects into a frenzied disorderly mass. He chuckled at the result and cleared his throat. From where they sat high on Hilltop Farm. they could view the entire width of the valley for several miles. It ran southward in an easterly direction. Each side of the valley had a creek running down it. The boys had named them Clear Creek on the west side and Hidden Creek on the east side. Hidden Creek was the one that ran through the Glade.

The creeks emptied into the Rock River several miles to the south, where the valley flattened out to a delta of sorts. The entire valley was a part of the Upper Rock River Basin.

John gazed at The Triangle Farm and said, "I like what you're doing with the land. Saw you clearing the berry patch yesterday after the storm. Good to see sons working alongside their father; Yep, good. The spirits must be happy with that."

He spat again. The boys followed suit, conjuring up juice from the grass stem they were chewing on. That made the farmer smile.

"What you are doing for the land makes the spirits happy. You can feel it."

"What spirits?" the boys asked. "The Indian spirits from the mound?"

"You mean mounds, not a mound. There used to be all kinds of them right here in the valley. They have plowed most of them under. There are two mounds here now. The one on your property and the one on VanRooden's. As for the spirits, I don't know. Maybe from the Indian Mound or those carried over here from Wales by the Lloyd's."

"Where is the other mound?"

"It's right there in front of the creek," John said, pointing way off to their left by Clear Creek.

"That's just a long pile of dirt that is dug up," Roy said with an accusatory tone in his voice.

John spat again and stared at Roy with a cool look. He then smiled and shook his head.

"Nope, son, that is a mound that has been looted. A long time ago, all the mounds that were not on the Lloyd Sisters' property were looted for artifacts, and skeletons, especially skulls. That is why it was no big deal to plow them under after they had been looted. After the Lloyds deaths the family that inherited the land sold it and the mounds were destroyed—a nasty business."

"What did they find, buried treasure?" Ross blurted out.

"Of course not, these mounds would have bodies, arrowheads, and beads," Roy said in a knowing voice. He had done a paper on mounds at school last year.

"I don't know what they found. The Lloyd Sisters told me looters would come to this valley in the summer. This was told to the sisters by their grandparents. They had firsthand knowledge and experience with the Native Americans. These were not the mound builders but knew of the builders. They called them the Ancient Ones. There were entire tribes of them, all the way down the big river, the Mississippi River, I guess. They came here because back then there was plenty of game, fish, and fresh water. They also came for the peat moss."

"The peat moss, why would they want that stuff?" Ross asked.

John was still gazing out over the valley.

"Look out past your property on the other side of the highway. See how the bog actually continues way up past the Jones place?"

The boys nodded.

"That is one large peat bog. The Indians used it for many reasons."

John abruptly stood up and brushed off the seat of his overalls, pulled the plug of tobacco out from the cheek of his mouth, and rinsed his mouth out with well water and had another drink.

"It's time to get the cows in the barn and start milking."

The boys imitated his moves and followed him to the barn to help until their mother called them home for dinner.

A couple of nights later, after dinner, Dad had his information from the library and Mom her calculations. Ross had referenced the encyclopedia. Roy had notes from talking to John. This is what the boys concluded.

The mound on their property and the one across the fields by Clear Creek were the last of a much larger group of mounds, according to the library, John, and encyclopedia. Dad had discovered they were built by a tribe of the Oneota culture, which was part of the much larger Mississippian civilization. It flourished in what is now the Midwestern, Eastern, and Southeastern United States from approximately 800 CE to 1600 CE, varying regionally. They were known for building large, earthen platform mounds, and often other shaped mounds as well. It was composed of a series of urban settlements and satellite villages linked together by loose trading networks. The largest city was Cahokia, believed to be a major religious center located in what is present-day southern Illinois. Dad was impressed with the sophistication of these civilizations. This agreed with the information Roy had prepared for his school paper last year.

John said that the Lloyd sisters told him that Native Americans returned to this area when the early Lloyd clan immigrated here, from the late 1700s to the early 1800s. There was a large number of mounds up and down the valley. They had been built by a group of natives that they referred to as The Ancients. These mounds were mostly looted and destroyed by settlers for the prize soil they were made of. The vast majority were the round dome type, like in their yard. A few were rectangular like the one with the top ripped open on the VanRooden's property. There are some mounds called effigy mounds which were in the shape of animals, birds, and reptiles at a state park called Aztlan. There were thousands of mounds in southeastern Wisconsin at one time.

Ross said that this information agreed with the information in the encyclopedia. Mom gave her calculations of the mound they measured just before the storm had hit. The measurements were six-foot radius and six feet high. The diameter of the mound was twelve feet (2 x radius) and the circumference was 38 feet (2 x π x radius). There is a volume of 432 square feet (= 4/3 π radius³/2).

"That is a large amount of dirt to be moved in small baskets. The mound was much larger when originally built. There has been a lot of erosion over as much as 400 years. It's a tragedy that so many of the mounds here were destroyed. We need to treasure the one we have," Mom said.

They all agreed and planned to make trips to some of the parks to see some of the other mounds.

Roy made a commitment that he was going to visit the looted mound on VanRooden's property and see if any artifacts may remain. It would be really cool to find a skull. He also was going to explore the land on the other side of the railroad tracks and Highway 16 and spend a few nights on their mound and see if there are spirits lurking there during the midnight hour.

It was then Dad said that maybe they should excavate their mound. There may be some valuable artifacts in the mound. Mom stood up and said that they would absolutely not desecrate the mound. It was to be treated with the same respect as a modern cemetery or church. She stood there straight and stiff-lipped and stamped one foot to put a point on it. Dad looked at her in surprise, shrugged his shoulders, and nodded in agreement.

The kids looked at each other in astonishment. Ross mouthed the silent word wow.

Roy was getting the feeling that Dad would sell whatever was not nailed down or of importance to him. This just added to the increasing contentiousness that was close to erupting between him and Dad. Roy was quickly developing a love for The Triangle and all its surroundings. He was becoming very protective of it. Some of this was a result of being a close companion of John Franger, a true product of the land and an ardent defender of it. Was Hilltop Farm the large dominant mound that was always present in the Ancient civilizations? Was John Franger its guardian?

The future was anything but calm. Time would tell all.

TALE NUMBER TEN

THE BOG

*"Good judgment comes from experience,
and a lot of that comes from bad judgment."*
– Will Rogers

The boys headed down the railroad tracks from the driveway crossover, walking toward the Glade. They were going to explore the bog on the other side of their property. This was the start of the investigation of the peat bog at the end of The Triangle Farm. The family had got together after supper and decided that the bog would be the next feature to be investigated. Dad was going to get info from the library and the county extension office, Ross would look in the encyclopedia, Roy would visit John, and the boys would also explore the total bog between the railroad tracks and on the other side of State Highway 16. Mom and Dolly would join them for the last part because of having to cross the highway. Dad kept mentioning that peat moss had a commercial value. Mom was ill at ease, as she knew there would be a major blow-up confrontation between Roy and Dad if he took any steps to sell the peat moss.

The boys stood on the tracks above the bog between the tracks and the highway. As usual, the bunny and Bootsie were with them. They located a small game trail going down the embankment and started down. The rabbit stayed up on the embankment. It never seemed to cross over to the other side of the tracks. Bootsie led the way down. Tail waving like a banner of a color bearer leading a military column. There will be lots of burr picking and brushing off Bootsie tonight. The going was easy, and they were on the bottom quickly. There seemed to be no difference between the brambles and burrs that festooned the embankment on those that carpeted the ground. It was tough going. Burrs, stickers, and scratches quickly covered them. Bootsie had disappeared into the tall brambles and stunted trees. Only the shaking of them told where she was. The boys stopped at the edge of the bog. The bog here appeared to be the same as the one on their property. To prove it, they planned to push through the bog to Hidden Creek, which formed the boundary with the bog the same as The Triangle. They began shouldering their way through the reeds and tall grasses, with Roy leading as usual. Ross navigated as best he could.

The going was tough and painful, but thankfully there were not any creepy sounds beckoning Roy on this side of the tracks, yet he was still very leery as they pushed through the bog. The footing on this side was spongy to goopy, and they sank up to their ankles. Their shoes were older pairs in anticipation of the muck. The odor was equally pungent, and the biting insects were just as vociferous and rose in clouds to feast on them. Blackbirds were present on this side as on The Triangle side as well. The birds were just as angry as having these large clumsy animals disturbing their nests. They buzzed the boys, making them duck and cover their heads with their arms, which gave the insect and thorns a clean shot at them, which wasn't wasted. They finally made it to the creek. The bog ran right up to the creek's edge, unlike on their side, where the Glade bordered the bog between the creeks.

Ross was sweating so much that his T-shirt was plastered to him, as was Roy's. The sweat made their scratches sting and itch. They looked at each other and turned to face the creek and gave a yell as they jumped into the water. The water was cold and clear, the current wasn't strong but was brisk. It was about three feet deep. John had told them that an underground river fed both creeks. This accounted for the clear, cold nature of this and Clear Creek on the other side of the Hilltop Farm. The boys had bent knees and sort of bobbed in the water, keeping in place against the current by using their feet digging into the creek bottom, which was sandy, not muddy.

"I wonder why the bog, which is right at the edge, doesn't make the water muddy?" Roy commented.

"I don't know," Ross answered.

Bootsie stood on the edge of the bog and nervously paced back and forth. She whined and even barked once or twice, unsure of what to do—obviously wanting to be with the boys. Ross encouraged her and then Roy did. She finally jumped in after a lot of coaxing by the boys. She nervously paddled with her front legs, splashing the boys in their eyes. They laughed and were careful not to get scratched by her flailing legs. They took turns holding her, and she quickly calmed down and seemed to enjoy the cold water. And she even took a drink, lapping up the clear water. The boys looked at each other and took tentative sips of the water. It was sweet and very similar to the well water at Hilltop Farm. They nodded to each other and drank deeply from the creek.

They let themselves be taken toward the embankment and the culvert pipe underneath it. Bootsie paddled comfortably alongside them. When they reached where the creek entered the culvert pipe, they halted and took hold of Bootsie. They were unsure if they should go through the culvert pipe under the tracks. They could see the other end as a small circle of light at the exit of the culvert. The creek discharged into the Glade. They looked up at the embankment and all the brambles, burrs and thorns they would have to wade through to get up on the tracks or float through the culvert with Bootsie. Just then, their damselfly appeared at the entrance of the pipe; Bootsie barked a hello to it. It seemed to beckon them, assuring them it was safe to go through the pipe to the Glade.

Roy took a deep, steadying breath and started through the pipe. Ross put his arm around the dog and let the current take him and Bootsie.

The pipe was four feet in diameter and over one half full of water. The minute Roy entered the pipe, the temperature cooled off considerably and all the outside sounds diminished dramatically. He could stop his forward motion by kneeling on the bottom of the pipe. He had expected the pipe to be covered with slimy moss and algae, but the pipe was smooth and clean. Ross pulled up next to him and look all around the dim interior of the pipe. Bootsie was fine if he held her close. The damselfly hovered close by as though questioning why they had stopped mid-pipe.

"This is pretty cool," Roy said.

His voice echoed slightly, and the Damselfly darted away at the strange sound.

Ross nodded agreement. "I wonder what a train sounds like here. I'll bet it is pretty wild with the echo effect."

The boys then let the gentle current carry them to the end of the pipe. The damselfly and the rabbit were waiting for them in the Glade, as was the spider. Bootsie swam over to them and got them all wet when she shook out her coat. The boys laughed at that. They were usually the recipients of that shower.

The boys stretched out on the bank and let the warm sunshine dry them off. They were quiet for several minutes as they lay there with their eyes closed. They both were pondering their early morning exploration.

"You know Ross, there weren't any damsel or dragon flies in the bog."

"You're right. I wonder why that is?"

The damselfly and the rabbit had drawn close to them as they began talking. Bootsie had rolled on the grass and gotten dry enough to come over and lie with them.

"Ewwww, Bootsie, you smell like wet dog." Ross complained and wrinkled his nose.

She looked at him with head cocked to one side as though to say, of course I do, I am a wet dog.

Roy studied the damselfly and asked it, "Why is that so? Why are there no other damsel or dragonflies on the other side?"

The damselfly just hovered in place and didn't respond.

"Maybe it is the fumes from the cars and trucks that we don't have on this side of the tracks?" Ross offered.

Roy nodded a tentative agreement. "There isn't a lot of traffic, but maybe it is enough. We need to get some advice from Dad and John about that; we need to do some more observation over there. Let's go get lunch and you can check the encyclopedia and I'll go talk to John this afternoon."

The boys got up and said goodbye to their companions, who seemed to appreciate that, and headed home.

Lunch was waiting when they got home. Mom was surprised by how clean the boys and Bootsie were. She didn't know the dip in the creek and the trip through the pipe and the boys didn't say anything about it. They all ate, and Mom was interested to hear about their morning exploration and was as puzzled as they were about the lack of damsel or dragonflies on the other side of the tracks. She didn't think it resulted from any pollution from the traffic. She wasn't sure about the water being clear, even though the bog ended up right at the water's edge. She guessed it was from the filtering feature of the peat moss.

She asked the boys to spend time with Dolly when she did the washing and cleaned the house. She only needed them to do it for a couple of hours.

The children gathered in the backyard. Dolly had her collection lined up for display in the cellar. The boys took the oldest reptiles that she had collected and let them go behind the barn. Dolly would replace them with new snakes or toads, frogs, and other strange creatures. She had one special snake that she always kept track of. It was a milk snake, with pretty, brown patches outlined in black on a silver background. It was a big snake, about three feet long, and was very comfortable in Dolly's hands. She left it loose and went and found it whenever she wanted to play with it. Dolly named it Milkshake but didn't seem to respond to that name at all. That didn't deter her from her love for the animal. The snake fed on rodents and other small snakes, that resonated well with Dad and Mom, that Milkshake even was tolerated in the cellar to keep mice under control. Dolly always enjoyed showing off her collection and having the boys help her. Roy was getting over his squeamishness around the snakes, although when Milkshake was digesting a meal, Roy preferred to be somewhere else.

The boys helped Dolly catch a couple of new candidates for the collection. The boys had convinced their sister to rotate members of the collection. They were wild creatures and would not survive in glass jars. Roy then told Dolly and Ross that he was going to go up to Hilltop Farm and talk to John about the peat bog. Ross was going to check out the encyclopedia and other books about peat bogs.

Roy headed up the driveway toward Hilltop Road. The afternoon was warm, and the sky was clear and high, thin wispy clouds floated lazily from west to east. He was enjoying the walk. The Corn was over his head high and at night he could hear it grow. The grass in the little field between the mound and the orchard was almost high enough to cut again. Roy was looking forward to swinging the scythe again. The air was clean and sweet with the faint scent of earth from the cultivating of the cornfields.

As he walked along, he passed the little orchard. It was still sad looking, but the care Dad had given it with clearing the grass and weeds from around the trees, and the application of some chemical he had received from the county extension, had started some trees to sprout fresh growth. Dad said they would begin pruning the trees this weekend to encourage more fresh growth and strength. Roy wondered about that. How could cutting stuff off the trees encourage fresh growth and strengthen them?

The berry patch was looking good after they had cleared the brush from around the bushes and mulched them with old newspapers and shredded cardboard the boys had cut up. Roy was looking forward to the fresh berries this fall, if the birds didn't get all of them. Dad said they might cover the bushes with some sort of netting to prevent the birds from eating all the berries. The birds were welcome to some berries but not all of them.

Roy turned up Hilltop Road toward Hilltop Farm. The gravel road rose sharply up the hill. The pitch of the steepness of the inclined had caused it to become "wash-boarded" from heavy traffic, such as the big milk truck the comes weekly to collect John's milk cans of fresh milk. John's tractors also contribute to the wash-boarding. Their large rough treaded tires murdered the gravel road. Wash-boarding was when a gravel road develops ripples and causes very uncomfortable rides. John would grade the road soon. This grading would have to be repeated frequently.

He looked at the surrounding fields deeply, breathed in the clean fresh air, and smiled to himself. He was growing to love this place and all the intriguing animals, history, geography, and legends made it appear he was living a dream sometimes. He rarely thought of the city anymore. As he approached the farm buildings, Stumpy, John's dog, came hobbling down from the house. He was wagging his tail but must always announce his presence with several halfhearted barks. He was quite the sight with his front legs gone just below where the paws would have been. They had been sheared off by a hay mowing machine many years ago. Normally, he would have been put down because no one would have cared for the permanently crippled animal. John had only the little dog for companionship, so he nursed the animal back to health and changed his name to Stumpy.

Roy reached down and scratched the dog's ears. He stood up and turned around to gaze out over The Triangle and the land past the highway. The bog continued along the creek for a long way and the total parcel of land that comprised the initial set aside was visible. The outline of the partial of land was clear. Fields of various crops butted right up to the fallow piece of land which, over a century ago, was pledged to be kept uncultivated, undisturbed. Now there was a railroad and a highway slicing the land into three pieces. The Triangle Farm, The Triangle between the tracks and the highway and a large square piece on the other side of the highway. The parcel had to be cut into three pieces. This was the betrayal of the legendary pledge made to the Fairy people who stowed away with the Lloyd Clan when they immigrated from Wales.

"I wonder if that has something to do with the lack of dragon or damselflies on The Triangle, the tracks, and highway they explored earlier in the day?" he asked.

"That's a good question boy," a voice said behind him.

Roy jumped, startled. John had walked up behind unnoticed.

"They are plentiful on the other side of the highway. Seems only the nasty, irritating ones such as skeeters and no-see-ems are on the land between. The other two pieces, your farm, and the land north of the highway, are open on all their sides but the tracks and road. That openness maybe the reason that those two parcels are alive." It's just the same with the fireflies. It's quite a show from up here in the summer. John nodded and eyeballed a line of busy ants. He loosened a long line of tobacco juice that violently disrupted them. He smiled and turned away.

"If you are on my hill to discuss something, come and help me get the mowing and baling equipment ready. We'll talk as we work. If we are going to use the air anyway, might just as well do something constructive, yep."

They walked up to the machinery sheds that were parallel to the enormous barn. In them were parked the International pickup truck, a car, two huge Farmall tractors, and every other piece of equipment necessary to plant, till and harvest crops on the farm. It was an amazing array of machinery filling two large buildings. The machinery was large and dangerous looking. He loved checking them over, maintaining, and repairing them and becoming acquainted with them.

Today they worked on the hay mowing, raking, and baling equipment. It needed to be lubricated. John showed him how to watch for the old grease to get pushed out of the joint and to keep pumping the grease gun until clean grease emerged. All the equipment had to be checked over for loose or missing nuts and bolts, damaged areas repaired or replaced. He learned much from John, who was patient and forgiving. Roy learned how to form metal with the use of an anvil and cross peening hammer. The best time came when they headed to town to get parts. They would hop in the pickup and head to Watertown. They'd pick up parts at the farm supply store and then stop by the Lopppy's Bar and Grill in Ixonia. There they enjoyed cold drinks, cheeseburgers, and local gossip. Roy got to meet neighbors and some boys his age.

While working on the equipment, John relayed what he knew of the bog. The peat was of no use to the farmers, so that entire piece of land was to be left fallow. Legend has it that the parcel of land was to be the home to fairies, trolls, gnomes, and such. It was to be kept fallow for them.

In the time before the Lloyd's and other settlers arrived, the whole basin is used by ancient native peoples partly because of the peat moss. They used the moss for medical purposes and dried it for fuel. Periodically there was talk about draining the bog and filling it with good soil, so it could be cultivated. That was never put into action, some say because of apprehension of the old legend to keep it fallow for the mystical beings. John didn't have any stated position on the legend. He just stayed clear of that land.

They used the afternoon up and John had to prepare for the evening milking, and Roy had to get home to prepare for a family meeting to discuss the peat bog. As he walked down the hill on Hilltop Road. The late afternoon was hazy and warm. There was no breeze, so the chittering and buzzing of insects created an atmosphere of serenity which lasted until he turned into the driveway.

While he had been at Hilltop Farm, Ross was to research peat in the encyclopedia and other material they had. Dolly had asked him if she could help him. Ross wasn't sure what she could do. They first put the snakes back on the stairs in the cellar. Mom made them some Kool-Aid and gave some cookies as they settled down in the living room to begin their research. It tickled Dolly to be included in the project and beamed her happiness. Dolly continued to ask questions that were surprisingly relevant. He enjoyed answering her questions and discussing peat with her. The two of them and Bootsie were waiting on The Mound when Roy turned into the driveway.

Bootsie was off like a shot when she saw Roy. She jumped and barked when she caught up to him. Roy laughed and tussled her fur and waved to Ross and Dolly who were running down the driveway to meet him. All three and the dog began walking home. The afternoon was slowly fading into evening and the western sky was taking on a purple and orange hue prior to sunset.

The quiet afternoon melted into early evening when Dad came home, and they all had dinner. They all gathered to go over the information on the peat bog. There was a cool breeze blowing through the house, and the sweet scent of lilacs was in the air. That's when Dad dropped a bomb on the peaceful evening. He opened the gathering with the announcement that during his investigation into peat, he found it had value to landscapers, so he sold many cubic yards of it. The buyer would come to get it that weekend. Everyone but Roy gasped in shock.

Roy got up, eyes blazing, fists clenched. His body was rigid with anger. Mom was afraid he was going to physically confront his father. Roy pushed his chair back and stepped away from the table. Dad stood up with his eyes fixed on Roy, his fists clenched, and a smirk on his face as though this was playing out just as he wanted.

Mom cried out to Roy, "Stop it!"

Roy hesitated and while staring at Dad with his eyes that icy pale blue they got when he was on the verge of doing something violent. He then turned and crashed out of the dining room through the kitchen and outdoors. He was heading to the Glade and the solace it provided him.

Dad told everyone to sit and finish the discussion. They all sat and there was a quiet hush that you could almost feel. Dad cleared his throat and restated the sale of peat, and that the buyer would be here Saturday morning, but he had to work in the city. Mom would provide directions to the buyer. They then went over the information he had collected on peat, and Ross said that it agreed with what he could gather for the encyclopedia. Dolly emphatically agreed with Ross.

Peat moss is the dead, decayed plant matter of sphagnum moss that settles and builds up in the bottom of bogs for thousands of years. Moss started growing some 540 million years ago, ages before even animals walked the land. Found to have anti-biotic effects, used during World War II, it is a useful species for humankind and is now used worldwide for multiple purposes. These are natural bogs, the decayed matter known as peat moss is usually not purely sphagnum moss. It may contain organic matter from other plants, animals, or insects. However, peat moss or sphagnum peat moss is dead and decayed when harvested.

Everything seemed to be subdued, even the outdoors seemed muffled and tense.

Dad got up and said, "Jean, let's go for our walk around the property."

Mom got up and asked Dolly to come with them. Dolly jumped up and down with excitement. Dad looked at her and began to say something, but Mom's icy glare brooked no comment from him, and they went out into the evening, with Dolly skipping along and asking questions. There would be no personal time between them tonight.

This worked out great for Ross. He grabbed a couple of light jackets and headed out after Roy.

Roy stormed about halfway to the Glade before he calmed down a bit. He didn't lose his anger, but it stilled his rage. *How could his father have done that? How could he have sold some of The Triangle? He knew his father would have his way with things, but to drag them all the way out into this strange country and then, just as they began to settle in and get comfortable, he began to sell pieces of it. How could he?*

He sat on the bank of the pond, and the sound of the water trickling over the rocks as it exited the culvert under the tracks was very calming. Several others accompanied the damselfly, some of which were dragonflies. The amount of insects that gathered when the boys were there was increasing with every visit. When the boys were there, the spider would come out. The little rabbit usually showed up as well. The peace and harmony that prevailed in this small glen was almost magical in its impact on Roy. He breathed deeply and let the sweet air cleanse his inside and refocus on what was in front of him, the future, and not what was behind him in the past.

The damselfly which hovered around him and settled down as he did. It brought calmness to him. The spider perched on the upper edge of its web radiated patience to him, and he absorbed it. The little rabbit was always on the alert for danger. He was prime dinner material for many predators. Roy relaxed and was clear minded but always alert for perils.

Ross joined him and gave him a coat. Bootsie came along with him and the little rabbit, and the assorted insects welcomed her. Their damselfly came over and perched on Ross's finger. The evening was sliding into night, and it was getting dark.

"How are you?"

"I am okay now. I always am fine when I am in the Glade," Roy said, as he looked Ross in the eyes to underscore his sincerity.

The gathering of fireflies amongst the trees and tall grasses signaled the beginning of darkness.

"I can't believe he did it, letting no one know—without even talking to us. Why does he do this?" Roy inquired rhetorically.

"I don't know."

Roy sighed, shook his head, and got up and stretched. It was getting darker and chilly. Crickets and nightbirds were beginning their night songs. The mockingbird was the loudest, but the nightjars were good competition.

After saying goodbye to their friends, the boys started home. Night had descended on them, the grass in the pasture was starting to dew up from the temperature change, and the nocturnal vestments clothed everything, changing the obvious and distinct to the obscure and capricious. This night world was the source of grand adventures and mystery, and the boys loved to wander the woods and fields with only moonlight to be their lantern.

As they passed by the bog, Roy stopped and stared at it. He smiled, then chuckled, then laughed so hard he fell in the grass. Ross was surprised and completely puzzled by Roy's radical change of disposition.

"Don't you get it, Ross?" he said when he got his breath back. "I am going to have a pond in the middle of the bog, just like I imagined and heard, but could never find. The guy coming here Saturday is going to dig it for me!"

"Little brother, The Triangle shape, the mounds, and now the peat bog all bridges from the ancient to today in one form or another. They are equally ingrained in legend and myth plus practicable application.

They both laughed and wondered at the strange behavior of this land. Roy once again assured him that this place was something special for him, and he stepped out across the pasture eager to see what tomorrow had in store for him and his family.

Drawn by: Abi Lynn Gordon

Aspen Glade

TALE NUMBER ELEVEN

GLADE, GROVE, COPSE, WHATEVER

"Don't part with your illusions. When they are gone, you may still exist, but you have ceased to live."
– Mark Twain.

The boys faced a dilemma. They wanted to find out about the Glade, what kind of trees it consisted of, where did the creek come from and where did it go, why is the ground not cultivated, whether there are any legends about it, and more? The dilemma was that while they had questions that needed to be answered, they also had kept the Glade private and not shared it with anyone. That's why they were on their way to the Glade, with Bootsie, to sit in its serenity and try to come up with an answer.

"He thinks he is getting away with something, ha," Roy chided.

Bootsie huffed her agreement.

"Who does, about what?" Ross asked.

"Dad, about selling the bog," he responded. "He thinks he is so clever. All he is doing is what the bog wants. He is creating a pond in the center of it just like I believed in the beginning, and you said wasn't there."

Bootsie huffed again.

"There wasn't any pond there. And I wish Bootsie would stop agreeing with you," Ross firmly stated.

"It was not there yet, and you need to take that up with Bootsy," his brother answered.

"Bootsie, stop agreeing with him, please."

Bootsie put her ears and tail down in submission.

"Thanks, good dog," Ross said and roughed up her ears.

Bootsie responded with a joyful bark and bounded up ahead of them.

"Are you telling me the bog was saying there was a pond coming?"

"Yep"

"If that is true, it is way too spooky," Ross said.

"You mean way too groovy? Remember day one? You said that the excavation was hurting the land, and I thought we should heal it?" Roy said.

"Oh yeah, and I asked how, and you said it would show us how. It would be a glorious adventure."

"That's correct little brother, that is absolutely correct. It is an adventure of the grandest scale!"

They were entering the Glade. And everything quieted down, including themselves. Bootsie had got there ahead of them.

The boys settled down on the bank of the pond as usual and greeted their animal friends: the damselfly, bunny, and spider. The animals acknowledged their greeting. Over their time at The Triangle, the boys developed a relationship with the trio. It was one component of the harmony of the Glade, along with the bubbling of the creek as it exited from under the railroad embankment. The cool freshness of the air, the gentle rustling of the leaves, and the dappled sunlight filtering through the foliage, wrapped up in the acoustic silence provided by the dense undergrowth—a harmony that echoed how it was in a time before.

Roy laid back lost in thought on how to get the questions they had about the Glade answered while keeping the Glade private to themselves. Ross busied himself trying to get the damselfly, which they named Queeny, to go from finger to finger with no success. Every time he tried to get Queeny to transfer from one finger to the next, it flew up and hovered until his hand quieted. When it did, Queeny would settle down on the index finger, her preferred finger.

There was a multitude of dragonflies and damselflies that visited the Glade since the boys had adopted it and it had adopted them in return. Every time Roy tried to coax one of the dragon or damselflies to land on his fingers, the spider clicked, and the flies would dash away from him and wouldn't return to being close to his outreached hand until the spider quieted down.

"I am going to have to have a talk with that spider," Roy sighed.

That brought a rash of clicking from the spider.

"Oh, shut up spider," Roy grumbled and patted Bootsie on her head. She has sidled down next to him. She huffed in response to the pat.

After several minutes of pondering, Roy sat up and stated that he had an idea and asked Ross if he had any. Ross looked away from playing with Queeny and stated that he had not come up with anything.

"Ok, here's the plan. We call a family meeting to investigate the Glade. This isn't on our property, so Dad can't mess with it. It's pretty far away so Dolly won't be interested in trudging all the way down there, and John isn't going to come down here, so we can check out the Glade without having people tramping all over this sanctuary. What do you think?" Roy put forth to Ross.

Ross pondered this plan for a while and agreed, then returned to working with Queeny. Roy laid back and petted Bootsie while he thought more about his plan. They spent the rest of the morning hanging out in the Glade chasing crawfish in the pond and looking for a good sample of the trees so Dad could identify the tree. They headed home for lunch with a sample of the trees.

Roy walked up Hilltop Road, after lunch, to spend some time with John. Bootsie stayed home to let Dolly brush her out. Dolly was *helping* Ross out in the living room, looking up the tree type in the encyclopedia, using the sample they brought back from the Glades as a guide. This helped Mom out, not having to monitor Dolly.

The summer was supplying everything the farmlands needed to produce a good harvest. Warm to hot daytimes with cooler nights and plenty of rains and steady downpours without torrents. There were fields with crops bursting forth as far as Roy could see, as he climbed the steep hill on his way to the Hilltop Farm. They filled the air with the scent of greenery, earth, and fresh-cut hay that lay drying in the fields. Soon the raking and baling would start, and John had promised to let Roy help; maybe even drive a tractor. He had graduated from mucking out the gutters in the barn and filling the manure wagon. He was helping with the milking; not only hauling full milk cans to the cooling house and putting them in the cold-water bath but also putting the milk machine onto the cow's teats and then stripping the teats of the remaining milk by hand when the machine was through. He had gotten to where he could direct a stream of milk into one of the several cat's mouths that were always begging for some. This was an exciting summer, full of grand adventures. Just the opposite of what he dreaded when they left the neighborhood some time ago.

He found John sitting behind the house under his favorite tree, enjoying some quiet time. Roy sat down on the ground and pinched a stalk of rye grass to chew on. John grunted hello, and Roy grunted back. He really enjoyed being addressed in the same manner as an adult and returning the hello in like terms. They just sat there not saying anything, looking out from the opposite side of the Hilltop Farm that The Triangle was on. The hill was much steeper on this side. There was a gravel road going down the hill. Water had partially washed it out. The steepness of the road would continue to make it a high-maintenance item. At the bottom of the hill, it crossed a creek that the boys had named Clear Creek, giving access to fields on the floor of the valley.

Stumpy came over to have Roy scratch his ears; he stretched out and promptly farted a foul-smelling missive. The lack of any dominant breeze caused the stench to linger, at least at Roy's elevation. It is so pervasive that he had to get up and move away from the dog.

John spat a stream of Red Man at an ant hill.

"Dog must have eaten some cat poop again," John chuckled.

"Phew, that smell is worse than anything I ever smelled before," Roy said as he coughed and wiped his eyes.

He coughed again and sat back down. A breeze blew from the west so Roy could sit upwind from the dog.

"Did you come all the way up here to sit and smell my dog's farts, or do you have some business with me?

"Have some business if you have time to answer a few questions."

"Yep, why don't you run out to the milk house and get us a couple of beers from the cold-water tank?"

"Ok, but can I have a root beer instead?"

"It's your life little pickle," John said, continuing to look down the valley.

Roy ran and got cold drinks. He opened them and ran back to John. He gave the farmer his beer and made sure he was upwind from Stumpy. He tried to figure out where to start with his questions. John emitted another tobacco juice projectile on the tiny industrious insects.

"Saw you and your brother coming back from the grove of trees at the end of your property. You two boys spend a lot of time there. Is it special?"

It was as if he knew what Roy was thinking. How did he do that? John was a strange man, the boy mused.

Without waiting for Roy to answer, he got up and said, "Let's move to the other side of the yard, where we can see it." And off he went. Roy scrambled to keep up with him. John found a place that suited him with an anthill within spitting range. He took a long pull off his beer, how he could drink beer and chew tobacco at the same time perplexed Roy.

"Well, boy?"

"What do you know about that grove of trees where the creek passes under the railroad track?"

"Well, there are a few things. They are part of the fallow land. If the tracks weren't there, your property would include them, and your property is part of the fallow land."

He said this as if Roy's family ownership did not matter.

"That is the only place around here with that type of tree. There are strange lights and sounds coming from there at nighttime sometimes."

"What lights and sounds?"

John spat at a line of ants heading their way. The wad landed right in front of the line and caused them to veer off in a different direction.

"Ha," he exclaimed in satisfaction.

Roy assumed by that exclamation he was ahead in today's battle with the ants.

"Well, I am not really sure. I never go down there at night, but sometimes if the wind is just right, it sounds like real faint singing, and there are steady lights flitting around in there, tiny little lights."

He was gazing down at the Glade with the look someone had when they recall a fond memory.

"I remember Miss Lloyd telling me about the fairies of the Lloyd homeland, Wales, and how some of them stowed away on their ships and came here with their ancestors, to look out for them," John said in a quiet voice with a smile on his lips.

"Do you believe that?"

"I don't know. It does not seem to hurt anything, and it helps me remember her and her sister. I miss them. It gets lonely up here. I am glad you folks moved in down there. The land is also, I can feel it."

"What do you mean, you can feel it?" I asked.

"Son, when you work the land, live with it day in and day out, you can feel it. When you run your hands through fresh dirt, it will talk to you. Tell you what it needs, when it's ready for planting, and its history."

"You're kidding me."

"Not a bit. If you stay here long enough and work the earth with me, it will speak to you as well. Your dad says he's from a dirt farm in Indiana. Ask him, he'll know." He spat again, and this time bowled over the leading ants. He chuckled and got up.

"Time for chores, lending a hand?"

"Sure thing John, be glad to."

Roy always felt a little strange calling him "John." He was an adult after all. But that's what John wanted.

Later that evening Ross, Bootsie, and Dolly went to the mound to sit and watch the evening turn into nighttime. The purple and gold of the horizon slowly faded into dark. One by one, the stars started to come out and share their light with them. The heat of the day faded, and the coolness of the evening came on. They seemed to be a matched pair, darkness, and coolness. It took a while for the earth to cool off so you could still have warm butt and goosebumps on your arms at the same time. It was a neat experience.

They were sitting on their mound and looking toward the looted mound that was one-half mile across the fields on the other side of Clear Creek. In the gathering darkness, the mound went from a distinct bread loaf shape to a dark, indistinct lump.

"We need to go to the looted mound and do some serious investigation to see if any artifacts are still there," Roy said quietly, in keeping with the growing quietness of the night.

"Do you think there would be anything left after all this time?" Ross asked

"Won't know until we know, will we." Roy replied.

"Can I go with you?" Dolly asked, "please."

Roy and Ross looked at each other. Ross shrugged his shoulders.

"Sure thing, snake girl," Roy said. "When we make that expedition, we'll take you along. You can be chief sorter."

Dolly jumped for joy and hugged her brothers, to their vexation.

Ross thought a moment and then added "I'll check the encyclopedia and see if there are some guidelines for an archaeological dig."

"Cool," Roy replied.

It was pretty dark now, and the fireflies were starting to make their appearance.

Dolly and Bootsie were off trying to catch the fireflies or maybe even a fairy according to Dolly.

The boys indulged her belief that there were fairies mixed in with the fireflies.

When Dolly was out in the field the boys shared what they had discovered about the Glade this afternoon. Ross was a little upset about the supernatural spin that John put on it. He shared one very special thing he had learned from the encyclopedia.

"It appears that the trees are really one tree," Ross exclaimed.

"What do you mean, one tree?" his brother's voice was filled with disbelief.

"I mean just that," Ross responded resolutely. "According to the encyclopedia, the tree is an Aspen tree, I think. It has a root system that is called a name I can't remember. It produces new shoots from its root system which spreads all over. These are the same tree, and they live thousands of years, just reproducing. It's like a mother and all her babies."

"Wow," Roy exclaimed, eyes wide in amazement. "That is wild. No wonder it feels so special there. It's like being cradled and protected by a mother. I wonder how old she is?"

"I don't know," Ross murmured.

He was glad that he was the one who discovered the special fact of this time.

"I hope Dad gets the same info when he's at the city tomorrow," Roy said.

Dolly came running back and was jumping up and down, "I caught one, I caught one!"

"Caught what?" the boys asked in unison.

"A fairy, I caught a fairy!" she shouted holding her clasped hands up. There was a buzzing and light flashing on and off.

"Come on Dolly," Roy said. "There aren't any fairies. You are going to kill that firefly."

Ross chimed in, "Dolly, let it go before you do injure it."

Bootsie was beside herself, barking, wagging so hard she hit herself in the face with her tail. Now she chased her tail.

"Here look for yourself." She held up her cupped hands for their study.

Roy bent down and tried to see into the tiny opening she made in her hands. What he saw was unclear. It was so bright it was hard to distinguish. It was flitting back and forth so fast it was a blur. Whatever it was, it sure wasn't a firefly, and it was mad!

"Let me take a peek," Ross said.

Roy backed up and started rubbing his eyes. They hurt a bit from the brightness.

Ross studied it for as long as he could until his eyes hurt him.

"See, I told you," Dolly said and held her cupped hands up to peer in at whatever it was.

"Don't worry she said, I'll take good care of you just like my snakes."

That set whatever it was into a frenzy. The boys could hear it loud and clear.

"What do you think it is," Roy asked his brother.

"I don't know, but it sure isn't a firefly."

"It can't be a real fairy, can it?" The older brother said.

Ross pondered that for a moment and then shook his head and looked Roy in the eye.

"The longer we're here, the more the unbelievable becomes believable," Ross sighed.

The captured thing was raising a real ruckus, and Dolly looked at the boys with bewilderment written all over her face.

"What do we do?"

"We?" exclaimed the boys.

"Yes, we're a family, right?" Dolly said with pleading in her voice. These were, after all, her big brothers. They are all wise and all strong in her eyes.

Roy stopped short with her statement about family. She was right of course. They were her brothers, and she was their little sister. They were supposed to protect her and share their knowledge and experiences. Roy's regard for Dolly changed at this juncture in time.

Roy stepped forward and grasped Dolly's hands in his own.

"Whatever you have in there is not happy, and we need to be in harmony with this land and its inhabitants. You need to let it free."

Dolly looked into her hands again and says, "I won't hurt you; I promise."

The captive was not quieted down at all.

Dolly looked at the boys and said, "I need a friend. I'm all alone so much."

The boys looked at each other. "We need to help out," Roy said.

Ross held up his hand and took Dolly's hands in his. He spoke into her hands. "If Dolly lets you go, will you be her friend?"

Amazingly, the captive quieted down, and there was a steady glow in her clasped hands.

"Really?" Dolly asked her captive and seemed to get the response she wanted. She opened her hands, and the light did a quick circle over their heads and was gone. Dolly had a big smile on her face and the boys looked at each other incredulously.

"I have a friend, a real friend!" she yelled excitedly while jumping up and down.

Bootsie got caught up in the spirit of things and joined in with barking and tail-wagging. She once again hit herself in the face with her tail and was absorbed in chasing it. When she caught it, she bit it, and yelped in pain. This got her mad at it all over again, and the silliness was repeated until she got tired out. It was quite a show.

They all headed to the house as the darkness of the night contrasted with the bright flashing fireflies, some not flashing but emitting a steady light and louder hum of their wings.

Each of the children looked forward to the coming day for different reasons. Dolly to got to play with her new friend. Ross looked forward to Dad verifying his findings on the trees being aspen. Roy was anxious to get to the Glade and experience the sense of well-being and refuge it provided him.

The next day brought summer thunderstorms, so the children were confined to the house and the sheltered front porch. Dolly wanted them to go to the cellar and play with the snakes. The boys countered with the board games Candyland, Sorry, and a really strange version of Monopoly. They spent the afternoon rolling dice, laughing, wrestling, and squabbling. Mom had to intervene several times and act as a referee. She also used cookies and milk to mediate. Chocolate chip and coconut cookies were the most popular.

They also spent a fair amount of time on the porch watching the storm. The thunderheads rose in the west preceded by a chilly breeze. They marveled at the goosebumps it raised on their arms.

The underbelly of the storm clouds was dark, even black and there were layers upon layers of foamy white filling edged with gray, and every so often a bolt of lightning would strike out of it to the ground. Dad had told the boys if they counted one Mississippi, two Mississippi, and so on until they heard thunder, the total number they counted was the distance in miles the lightning was from them. The kids liked tracking the storms as they approached. There were some storms that were so strong and fast that they were almost all black and roiled upward to cover the whole sky as they raced across the horizon. Multiple lightning strikes emitted from the turbulence, so it was impossible to count the distance. These were the ones that could become dangerous, and they needed to keep an eye on them and stay close to the cellar.

This one was like the first one and the rain was gentle and the lightning infrequent. The kids enjoyed watching it approach and occasionally they would dash out into the rain. The afternoon was spent in this manner, with pauses to enjoy snacks their mom delivered.

Mom would take time out of her cooking and cleaning to share the snacks and tell them tales that her mother would tell her when she was a young girl in Wales.

The afternoon zoomed by and before they knew it Dad came home, and it was time to get ready for dinner. Roy was surprised that he and his brother had spent all afternoon with Dolly and had a great time.

After dinner, Dad presented what he had found out about the trees in the Glade. They were indeed Aspens. His info matched up with what Ross had uncovered in his research. Dad had some new info about the Aspen. These aspens were called Quaking or Trembling Aspens because their leaves were flat and attached to branches with long slender stalks which allowed them to "quake or tremble" in the slightest of breezes.

"This is a very interesting tree. I'd like to check them out," Dad said.

Roy stiffened; his mind went into a swirl. He could not let Dad into the Glade! He would ruin it with his attitude of strictly business. The direction of this conversation needed to be changed. Then he remembered what John had said, "When you run your hands through fresh dirt, it will talk to you. Tell you what it needs when it's ready for planting, and its history," and asked Dad if that was true.

Dad was taken aback at the question. It changed the subject entirely. He thought about it for a while. His eyes took on a vacant stare as though he was watching a movie in his head. The same look John had had.

"My dad, your grandfather, would tell me and my brother the same thing."

Then Dad went on to tell them how his dad would take a handful of soil and crumble it in his hands, smell it, and put some on the tip of his tongue and taste it. Then slowly let the soil trickle through his fingers.

"The soil talked to him," he told me, just like John said. "I could never do that. I didn't believe in it I guess," he said almost sadly and looked down and sighed again.

"Well enough of that, I need to get busy with the things that need doing around here."

Roy looked at Ross and winked. That was a close one. So, the Glade is a special place with special powers, or at least it seemed that way, and Roy believed in it. It was his refuge that protected him.

TALE NUMBER TWELVE

A BOG TOO FAR?

"Life is a daring adventure or nothing at all."
– Helen Keller.

Roy peered through the binoculars. He had borrowed them from his father to use to check out the bog on the other side of the highway. He and Ross were at Hilltop Farm sitting on the hillside overlooking The Triangle and the land beyond. They were considering investigating the bog on the other side of the highway because it and the bog on The Triangle were all part of the same bog. When the highway and the railroad tracks were built, they divided the bog up.

The bog and related land had been stipulated to remain fallow or unworked. Legend held that that had been done to provide a piece of land reserved for the fairies and other magical creatures that supposedly had stowed away with the Lloyd clan when it immigrated from Wales. With the highway and railroad being constructed through the reserved land the promise has been broken. The boys wondered if there were consequences because of that violation. They also wondered if the bog on The Triangle was any different from the bog on the other side of the highway as a result of them being separated.

That's what the boys were studying. From the vantage point of Hilltop Farm's height and their father's binoculars, they hoped they would have a clear view of the bogland on the other side of US Hwy 16. They had hoped to see some differences so they could convince their parents that they needed to cross the highway.

"Here Ross, you take a look," Roy said as he passed the binoculars to his brother.

Ross adjusted the width of the instrument and studied the land across the highway. He slowly moved them back and forth getting them adjusted to his liking. He sat quietly for quite a while, slowly panning his view around the land. He grunted every so often.

"Well?" Roy queried.

"Hmmm," was the only response Roy got.

"Come on," Roy jabbed Ross in the ribs.

"Stop it!"

"Then tell me what you are seeing."

"Ok, I don't see anything that is very different from our bog, other than it is much bigger."

"Nothing?"

"Nothing except there are a lot more dragonflies and damselflies there. Everything is much greener and looked much more alive than the middle area between the highway and tracks," stated Ross.

"Well, that is something," Roy hopefully said.

"I don't think it is going to be enough," Ross said ruefully.

The boys had asked permission to go explore the bog on the other side of the highway to compare it to theirs. Their parents originally told them no because the highway was dangerous, and cars drove at 65 miles an hour or more. The boys kept asking, looking for some way to change their minds. Finally, at the point of losing his temper, Dad relented and said that if they could find some evidence of a difference, they could explore it. They also had to convince Dad or Mom to take them across the highway.

That is why they were sitting on the Hilltop Farm's height with Dad's binoculars.

The main motive that was driving Roy in these explorations and investigations was that he was compelled to learn what this land looked, felt, and smelled like, during the before time. He felt attached to that land or maybe not the land but the Spirit of that time. Only getting in touch with the period or Spirit would satisfy the persistent urge; "scratch that itch" is what his Uncle Ross would say.

"Well, we'll have to make it work. I need to think about it," Roy said.

Ross got up and put the binoculars away.

Roy got up and stretched as John was coming across the drive from the barn.

"Find what you were looking for?" he asked.

Stumpy was with him and when he saw the boys, he half ran, half hobbled over to them with a happy little bark. Roy turned to Ross and told him how the little dog loved having his belly rubbed. Ross knelt to get down to Stumpy. Roy backed slowly away from them. The dog rolled onto his back, proffering his belly for a good rub. Ross obliged and started to rub his belly. Stumpy sighed and stretched out. Right on cue, the dog unleashed a fart of grand proportions, "Baaraaap!" Ross was immediately enveloped in the canines close to lethal smelling flatulence.

"Aaaaaahg!" Ross cried out and leaped back and continued to yell.

"How can he do that and be alive, my eyes are watering, and I can't breathe."

Stumpy got up and followed Ross for more belly rubs. Ross ran down the hill toward home, and the dog looked wistful (if a dog can look wistful, Roy believed they could) after Ross.

Roy was laughing so hard that he collapsed. Unnoticed to him, Stumpy sidled up to him and replicated its last gaseous missive.

"Awwww!" Roy moaned and moved upwind. Stumpy looked confused and forlorn. Roy cautiously inched up to the dog and scratched his ears, making sure to stay upwind.

"That's okay boy, I still love you."

Ross witnessed the gassing that Roy experienced and yelled up the hill that Roy deserved it. He then turned and continued homebound.

"You'll get used to it," John said with a broad grin on his face.

"No, I won't, nobody can," Roy declared.

John shrugged and changed the subject. "We're going to start baling next week, you want to get set up to drive the tractor?"

"You bet."

"Well come on up to the machinery shed, and I'll start getting you familiar with the equipment."

The rest of the day was a blur of learning the different functions of the equipment and actually sitting on the tractor, starting it up, and making sure he could reach all the controls. *This is way better than the city Roy thought.* A lot of time was spent on the dangers of the equipment and the baling process. John highlighted these points by exhibiting the scars, a missing finger, and a semi-crippled left leg. The emphasis he placed on safety was in keeping with his first instructions to the boys.

"You can go wherever you want and do anything you want just as long as you don't hurt yourself, my animals, or things. Have fun and learn."

John's consistency was reassuring to the boys, Roy in particular. His yes was yes, and his no was no. Roy tried to live his life in that way but slipped many times.

That night at dinner Roy shared how John was getting him ready to help with the baling, maybe even drive the tractor. Mom gulped and looked at Dad.

"It's all right Jean, John spoke to me about it last week. I'll check it out before the boy is turned loose."

Mom didn't appear totally assured. She wasn't done with the subject just yet. Roy took note of the fact that there were conversations between John and Dad he was unaware of. He needed to remember that.

"Did you boys note any major differences with the bog on the other side of the highway?" Dad asked.

He had noted the binoculars were back and assumed they had finished checking the bog out.

Dad continued, "I drive past it every day and other than bugs, dragonflies spattered on my windshield, I don't see much of a difference.

The statement about dragonflies being splattered on the windshield startled the children.

"Oh no!" Dolly exclaimed. Her eyes were wide with fright. "Daddy, you can't do that. They may be fairies, my friends." "Daddy" was her special name for Dad, and he loved it.

Mom put a hand on Dolly's shoulder and tried to comfort her before there was a meltdown.

"Not to worry little one, the ones that get spattered on windshields are just bugs that know no better. I'm convinced that fairies are far too smart to get caught on the highway. Right boys?" His look at the boys clearly indicated he wanted a prompt and vigorous agreement.

"That is right, absolutely correct!" they both chimed in.

That seemed to settle Dolly down, but Roy knew he and Ross were going to be expected to provide some sort of evidence later.

That gave Roy an idea—a brilliant idea.

"Dad, Mom, why don't Ross and I take Dolly to the bog across the highway, and we can check out the fact that the fairies are too smart to get splattered on windshields? Ross and I can also check that bog out for differences from ours." Roy eagerly put it forward.

Dad looked at him with narrowed eyes and a thin tight mouth. He knew what Roy was up to but couldn't stop it without being the big bad guy. Mom was already shaking her head no; Ross was staring at him wide-eyed like he thought Roy was crazy: Dolly was almost overcome with joy.

"Yes, yes!" she yelled. "Tomorrow morning we'll go and take Bootsie with us. Yes, a great adventure like you're always talking about big brother, yes, yes."

"Whoa, slow down little one," Dad said, holding up his hands for emphasis.

"Yes, that is not going to happen," Mom added.

Dad and Mom knew they had been trapped by Roy, who sat at the table with the most innocent face that he could muster. Dolly was hugging him.

"I love you, big brother."

Roy hugged her back.

"You too, Ross," she hugged him also, then returned to Roy.

Bootsie, hearing her name mentioned and with the excitement happening in the kitchen, joined in with Dolly. She performed her famous swat nose with a wagging tail and then chasing it routine, and then barked happily for whatever reason.

Ross looked at Roy shaking his head with an incredulous look pasted to his face. *His big brother must have been made crazy with that stench from Stumpy. Luckily, he had run away.*

Dad knew that if he refused to let them go, he would be a villain in his sweet little daughter's mind. She was his favorite, and she showered him with love. He did not want to jeopardize that. Roy had trapped him plain and simple. He hadn't helped his position with that bit about splattering dragonflies on his windshield. How was he to know the bugs might be fairies for Pete's sake? He had to come up with some sort of solution.

Mom was amazed at how quickly everything spun out of control. She knew Roy's idea was a trap that she and Bill had blindly stepped into. They needed to counter with something that was ok with the kids, especially Dolly, tantrum city. They had gone from not crossing the highway to crossing it, in the blink of an eye.

Mom and Dad both looked at Roy while he was smiling innocently and hugging Dolly. He knew that he would need to keep on his guard for payback from Mom and Dad.

"All right, here's what we are going to do," Dad said. Holding up his hands as a sign that order was to be restored and they were to pay attention to him.

"Mom will accompany you across the highway and supervise your time over there. Maybe she can prepare a picnic lunch for all of you. There is some high ground and a couple of trees for shade."

Mom glared at Dad who also had assumed an innocent, well-intentioned look. Dolly erupted with glee. She ran around the table and hugged Dad who looked at Roy and nodded. *Well played son,* he thought.

Dolly now descended on Mom.

"You are the best mother ever. Don't forget to pack lunch for Bootsie. Last time you didn't, and I had to share my sandwich with her," Dolly exclaimed hugging and jumping up to kiss Mom.

Mom knew she was boxed in, but this was not over, she was not without a move of her own.

"Dolly, honey why don't you sleep upstairs with me tonight and we can make plans for our great adventure? You can also make plans with the boys.

"Yippee!" Dolly squealed.

Dad said "Hey, tomorrow is a weekday, I have to get up early to go to work."

"She'll mess with us all night," Roy complained.

Mom cocked her head, and it was her turn to look wide-eyed innocent. Dolly and Bootsie were already on their way upstairs.

Ross looked around and said, "What just happened."

The next morning the children, Bootsie, and Mom stood at the edge of the highway. Roy carried the picnic basket, Ross had the water jug, and Mom held onto Bootsie's leash. She also held onto Dolly's hand. Both the boys were yawning. They had been bugged until late into the night by Dolly relaying plans, she and Mom had made. Dad had eventually moved downstairs to sleep.

"It is clear now; everyone let's get across quickly," Mom said.

They all hurried across the highway and proceeded up the small rise onto the land across from them. The day was starting out perfectly. Big, pure, white cotton candy appearing clouds drifted slowly across a pale blue sky. There was a steady breeze that would go from a refreshing cooling one to a muggy warm one as the day wore on.

The family continued, staying on the high ground which was on the west side. Jean sized up the piece of land. This was a big piece of property, approximately 40 acres. The highway cut off about 25 percent of the original parcel so it could easily have been 50 acres. That was a sizable set aside for a supposed group of stowaway mythical creatures. But those were different times when the Lloyd Clan immigrated here in the Eighteenth Century. The majority of the parcel was untillable without some major drainage work which wasn't an option when the land was originally settled.

Up on the high ground, where they were, it was dry and open; the picnic should be pleasant. As the terrain dropped down into the peat bog proper, she guessed that the environment would not be as pleasant. She was glad that she would not have to experience it. That was the kid's responsibility. She gathered them around.

"Pay attention now children. I'll only say this once. If you don't obey me, we're going back home, period, no talkback, understand?"

There was no doubt in the kid's mind she was not kidding.

"You've got about an hour to explore before lunch, I'll call you for lunch, once just once. Got it?"

They nodded that they got it. Bootsie even barked assent.

"Okay, take off, I'll set up the picnic under this tree, okay go."

Roy led the way as normal with Bootsie bounding ahead, Dolly in the center, and Ross bringing up the rear. They descended down the incline through grass and scattered bushes and then into the bog. The surroundings went from an agreeable one to hot, smelly, and full of biting and stinging insects. The reeds and brambles grew tall enough to prevent them from seeing where they were, just like their bog.

Roy started hearing the splashing and sounds of frogs, the same as he had heard in their bog. He stopped, confused and a little afraid. He hoped he wasn't going to experience the disquieting events he had in their bog. He stopped and turned around to look at Ross. His disturbed state of mind was obvious.

"Don't worry, I hear it too. I think it is a real pond," Ross said.

Dolly said that she heard it also.

With a sense of relief, Roy started off in the direction that the sounds were coming from. After a tough few minutes of fighting their way through dense reeds and stunted bushes, ankle-deep in foul-smelling water that seeped up from where their feet sank in the sponge-like peat, they arrived at the pond.

They lined up at the edge of the pond. Everything seemed brighter, cleaner, and had the smell that reminded Roy of being lakeside. A fresh beckoning scent recalling the first night, driving through the lake town Oconomowoc and smelling the lakes, wanting to go jump in them. It made him smile.

Ross murmured, "This is really a difference. The pond makes it totally different. Doesn't it Roy?"

"Uh huh," Roy agreed.

"Wow," Dolly said.

Bootsie whined.

"Are you kids all right," they could hear their mother call.

"Yes," they all shouted in unison. Bootsie barked.

"This is really neat," Ross said. "I wonder if we can go swimming in it?"

"I was wondering the same thing, Ross."

"Me too," Dolly followed.

Roy gestured out over the pond, "Look at all the dragonflies and damselflies. They are everywhere.

Dolly was all excited.

"Look at all the frogs, and I can see some tiny little fish also. Wow, this is so neat. Can we go swimming?"

"No," the boys said together.

Mom would have a conniption if they brought frogs home.

"The pond makes all the difference in the world. That's what happened when the highway and railroad tracks were put in. It cut the rest of the land off from the pond and its life. Our bog needs that pond that Dad is unknowingly going to give us," Roy proclaimed.

"What pond," Dolly asked looking up at Roy. "We're getting a pond?"

"Now you've done it, Roy."

"Zip it, Ross."

"What Pond?" Dolly insisted.

"When dad has the peat removed, by the man he sold it to, it will create a hole in the bog that will fill with water creating a pond," Roy explained to her.

"What I must do, with Ross's help, is to get the hole where we want it. This is a secret. You can't tell Dad, or he will mess it up."

"I can keep a secret" Dolly piped up. "You can trust me. I'm going to see if there are any fairies around here, and any snakes, maybe catch a frog. Will you teach me how to put it to sleep?"

She started to look around. Bootsie started sniffing around as if helping her.

Roy and Ross looked at each other after she prattled off all the things she was doing at once and just shrugged.

"Let's work our way to the creek," Roy directed.

They all started edging their way along the pond heading toward where the creek should be. As they moved along in standard caravan order, Roy-Dolly-Ross, Bootsie roaming, they eventually made it to the creek's bank. Roy and Ross would have jumped in if Dolly wasn't along.

Ross looked around, "You know this bog feels and smells better than ours does. It must be because of the pond and creek being part of it. Ours doesn't have those."

Roy looked at his brother. He constantly surprised him with his insight on matters that completely were overlooked by him.

"You are right."

Roy looked toward the highway and suggested they check out the culvert that ran under the road. Off they went.

When they reached the highway, they could see dragonflies and damselflies going and coming through the pipe. Every once in a while some would go over the culvert and cross the highway, running the danger of getting splattered.

They studied this for a while and Ross commented, "The smart ones go through the pipe safely, the not so-smart ones go up and over into danger."

Dolly sighed and said, "I understand now. The fairies are smart enough not to go over the highway. Good, I'm hungry."

Bootsie agreed with a couple of barks, and they all started back up the hill toward Mom and the picnic basket.

Roy was amazed at how everything was tied together and made sense if you gave it time to reveal itself. It was a wonderful place they had arrived at. He now understood why the bog on The Triangle was calling to him. It needed a pond to come to life. Now he understood, all the spookiness and silliness made sense after all. Life's Principle: Trust your gut. And be patient.

Now it was time to have a picnic and play card games that Mom always brought to picnics.

Next was to figure out how the town, Ixonia, got its name and how it started. This was their new hometown after all.

Tomorrow would bring a new set of adventures and maybe even some dangers. But today had enough of its own to focus on. Tomorrow was another day.

Feed mill & Grain Elevator   Ixonia

TALE NUMBER THIRTEEN

WHAT IS AN IXONIA?

"One man alone can be pretty dumb sometimes, but for real bona fide stupidity, there ain't nothin' can beat teamwork."
– Edward Abbey

When Roy heard that they were going to move to a place called Ixonia, he thought they were moving to a foreign country. In his geography class, he heard names of small little countries that sounded like it. He was surprised to find out that was the name of the town they would be living close to, about one-mile due west. When they moved to the area, Ixonia had a thriving population of 100 souls, according to the signpost when you entered the town on US Highway 16. That sign never changed the whole time he lived in the area. He figured that the reason was the death rate equaled the birth or new resident's level. He maybe should have asked someone about that.

It was a quiet, friendly town that was clustered along the highway. Surrounded primarily by dairy farms, it reflected that lifestyle. The biggest structure in town was a feed mill/grain elevator named Farmco, flanked by two bars. These establishments were frequented by the farmer before, after, or during the conducting of business in Farmco. Roy had observed the behavior of some of the farmers in the bar and he had little doubt of the reason for some of the maiming that took place in the farming vocation.

It was interesting how certain farmers always went to the same bar. Roy thought maybe it was because of a particular beer, bartender, or the pickled pig's feet brand. Not so, John informed him, the segregation was because of where their farms were located. Everyone east of Farmco went to the bar that was on the east side and vice versa on the west side. That made common sense to them, Roy supposed. In fact, the bartenders who also were the owners used to be farmers from, you guessed it, the same side that their bar was on. Everything in its place in Ixonia, there was little tolerance for disorder.

Farmco was alongside the railroad tracks, fronting US Highway 16. It was the prime focus of the town if not the reason for its early growth. Everything in town spread out from it. Across the highway was the general store, a bar/restaurant (great fish fries on Friday evenings) which were frequented by farmers from both sides of Farmco. There were several houses, a block deep, along that side of the highway, and a gas station/ repair shop on the east end of town. There was a volunteer fire department located behind the block of homes. It was the site of the Annual Fireman's Picnic every summer, which was a big deal with a carnival. Leaving town and headed west, toward The Triangle Farm, the highway rose up a hill, and at the top of it was the two-room Ixonia State Graded School. This is the one the children attended until 1956 when a new one with four rooms was built in town.

The boys, with help from Dad contacted local officials and with some input from John's memory, put together a simple history for this strangely named town. The present bustling town was proceeded in the 1600s by the Winnebago and Potawatomi Indian tribes. Signs of a much earlier civilizations are still visible in the area. Mounds, settlement remains, and burial sites were plentiful in the early years of settlement, and some remain, like their mound. The construction of a wooded plank road from Milwaukee to Watertown was done in the early 1800s; it was called the Watertown Plank Road. Legend has it that their driveway is part of the remains of it. US Highway 16 travels a similar path to the old plank road.

Roy, upon hearing this, made a mental note to dig part of their driveway up to see if any planks remained. The railroad, originally called the Milwaukee and Watertown Railroad, was constructed in the late 1850s to early 1900s. Payment for the construction was made in the manner of each subscriber's particular line of work, such as carts from wagon workers, harnesses from harness makers, cattle, horses, pigs, and various crops of grains. Most of the subscribers were people in the area who would benefit from the railroad service. The first train station, which was part of the grain elevators, was constructed in the late 1800s and has moved several times since then. There was even an electric railway further south of the railroad (a streetcar) that ran from Milwaukee to Watertown from 1904 until the increased use of cars and trucks with increased roadways eventually caused the electric railway to close.

The strange name, Ixonia, turns out to mean absolutely nothing. When the town was organized, an agreement couldn't be reached on a name for the newly established town. To simplify matters it was agreed to put all the letters of the alphabet on pieces of paper, put them into a hat and have a young lady draw them out at random one by one until a name was formed. "Ixonia" was born on January 21, 1846. John's comment on the process was that it was all kerfuffle.

As with all the other unique features of The Triangle Farm, they would need to experience it and put boots on the ground as it were.

Roy and Ross sat on the mound watching the setting sun sink into the early evening dusk that was then blanketed by the dark of the night. They continued to wait for the full moon to rise, bathing the countryside in the pale light of the sun's reflected rays.

Dad and Mom knew they were spending the night outdoors as they did many times before and would go prowling the woods, creeks, and hollows all night long. Their parents were comfortable with the boys doing this if they didn't cross the highway, which the boys didn't (so far). Bootsie usually went with them.

Tonight was going to be different. While they were not going to cross the highway per se, they were going to get up on the railroad tracks and walk into town by the light of the moon. They hadn't shared that fact with their parents, mere details Roy and Ross agreed.

They were a little concerned about Bootsie, so they talked Dolly into having the dog spend the night with her. They also had their hunting knives with them as usual and matches along with a small tarp in a backpack that had a water jug in it. This was the normal gear for a night's exploration. They had planned for this night because they would benefit from an almost full moon on a clear night.

They reviewed what they had discovered about Ixonia so far. This was a special little town with a long and special history and all that was necessary to wrap this subject up was to walk the grounds, touch, feel, and sense what it was that Ixonia was and is. It was their hometown now.

The moon came up, and the night was clear. While not quite full it was gibbous and provided plenty of light. They quietly walked down the driveway and up Hilltop Road to the railroad tracks. After putting their hands on the tracks to ensure there weren't any trains coming, they began walking toward the town. The light from the moon glinted off the tracks that had been worn smooth and shiny by the train wheels. The tracks as they disappeared into a single point in the distance were like a guiding light for their journey into the night. The moon seemed to be benevolently radiating the reflected sunlight on them.

The nighttime brought with it a totally different atmosphere than the daytime. There were different sounds from different animals that were about. There was a different smell in the air. The cooling air will leave dew on the grasses and other exposed surfaces. This moisture subdued daytime dominant smells and allowed the scent of the unaffected items to come forward and change the bouquet of the air. At first, the night seemed to be without sound, but that wasn't true. The sounds of the night were a different timbre than those of her louder, brighter brother, daytime. It required a quiet posture, then you could hear all the denizens of the darkness.

John had told him that it was in the dark of the night that we are who we really are. During the daylight, it is our reputation that is seen. In the dark of night, the imaginations of our minds; the thoughts of our hearts; the habits of our bodies are revealed. These are the things that we keep to ourselves and solely in the dark aloneness do we allow these to show.

The chittering of nesting birds and scurrying of insects. The night was the time for the hunters. The predators such as coyotes, weasels, badgers, and foxes lurked in the shadows searching for their prey. They would sometime vocalize in an attempt to scare the quarry into flight and then the chase was on. The success of the chase was made known by either howls or barking and the shriek of the unfortunate victim. Failure was punctuated with silence. Owls sat immobile on their perches waiting for their prey to reveal itself and then launched a silent winged attack with extended talons. Success or failure was marked in the same manner as with the coyotes and foxes. Deer came out and grazed in the fields alongside of wooded marshlands. They frequented the recently harvested fields feeding on the bits and pieces of crop that always was left behind. The opossum scrounged the earth for worms and grubs, raccoons quietly washed their captured food in the creek. Added to this was the distant sound of passing cars and the faint glow of their headlights. Trains would dominate all when they infrequently made their scheduled passage.

Roy liked the night and tried to blend into it the way the predators did. From this vantage point, he was able to observe as opposed to being observed. He was able to find this action of "blending" in the normal day-by-day activities in broad daylight was a major advantage.—a tool or weapon depending on circumstances.

The railroad tracks provided a clear smooth pathway for their trek, providing they kept their stride in sync with the cross ties. Another life lesson, harmony with the lay of the land makes for a smooth journey. The elevation of the railway allowed them an unobstructed view of the surroundings, except when the railway encountered the hill on the west side of town. Due to a normal train's limitations with elevation changes, the builders needed to go around or through the hill. Based on the glaciated topography, it was decided to go through. This resulted in what is referred to as a cutback.

Now the tracks were overshadowed by the land, and the boys moved quickly through this portion of the walk uneasy in the almost total darkness. When they emerged back onto an elevated portion they were on the outskirts of the town. There were darkened houses across the highway, ahead was the center of town, as it were. The main item of interest was Farmco and the business' clustered around it. If they had time, they'd like to check out the volunteer fire department.

They eventually came to Farmco. It was the tall elevators that particularly intrigued them. They were anxious to climb up atop them. They left the tracks and slowly walked onto Farmco's yard, keeping to the shadows. The smell of animal feed made of ground grains and some supplements was pleasant and hung in the air all over this area of the town. When mixing the feed for each farmer the blend was different, but the aroma was basically the same to an uneducated nose. When the stored grain in the elevators is loaded into a boxcar or the farmer delivers grain to the elevator the transfer process is an extremely dusty one, breathing is difficult, and standing too close will result in choking and gasping.

Everything in town was closed except the bars and it was unlikely anyone from there would wander over here, but they would be as quiet and hidden as possible. This was very exciting and a great adventure as they always sought to have.

There was a ladder attached to the side of an elevator, but it stopped several feet above the ground—a safety feature no doubt.

"They must have a ladder somewhere they use to get up to that ladder," Ross observed. "I guess we can't go up there without it."

"I'm not going to be stopped by that. It must be around here someplace. Let's go find it," Roy said.

Ross was hesitant to start nosing around the whole layout. He was afraid they were going to be spotted and caught.

"I think maybe we should be satisfied with just walking around the place," Ross said.

"Are you afraid to climb up there?"

"I'm afraid of getting caught."

"It's dark out, we can disappear if we have to."

"When we're on top of the elevator? We'd be trapped up there Roy, one way up and down."

"Maybe you're right about that, but that's what makes it exciting. I'm going up, you don't have to. Help me find a ladder." And he started searching around the buildings.

They found a ladder in an unlocked shed that appeared to be a storage facility for maintenance equipment. The boys were wary of every noise they made. Even the slightest sound seemed to reverberate through the whole area like an alarm of some sort. They would freeze, hold their breath, and crouch, ready to break and run.

They finally got the ladder in position, but it didn't reach all the way to the elevator ladder. Roy was sure he could reach it from the ladder they had found.

"Hold it steady Ross."

"I got it."

Roy climbed up it and stretched as far as he could. He was able to get ahold of the second rung of the elevator ladder.

"Hold it good and steady."

"I got it I said!"

Roy pushed off the ladder and grabbed the third rung and started to pull himself up. The force of his push-off kicked the ladder sideways, and it knocked loose from Ross's grip.

CRASH!

The ladder fell on some piece of equipment. Both boys froze.

"What do we do now?"

Just then, the door opened to the bar next to Farmco.

"What the hell was that?" a man asked.

The back door of the bar opened and showed a light in the backyard of the bar with empty beer kegs and various boxes and crates. There were toddlers' toys scattered around. Someone must live above the bar.

"Nothing back here," a second man called out.

"Maybe it's at Farmco?" the first man said.

"Let's look. I'll meet you there," said the second man.

Ross hissed up to Roy. "Oh crap, what do we do now? I told you this was a bad idea. You're stuck up there."

Roy could hear the fear in his brother's voice. He needed to calm him down.

"It's ok they haven't seen us yet. Carry that ladder back toward the tracks, into the shadows and hide," Roy whispered down to Ross. "Remember, carry it, no sound. I'm going up to the darkness. They are half drunk and are not very observant. Just be quiet."

Ross did as he was told, and Roy scampered silently up the side of the elevator. It was dark half the way up. Farmco's yard lights were mounted at building roof level, they were not concerned about the top of the elevators, just the yard. When he got to the top, he crawled onto the catwalk so as not to be profiled against the night sky. He had learned that from observing the night hunters.

He squirmed around so he could watch the men.

This is so cool he thought. *I'm invisible up here.*

The men walked around the yard and looked casually at the lighted portion of the yard and shrugged their shoulders.

"Must have some coons or a possum or even a rat. They are huge in the mill," one said.

The other shuddered and looked more closely at the shadows.

"Let's get back into the bar. I don't want anything to do with giant rats."

The men hurried back to the safety and comfort of the bar, looking furtively over their shoulders. Roy started silently laughing.

"Did you hear that? In one second, it went from huge to giant. That's crazy. You need to verify everything you hear if it affects you," Roy whispered to Ross.

"By the way, where are you?"

"I am right here," Ross stood up and emerged from the shadows. "Let's get out of here."

"No, I am going to finish. If you want to go home, go ahead."

After a short pause, while Ross considered the walk alone, he said, "Okay, I'll stay."

"Good, I'm going to finish checking this out, why don't you check out the buildings?"

"What about the ladder?"

Roy sniffed, "Leave it, for crying out loud."

He could barely make Ross out as his brother crept along in the shadows. He crouched and began walking down the elevator catwalk. There wasn't much to see from the elevators, but the view of the rest of the countryside was amazing with the special effects of the night. It was like an animated shadow box. He could see miles and make out the dim outlines of farm buildings. Across the street, he could see into some houses that had their lights still on. The bar/restaurant directly across from the elevators had a big bay window facing him. The dimly lit room allowed him to see right in like watching TV. He felt strangely excited but at the same time embarrassed, like when you walk into what you think is an unoccupied bathroom that isn't.

There was a young couple silently slowly dancing, holding each other very close. The young man must have done or said something that was wrong because the girl pushed him away and walked out of the room. The boy walked to the window and looked out. Roy thought the boy was looking straight at him. The boy started to closely peer and Roy realized, *He can see me!*

Roy dropped flat and squirmed slowly back off the catwalk. Suddenly he was sliding down the slanted elevator roof. He still had hold of the bottom angle of the catwalk and that stopped him from falling almost 40 feet onto Farmco's railroad siding. He tried to get traction with his feet, but everything was covered with a layer of super fine dust from the grain, making the surfaces as slippery as ice. That is why the catwalk used expanded metal as its base, for traction. Every time he tried to get back up to his feet again, they slipped out from under him, and he slid down. His arms were getting tired. There was an upright angle that the railing was attached to that Roy thought would help him get back up. He hoped so because his arms were close to giving out.

Roy lunged out with one arm and got a grip on the upright of the catwalk railing. He then shifted the other hand over. With the advantage of the vertical handhold, he was able to swing his legs back onto the catwalk. He laid there for a moment, to catch his breath. He had been very close to falling. He looked over the edge to where he would have landed. He wondered why he was not terrified. The fall could have killed him. He then looked over to the apartment window and expected to see someone sounding an alarm. To his surprise, he saw the young couple dancing again, lost in their own little world. It seemed unless the interruption continued, things quickly returned to the enjoyable as opposed to the unenjoyable. A Life's Principle? Maybe.

He continued to the other end of the catwalk. The layout was the same, nothing to be learned that he hadn't already learned. The ladder on this end of the elevator joined another catwalk, about halfway down, that went to the feed mill.

"Now this may be interesting," he muttered to himself and began down the side of the elevator.

The catwalk to the feed mill ended at a door. Hopefully, it was not locked. Roy didn't want to have to go all the way back the way he had just snuck along. He cautiously crept to the door. There wasn't a doorknob on the door, just a small handle. That was a positive development. Unless there was some sort of latch on the inside the door wasn't locked. Just as he reached for the door, it started to slowly open.

"Crap," Roy said to himself. Ross was right, "one way in, one way out." That is unless he jumped. He started over the handrail deciding to take a chance on jumping from there. He guessed this catwalk was halfway down the elevator. That's about 20 feet. He could do it, maybe. He hadn't jumped from that height before, but if he didn't land on some junk that was scattered around the elevators, he might make it in one piece. If he didn't, he would have the sympathy card to play. He took a deep breath and…

"Roy, what in the world are you doing?"

Roy froze, turned around, and stared. It was Ross who came through the door.

"What are you doing here?"

"I was checking out the feed mill when I saw some stairs leading to this catwalk, and I thought I'd see where they led. Were you going to jump from here?"

Roy climbed back over the rail and took a deep breath.

"Yeah, I thought I was trapped, just like you said, "one way in, one way out." The only chance I had was to jump and hope I didn't break something," Roy gasped, still short of breath.

"That was a crazy idea. Come on, follow me and let me show you how neat this feed mill is," Ross said as he went back through the door.

Roy took another deep breath and followed Ross through the door. There were only, what he guessed, the night lights on so everything was dimly lit, and shadows dominated everything, everywhere. It was at the same time spooky and beckoning. It was as if one could totally meld with the shadows and become one with them. The building they were in was huge, the upper reaches were enveloped in complete darkness. The width and breadth were also wrapped in darkness and accentuated by shadows reaching out toward the boys from the various large pieces of machinery.

There were rustling and flapping-type noises high up in the building. The boys both froze and tried to make out what was making that noise. Visions of "giant rats" filled their heads.

"What is that?" Roy asked, backing back toward the door and out to the catwalk.

They were ready to run when they heard a "cooing."

"Those are pigeons," Ross said.

"Whew," his brother expelled a breath of relief.

"Come on, follow me," Ross whispered and started down a steel stairway to the floor.

They descended to the floor. And Ross pointed to a huge piece of equipment that was looming up in front of them.

"I think this is the equipment used to make the feed.

The piece of equipment in front of them had big tubes feeding into it and a spout on the bottom with lots of what looked like the feed John fed his herd scattered around the floor. There was also a thick layer of fine dust everywhere. The building had an almost sweet smell that was pleasant but probably overpowering.

Roy and Ross both were amazed and a little spooked at their dimly lit surroundings.

Ross looked at Roy and jerked his thumb indicating moving on. Roy nodded and they worked their way out of the building, careful not to trip on unseen obstacles in the dark. They could not use their flashlights for fear of being seen.

"I think that's enough for tonight," Ross said.

"I agree, that close call up on the catwalk and you surprising me at the feed mill is all I need in the way of excitement. I declare this adventure complete."

Ross nodded his agreement then said "What, wait, what close call?"

"I'll tell on the walk home. We need to move right along; the moon is about to set. It won't be any fun walking home in the dark."

They made their way to the tracks and started home just as the bar closed and people started to leave. A couple of cars were parked in the Farmco's yard, and they lit up the grounds with their turning around to head in the direction of their homes.

The boys had gotten down on the far side of the track's embankment to stay out of sight. When the way was clear, they got up and started to walk home.

On their way home, they shared what each of them experienced during the Farmco excapade and how the little quiet town was aptly named. It named itself by having random letters drawn by a young girl, and its legacy was not beholding to anyone or thing. It just was simply, Ixonia.

Like the other features of this land, it was woven into the fabric of now.

Hilltop Farm

TALE NUMBER FOURTEEN

HILLTOP FARM

"Ask a sage, he will explain.
Ask a fool, and he will complain."
– Toba Bet

"Answer not a fool according to his folly,
lest you be like him yourself."
– Proverbs 26:4 (ESV)

igh above the surrounding countryside, sat Hilltop Farm which is located at the termination of Hilltop Road. The road is constructed of gravel, well-worn and severely "wash boarded" on the sharply inclined portion. The hill was actually a ridge, running north and south. The northern end was the maximum height of the ridge and the widest. This is where the house and farm outbuildings are located. The ridge narrows as it heads south and decreases in height as it blends into the elevation of the valley. The formation, which is locally referred to as a drumlin, is commonly accepted to be a result of the receding glaciers of the Wisconsin glaciation period—a period 20 to 15,000 years ago.

Roy envisioned a structure that utilized an existing formation as its base and was added to and modified by the ancient mound builders. This was the case in many ancient and not so ancient structures. The descending southern portion was used as a ramp which ascended from the south northward and culminated in the highest elevation in this portion of the valley. It was narrow which allowed control, and the sides were steep for the same reason. The northern end was formed into a large base to accommodate temples, palaces, and defenses. In ancient times the grounds surrounding it could have been populated with other smaller mounds and various groupings of families, clans, or maybe tribes. Plentiful clear water, rich soil, and bountiful game and fish, along with the peat bog would have contributed to the success of this civilization. Roy's vision was based on illustrations of such civilizations he had seen during their research of the mound in their backyard and the paper he had done at school before they had moved here.

Dad called this a crazy idea not based on fact. Ross agreed that it was farfetched. Roy and Dad got into a big confrontation regarding this. While Dad continued to maintain it had no basis in science or fact, he refused to consider the fact that there was one in their backyard, and another mound on the neighbors' property. This area used to be full of mounds that had been destroyed. These were facts.

"The whole idea, it is pure bullshit, a total waste of time; and I can use that time you're wasting to get this farm into shape." Dad shouted into Roy's face, so close that some of his spittle hit Roy in the face.

"The Aztalan State Park is just 35 miles away and is the location of a complete ancient settlement. It includes stockades, temple mounds, and effigy mounds. It is fully documented," Roy responded. His eyes a hard ice blue, with that wry smile on his face, as he wiped the spittle off.

Dad stepped into Roy and knocked him down.

"That's enough of this crap," Dad roared standing over Roy and glaring at him.

Dolly screamed, and Mom yelled at the top of her lungs for them to quit it. Ross grabbed Dolly's arm and ran outside, both crying. Bootsie was close behind them.

Roy started to get up; he was trembling in rage. Dad's eyes were mere slits, and his face was set and hard. The air was almost crackling with rage and pain.

"OK boy, bring it if you think you are big enough." Dad taunted.

Roy stood up and stared at him.

"Not yet, but soon," Roy whispered just loud enough for Dad to hear.

Then Roy spun on his heel and went outside and sat on the mound. It was a beautiful clear evening, and it didn't take long to calm down. It was as though the mound absorbed the anger and adrenaline that had been pumping through his system. He looked up at Hilltop Farm silhouetted against the dark blue sky and imagined fires and rituals being performed by ancient priests and kings. He would go up and talk to John about his vision of the Hilltop as an ancient settlement. From Roy's perspective that was in keeping with the spirit of his land. It was an ongoing, evolving story with a destined ending.

Ross and Dolly showed up and silently sat with him. Bootsie came and curled up in front of him with her head on his lap. They sat there letting the night slowly engulf them into the quietness and coolness of its essence. The shroud of darkness was almost like a cocoon that wrapped around them in protection. After a while, Mom called for them to come in for the night. They got up and silently filed into the house. Dad was outside working on something. They kissed Mom goodnight and went to bed. The boys didn't speak a word the rest of the night.

Roy was up early and after a hastily gulped-down breakfast of cold cereal and milk, he was off to Hilltop Farm. Ross and Bootsie joined him. It was going to rain later today because of the dark clouds gathering on the western horizon. The farmers would welcome the rain, just so long as it wasn't a torrent that caused flooding. Stumpy came out of the barn to greet them. Bootsie barked hello, and the two of them engaged in the traditional canine greeting of sniffing each other. Ross warily kept his distance from the little dog and kept track of it out of the corner of his eye. He did not want another close asphyxiation. Roy witnessed Ross' actions and smiled. It was the first time he felt like smiling since the encounter with Dad last night.

"John must be inside," Roy said as he headed into the barn's lower level where the cow stanchions and pens were.

John was occupied in shoveling the manure from the troughs that ran down each side of the barn. They were specifically and scientifically located in just the right spot to receive the bovine's urine and bowel deposits. The cows apparently were unaware of these facts or just didn't care. They missed the troughs at least 50 percent of the time. This manure removal was a twice-a-day routine. The boys waited for their eyes to adjust to the change in brightness from full daylight to the dimness of the enclosed barn. They also needed a moment for their nostrils to adjust to the odor of fresh cow manure.

The lower area was where the cows were milked. That's where all the manure accumulated that needed to be removed so the barn could be cleaned and prepared for the next milking. There were specific requirements that must be met and maintained to keep a top grade for quality and top price. Random inspections were frequent and the driver who picked up the milk was also attentive to the state of cleanliness. The most critical inspection was the grading of the milk itself and was done at the dairy. There was a lot of money at risk. If you lost your top rating, your price per 100 weight (cwt.) was reduced and it took quite a while to get the grading back up.

Roy walked over to the side wall where the shovels, rakes were stored, along with several pairs of rubber "wellingtons".

"Here, take this shovel and put on a pair of boots," Roy instructed as he did the same.

"Why?" Ross asked.

"Because if we want John to sit and tell us about Hilltop Farm, we need to help him finish his chores."

"Crud."

"Yeah, maybe so, but we'll get to ride along on the tractor when he goes out to spread it," Roy said. "Come on, Let's get after it."

They booted up, grabbed shovels, and headed down the barn to where John was shoveling the slop into a manure spreader wagon that was hitched to a tractor.

"Good morning boys," John greeted them.

"Good morning," they said in return.

They spent the next 30 minutes, or so, helping load the manure spreader wagon. Once it was loaded and pulled out, they helped John finish cleaning the barn. That included spreading barn lime on the floor and in the troughs and putting fresh bedding in the stalls and pens. The bedding straw was in the upper level. On this level, there were years upon years of hay and straw stored, stacked on different sides of the barn. Straw for bedding and hay for feed. The rectangular bales weighed about one hundred pounds and were stacked up forty feet high. The upper level was also where the oats were stored in a huge bin. That bin was where Roy, on a prior occasion, also almost drowned. That's in another tale.

Roy and Ross ran up the stairs to the upper level for the bedding straw. It was a race to see who could get to the top of the stack first. The rule was that you were not allowed to use the ladder. You had to freestyle up the face of the straw loft finding hand and footholds between the bales. It was fun but dangerous.

Over the years, several nasty falls have occurred. Ross won this one; he usually did and started throwing bales down to the floor. The bales then were dragged over and pushed through a flap door that led to the lower level in front of the stanchions. You had to be careful in this area because over years and years of sliding bales through the flap door the floor had been polished as slick as ice. If you didn't watch your step, you would join the bale in the lower level. The fall was about 20 feet. You could end up flat on your back looking up at a cow.

The boys would then go down to the lower level and drag or carry bales to where they were going to be used and then use their pocketknives to cut the two restraining strings. Using a pitchfork, they would shake the compacted straw loose and spread it as bedding in the pens and stanchion areas.

That finished, the boys looked down at the length of the pen and milking area. It was fresh smelling; the barn lime deodorized the manure smell and provided a white covering to the floor and troughs. The fresh straw gave a soft, clean odor. It was ready for the next round of milking later in the afternoon.

John called to them from the other end of the barn, and they ran over to him.

"You want to ride along and work the controls as I spread this stuff?" He nodded toward the manure spreader.

The boys beamed and scrambled up on the tractor and sat bracing themselves against the fenders. John drove out to the field in the back of the farm. This was the long ridge down that Roy envisioned as a ramp to the elevated base for the temples and palace where the current farm buildings were located. When John turned down the side of the steep ridge the boys had to hang on to the fenders tightly.

"OK, let her go!" John shouted.

Roy pulled the cord that was attached to the lever that engaged the mechanism that moved the manure to the back of the spreader and into the spinning tines of the spreading mechanism. He passed the cord to Ross who would pull it to disengage the spreading mechanism when the spreading was complete. Manure flew everywhere. The rate of spinning of the tines was determined by the rate of travel. The faster John drove the tractor, the further the manure would be projected into the air. If they stayed upwind, the stench was tolerable. If John drove too fast the spreader could rain manure down on them. That was nasty and only happened once.

"Feed and speed boys, feed and speed. There always is a correct ratio in life whether you are kissing a girl or spreading shit. Life Principle, remember it or you could get covered with shit," John stated.

Roy did. It was the life principle in play with Dad during last night's physical encounter. He needed the right time and size to settle the situation.

When they pulled back into the barnyard and put equipment away Roy asked John if he had time to talk to them. John said sure. He had time since they had helped him.

Roy winked at Ross as a means of saying *I told you so.*

John led them over to the windmill to get a drink of water using the tin cup that always hung there and then rinsed the old chew out his mouth to make room for a fresh one. The boys followed him and shared the cup for a drink of the ice-cold sweet artesian well water.

As good as any soda, Roy thought.

John picked a spot on the hillside under a huge ancient elm tree looking over The Triangle Farm side of the valley. The other side probably stunk of the fresh manure they had just spread. Bootsie and Stumpy appeared from somewhere and stretched out looking for pats and scratching, which the boys delivered. Ross was wary of Stumpy whom he viewed as a ticking bomb of stifling, nauseating flatulence. He kept his distance from the friendly little dog. Roy admired the animal's courage and perseverance in surviving the terrible accident and the love that John obviously had for the dog revealed some of the farmer's warm soul.

"Well boys, what do you want to know?" John asked as he cut a chew-sized piece of the plug tobacco he had in the Red Man bag. His pocketknife was kept sharper than a razor and had been sharpened so many times that a lot of it had worn away. He put the chew in his mouth and put the tobacco pouch in a bib pocket on his overalls.

"Can you tell us of any legends about this hill? It's so dominant in the valley. It must have been special to the early settlers," Roy said.

John spent a few moments getting his chew started. He spotted an anthill a little way down the hillside where the Hilltop Road had been cut into the side of the hill as it climbed up from the valley floor and ended in his front yard. He pursed his lips, and an amber stream of tobacco juice was projected at the industrious little insects landing right on the anthill. Chaos erupted as the disorganized little workers scurried around in confused panic.

"Gotcha," the farmer said with satisfaction. "That'll keep them busy for a while."

Boy, he sure doesn't like ants Roy thought. Ross stared at the tobacco-drenched anthill with a perplexed look on his face. He hadn't experienced John's predilection for drenching the insects with tobacco juice.

"So, you want to know the legends of Hilltop Farm, do you,"

"Yes," both boys said at once.

"Catherine told us a few stories before she died," Ross added.

John gazed out over the valley with a faraway look in his eyes and sighed.

"What I know is what the sisters told me and what the manager Zacharias shared with me. His family went back as far as the Lloyd family did."

There was a cool breeze coming up the backside of the hill and skipping over the top. The breeze was compressed being forced up the back face of the hill, so it accelerated over and around the top. It then spread back out after it crested the top and slowed down. This was the same action responsible for the depositing of snow during snowstorms. On a larger scale it was the same principle that accounted for the rainy side and arid side of mountain ranges.

'Who was Zacharias?" Ross queried.

"He was the farm manager when I came here from Europe as a young boy." John said.

"I was his assistant. The farm was much larger at that time, and it took two of us and the sisters to manage it. We milked twice as many cows and tilled over twice as much soil. The VanRidden place was ours back then and most of the Haggans. And we used horses instead of tractors when I first started. Daisy and Maybelle are the leftovers."

Daisy and Maybelle were two old draft horses that literally had been put out to pasture. They were great friends of John and would follow him around when he was in the field with them or close to a fence in the field where they were pastured. They still wanted to get harnessed up, John had told the boys. Draft horses were huge and had large hooves. This feature helped when the ground was muddy or slippery.

John released another brown stream of juice toward the anthill and continued.

"The Lloyds settled on this farm around the early to mid-1800s while there were still Indian wars going on. The one they spoke of was led by Chief Blackhawk and was not settled until the 1830s. That's when settlers really started moving in. There was a lot of lead mining going on here, gray gold it was called. The Lloyds had immigrated to the United States from the coal and peat mines of Wales to get away from mining; so, they looked for good, rich tillable soil. They said there were several families that migrated and settled between here and Watertown, along with the rumored fairies," he added, when he saw the boy's mouth open to say something.

"There was still the occasional Indian group who would pass through and trade with the settlers according to the sisters and Zacharias. It was from them that they heard stories of the ancient ones who had built the mounds scattered around the valley and used this big hill for their ceremonies and rituals. They also could gather here for defense when necessary."

Roy almost jumped up with excitement, he had been right about Hilltop Farm. He could not say so to Dad. That would start another fight. There was going to be a showdown when the time was right, but not now.

It was time for another bombardment of the beleaguered anthill. Ross seemed to be paying as much attention to the battle as to what John was telling them. The little foragers were battening down the hatches and going subterranean for protection just as the last missive splashed on the mound. John grunted with satisfaction.

"Now you must understand that the sisters were repeating what they had been told by their folks. It's not firsthand and they were youngsters when they were told this. I'm sure that what I'm telling you is not absolutely factual, but it represents a general idea of what they were told and believe."

"That protection and view on top of this hill are why the sister's folks settled up here and built their farm. Initially, the road passed around the base of the hill and came up the rear side ramp that we drove the tractor down this morning. It wasn't until several years later that Hilltop Road was built. It is obvious that there had been natives or even ancient people on this hill. I still plow up stone artifacts when turning over a field."

"What do you do with them?" Roy almost yelled in his excitement, looking all around hoping to spot a pile of them close by.

Ross was still engrossed in watching the ants start to emerge from their tunnel. He glanced over at John who also witnessed this activity and smiled in anticipation, and so did Ross.

"Spit-teewy!" John loosened another liquid projectile that was on its way to the just now cautiously emerging eusocial insects.

"Splat!" a direct hit. The tiny scouts were drenched in tobacco-laden spittle and rolled back into their tunnel. Ross looked up at John and smiled.

John focused back on his story. "I put artifacts with the rest of the stones in the corner of the west field. You are welcome to look through it. Other people have."

Roy knew he would be doing that soon.

"Do you ever worry about the ants retaliating?" Ross asked.

John scratched his beard and pondered that.

"I guess I haven't," looking concerned. "Do you think I should?" He then laughed and shook his head.

Ross continued to look concerned.

"What else did Zacharias have to say about the legends?" Roy asked, trying to get the conversation going again and stop focusing on the ants and potential retaliation.

John went back to looking out over the valley. "This hill has always had some sort of occupation. It is a natural lookout point and defensive position. The valley was a bountiful place back then. Other than that, I don't know much more. As far as ceremonies or rituals are concerned, I don't have any knowledge, although I expect there was, if the ancients lived here. Haven't found any skulls or things like that."

Roy looked out over the valley also and imagined it populated by the ancients, campfires burning, children playing. It looked like the pictures that he had seen in the books he had looked at when writing his report.

The rest of the afternoon was spent discussing what the sisters had done with all the land they had. When Zacharias retired, the sisters decided to rent out a lot of the land to local farmers. The sisters bequeathed to John the farm and land that he now farms. They bequeathed the balance of the property to their family who promptly sold it. The sisters kept the pledge to keep the set aside property uncultivated even when the government took the land for the road and railroad. It was in some sort of trust.

Roy was fascinated. There was so much that was extraordinary about this place, and it all was connected in one evolving story. A story that he and Ross were now a part of.

EPILOGUE
— PART TWO —

FACTS, MYTHS, AND LEGENDS, THE COMPROMISE

"The supernatural is the natural not yet understood."
– Elbert Hubbard

"If you have two competing ideas to explain the same phenomenon, you should prefer the simpler one."
– Occam's razor

Roy and Ross spent many afternoons in the Glade putting all the information together they had collected from their father (the Scholar), John Franger (the Sage), the encyclopedia, their mother (both scholar and sage), and their own experiences, plus their "gut." They needed to bring together all the elements and gain a solid perception of the environment they lived in, with all its peculiarity. Not just the physicality but the smell, sound, and spirit to put everything in the context of their habitat.

They had identified seven unique features of their habitat. The "triangle" shape of the farm, the "mound" of the ancients, their portion of the peat "bog," the "glade" of aspen, the balance of the peat "bog," and land that was pledged to the perceived fairies and other spiritual beings by the early settlers from Wales, the Hilltop Farm, finally the town of Ixonia itself. There was no doubt in Roy's mind that all these items were one contiguous body. A remarkable realm that he was destined to abide in and learn from for a time.

The conclusion, after the hours of discussion, was that they were not quite aligned in their mindsets. Ross was less inclined to the capriciousness and impulsive nature that Roy had. He was pragmatic by nature but accepting of his older brother's openness to a supernatural, spiritual component of the nature of their environment. They were comfortable with the variance in their conclusions. The smooth intertwining and acceptance made them stronger when together. Roy's visionary nature opened many opportunities. Ross' pragmatic nature kept them from going over the edge. They both were sensitive and accepting of each other's intuitions. The Cheesman brothers would be a factor throughout elementary and high school, after which they parted ways.

Their time had been intermixed with playing with dragonflies and damselflies, Roy trying to make peace with the cantankerous spider, catching crayfish (while receiving lots of painful pinches), and rubbing frogs' bellies, coupled with defending The Glade against Indian attacks and alien invasions. The usual distractions.

The Triangle: They agreed that the shape of the farm was caused by the construction of the railroad tracks. A railroad laid out its tracks in the straightest line possible from starting point to endpoint. In this case Milwaukee, WI, to Minneapolis/St. Paul, MN. The fact that it crossed land that was promised to remain fallow was incidental to the builders. Roy maintained that the tracks breached the promise and disturbed the harmony of the land. The fact that the odd-shaped piece of land they lived on had remained separate and not included with a tilled land adjacent to it was strange. It was like the property was destined to remain separate. That the mystical, supernatural features of The Triangle may be involved, Roy considered a possibility.

The Mound: They agreed that the structure in their backyard was created by an ancient civilization and was one of many originally in the area. Only a few were left. It was an interesting artifact. Roy pointed out that the fact that it was located on The Triangle was pertinent to its survival. It brought together ancient and modern cultures, with one overlaying the other. Even though the ancient was overlayed, it was not erased. It was part of the whole.

The Bog: The peat bog on their farm was separated from a much larger bog by the railroad tracks and highway. The bog was formed hundreds or even thousands of years ago. Peat moss was used by the ancients for medicinal purposes or dried for fuel. This has continued to this day. The bog was a practical feature of the land both boys agreed on, and Roy maintained the inclusion of the bog with the farms' land was special.

The Glade: The uniqueness of the copse of aspen trees at the end of the property and the almost magical ambiance was something they both shared. Ross was intrigued by the familial composition of the aspen tree and Roy saw it as contributing to the peaceful and protective nature of the Glade. The creek and tiny waterfall, and the heavy barrier of grasses and trees, contained within the Glade, enhanced the feeling of quiet and harmony. The demeanor of the creatures that inhabited it reflected the special environment of the place.

The Balance of the Bog: The land on the other side of the tracks and highway was the bulk of the land set aside by the original Lloyd settlers from Wales. The set aside was to remain uncultivated and home to perceived fairies and other mythical creatures that supposedly stowed away on ships and wagons used to travel to the new land.

The set aside was a fact, but the actuality of little magical flying creatures was very dubious to Ross and his parents. The possibility of their existence was real to their sister's mind and a possibility to Roy and John.

Hilltop Farm: John Franger owned and operated the 90-acre dairy farm that he inherited from his employers, the Lloyd sisters. The Lloyd sisters were direct descendants of the Lloyd clan that settled here in the early eighteenth century. The Lloyds emigrated from Wales. Roy noted that he, his brother, and sister were 25 percent, Welch, from their mother's mother. According to legend a complement of fairies and other supernatural creatures immigrated with the Lloyds. The early Welsh were strong believers in such folklore. The farmhouse, barn, silos, and other outbuildings were located on the highest elevation in this part of the countryside. Roy imagined what that looked like in ancient times with the ancient mound builders occupying the land.

All the mounds and effigies that populated this land would make the hill another huge mound or temple. He recalled the illustration of some of the excavated settlements he had seen and envisioned the same here. The high elevation, whether existing or enhanced by the ancients, was a perfect location for keeping watch on the surrounding land and would project the dominance of its occupier.

Ixonia: Ross and Roy because of their moonlit night expedition to Farmco, both had a similar view of the small town. Their experience at the Farmco facility was both exhilarating and frightening at the same time. While Ross was afraid they would one day be exposed for the "break in," Roy was proud of the courage it took to climb, hang from the railing, crawl, and check out the mill. The close call involving the bar patrons and almost being sighted by the dancers had got his heart beating faster. He was proud of the escapade.

The town from Ross's point of view was a strangely typical small farming community with a one-of-a-kind name arrived at in a crazy manner. Roy was in agreement with his brother, but the manner in which the town came into existence was like the town directed the selection of its name. It was like the name Ixonia was destined for this place.

The Old Man could now recognize that the seven features were not seven individual units but were part of a single entity. The event, or adventure occurring in one of the seven areas really needed to be considered in the context of the totality of the seven to properly be understood. They were segments of a realm. This was the beginning of Roy's spiritual awaking. It would take years to fully develop including many misconceptions that were briefly strongly held and just as strongly rejected. It was from his present position of experience and maturity that he viewed these tales and items.

He was beginning to learn that looking at something from the outside was far less meaningful than being inside it and experiencing it. Abiding in it and it's abiding in you was the condition to be sought after. C.S. Lewis likens it to the experience of standing in a toolshed and looking at a sunbeam shining in through a crack in the door, compared to the experience of having the same sunbeam hitting his eyes and looking along it to the universe outside ("Meditation in a Toolshed").

Roy was to learn and unlearn so much over the next few years on The Triangle Farm. It would be a daunting journey that Roy faced. The next step was his choice, each one a choice from a predestined selection, which was like a thread being woven over, under, and alongside other threads. I can gather from and give to these threads as I will, but the length and destination of my thread is already determined by the weaver. In this tapestry of life, every choice a thread makes impacts all its adjacent threads, which impact their adjacent threads and so on, but the beginning and end of the strand is already determined.

"Man did not weave the web of life; he is merely a strand in it. Whatever he does to the web, he does to himself."

– Chief Seattle

Tomorrow awaits.

TRIANGLE TALES

PART THREE

PROLOGUE

ASSORTED TALES OF LIFE, LIVED OUT TO THE MAXIMUM.

"Let no one be slow to seek wisdom when he is young nor weary in the search of it when he has grown old. For no age is too early or too late for the health of the soul."
– Epicurus

"Early in life I had to choose between honest arrogance and hypocritical humility. I chose the former and have seen no reason to change."
– Frank Lloyd Wright

T he Early Years are a very defining period of time in Roy's life as it is for most boys. Not only is he growing in size and strength, he is growing spiritually and intellectually. He is forming, or perhaps being formed into what eventually will be a man taking his place either as a member or a leader. That position will not only be determined by him but perhaps more importantly by those and what destiny has chosen to put him next to, behind of, or in front of him. It also will be determined where and when these occurrences happen and what his reaction is to them. This is the complex sometimes chaotic series of events that takes place in the maturing of children into men and women and the playgrounds into society, workplaces, and unfortunately battlegrounds.

"It was what it was. It is what it is. It will be what it is to be."

– A Life Principle

The Old Man would occasionally flash back to times in the city and The Alley Adventures to provide backstory or maybe just because he felt like it. It's his story anyway. As in prior parts, there is not necessarily any chronological order to them. They are recorded as they come to his mind. There are many adventures ranging from the exciting and informative to the totally stupid and dangerous. This all follows in The Early Tales.

TALE NUMBER 15

THEY ARE ALWAYS LOADED

"Every bullet hits something."
– The Old Man, Life Principle

There are three kinds of men. The one that learns by reading. The few who learn by observation. The rest of them have to pee on the electric fence for themselves."
– Will Rogers

Roy was horrified at what had just happened. He was shaking so badly that he dropped to all fours and struggled to catch his breath. He stared at the revolver that he had just fired. It was supposed to be empty! He was positive that he had fired all the bullets at the target. His brother Ross slumped on the ground, his mouth open in a silent scream.

When Ross had finally caught his breath, the scream was more of a grunt, like being punched in the stomach. "Oomph," he grunted.

"Roy, what the hell?" Ross sobbed.

"I'm sorry, Ross, honest to God, I'm sorry, I didn't think it was loaded," Roy shouted.

His ears were still ringing loudly from the revolver's thunderous report. It was only a .22 caliber, but it was deafening. They were walking through John Franger's pasture on the way home after spending all afternoon at the Glen, lying in the shade and soaking in the cool water of the creek.

They had been practicing with the .22 caliber pistol that their dad had given them. He did it only after a lot of safety training. Roy had just violated the two most important ones, "don't point a gun at anyone and treat a gun as if it is always loaded."

He had thought it would be a great prank to scare Ross by acting as if he would shoot him. Upon reflection, he could not imagine why he had felt that. He had drawn the pistol from its holster and pointed it at Ross. Roy's hand felt as if it had been pushed aside just as he pulled the trigger. Ross's eyes had opened wide, and he had thrown up his hands in a defensive reflex and fallen to the ground when the gun roared.

The bullet had hit one of the cow's hindquarters that was grazing in the pasture. The dairy herd that had been peacefully grazing in the quiet of the late summer afternoon was now in a headlong flight up the hill to the barn. Neither Roy nor Ross could pick out the cow he had shot. They were black and white Holsteins and sort of like zebras. Their black and white patterns made it impossible for them to pick one out of a stampeding herd.

The field was returning to normal after the gunshot and the stampeding herd. As the boy's senses returned, they became aware of their surroundings. The aroma, a mixture of the pasture's grass, soil, and manure, was peculiar to dairy cattle pastures and was accentuated by the heat and humidity. And when combined with the sound of crickets, grasshoppers, cowbirds, and cicadas in the trees that boarded the pasture, it made for what should have been an almost idyllic late summer afternoon. But Roy's foolhardy, almost tragic stunt had destroyed that setting.

They both looked at the revolver lying in the grass between them. The barrel was still smoking. A dragonfly lazily hovered close to it. Roy was conscious of the force that had pushed his arm away and prevented him from shooting his brother and possibly killing him. That was not the first time something like this had happened since they had moved from the city to this farming community and the five-acre "truck farm" they now called home.

Ross saw the peculiar look on Roy's face and said, "It happened again?"

Roy nodded, crawled beside his brother, and laid down on his back. Ross laid down also. They both stared up into the blue sky.

"What are you going to do now?" Ross asked.

After a long pause, Roy said, "We're doing nothing about it. Nothing about the shooting, or we'll lose the gun. "

"What if Franger sees the wound?" Ross said.

Roy stood up.

"Let's go home," Roy said, and they headed home. As usual, Roy said nothing more on the subject and was prepared for whatever may come of it.

That is the way the Old Man remembered it. He grinned that wry grin no one knew whether it would end in a fearsome snarl or a warm smile. It had become his trademark, and it had served him well over the decades. He was in the backyard sitting on the ground under the grand Newport maple. He wondered if he could get back up again. "I guess I just don't give a damn. It'll be what it'll be," he muttered as he leaned back against the huge old maple tree trunk.

Nothing ever came of the shooting, and Roy and Ross spoke of it no more. From then on, Ross wore the holster and gun and oversaw its use. They never knew if John had seen the wound or not. Whenever Roy helped John with the milking, he surreptitiously checked the cows out for wounds and came up with a couple of possibilities, but nothing positive. To this day, it bothers him that he never came clean to the best friend he ever had except Ross. It will always be in his mind that he was not as good a friend in return to John Franger. The tsunami of life swept him up and he never got back to John and confessing before he passed. Roy's father and mother spent some of their last years at Hilltop Farm. His father died in that house years later. Roy had not been honest with John. He tried never to let that happen again. It was easier to come forward with the truth than to let the lie gnaw away at his peace.

TALE NUMBER 16

UTFO (UNIDENTIFIED TRIANGULAR FLYING OBJECT)

"I believe in everything until it's disproved. So I believe in fairies, myths, dragons. It all exists, even if it's in your mind. Who's to say that dreams and nightmares aren't as real as the here and now?"
– John Lennon

"The truth is out there."
– Fox Mulder, TV Series The X Files

The boys and Bootsie were sound asleep. They were huddled together under a heavy blanket on the side of the mound. Sleeping outdoors was commonplace for the boys during the hot summer nights. Their attic bedroom was like a sauna during this time. With no circulation and minimal insulation, the room heated up during the day and stayed hot until the early morning hours.

A heavy quilt separated them and the ground to stave off the chill and dampness of the early morning hours. They loved to watch the final setting of the sun with the glorious colors of purple and scarlet. Then came the forerunner of nighttime, evening. The initial soft shadows lengthened until they merge, and darkness rose to reign until Sol bursts forth, and light relieved the earth and its inhabitants from darkness and the fear that was its natural companion.

Bootsie was the first to notice something was amiss. She snuggled close to the boys and whimpered softly. The whimpering woke Roy.

"What's wrong, girl?"

Bootsie continued to whimper and nuzzled her nose under the cover.

"Bootsie, what's wrong? "

Roy talking to Bootsie, woke his brother Ross.

"What's going on?" Ross inquired sleepily.

"Something is bothering Bootsie," Roy answered.

The boys both grabbed their hunting knives and flashlights. But before they turned on the flashlights, they became aware of a deep heavy droning. It wasn't loud but steady and prevalent, bordering on ominous. Bootsy's whimpering had become a low growl, and she bared her teeth. Her growling made the boys tense, and they huddled close together.

A dark shadow began covering them, coming from the east. It increasingly grew wider and wider as it slowly moved past. The boys looked up at it with trepidation. The object was blacker than the night sky; it seemed to absorb the light around it. It blotted out the sky from horizon to horizon when it was overhead. It was a triangular shape with three colored lights, one on each of its tips—a white one leading in front and a red and green one on the other corners. The droning kept going on without interruption. When the front end had moved to above the looted mound, the white light radiated down something like a spotlight, but not the same. It was more like a narrow beam. The droning increased while the beam was on.

The boys looked back and forth at each other with wide eyes and open mouths; they were stunned, paralyzed by the utterly otherworldly event they had witnessed.

The beam from the front tip of the object stopped, and the droning reduced to the prior level. The triangular object banked to the right and pointed vertically; with a blur, it was gone, and so was the droning.

Finally, Ross spoke up,

"What the hell was that?"

"I don't know," Roy answered.

They both were shaken up, and their voices trembled. Bootsie was barking and jumping around in what could have been a victory dance as if she had run it off all by herself.

"OK, girl, settle down, settle down." Roy tried to calm her down by petting her and telling her what a brave dog she was.

"I think if Bootsie hadn't woken me, we would not have even seen it," Roy said. "I wonder how often this has happened that we don't know about?"

"I don't know."

"Let's go tell Dad," Ross said and started toward the house.

"Hold on," Roy said and grabbed Ross's arm. "It's 4 a.m. He'll never listen to us seriously when he gets over being upset at us waking him. Let's wait until morning, check out the looted mound, and see what's so special about it. We haven't been there since the construction company filled it with tree stumps."

Ross agreed with Roy. He started to gather up the blankets.

"Whoa, what are you doing?" Roy asked.

"Picking stuff up to take back into the house."

"No, we are going to finish sleeping out here."

"After what just happened?"

"Yes, it just happened; it's over."

"Are we going to be safe with that thing around?"

"It didn't pay us a mind. We don't have anything to fear from it."

"Are you sure?"

"Yes, let's get settled back in. Bootsie will let us know if anything comes close."

The boys went back to sleep eventually, after spending a lot of time excitedly recounting what happened.

In the morning, they were up early, as most mornings when sleeping outdoors. They were in a hurry to finish breakfast and do any chores Mom wanted and Dad may have left for them. After weeding Mom's vegetable garden with Dolly's help, they cut the lawn and picked apples on the ground. These apple trees were in the backyard, between the house and the barn. They were Wolf River apple trees. The Wolf River apple was gigantic, up to five plus inches in diameter, and weighed one pound. The trees are also giant, the size of a big elm tree. There were two of them. Being so big and tall, when the huge apples fell, they would often spit from the impact. The boys needed to clean up the mess and the good apples given to Mom. She made excellent pies and turnovers out of them. Occasionally, a falling apple would hit one of the chickens, ranging free in the yard, and kill it. There would be a loud squawk, and it was chicken for dinner. The dumb birds never learned.

The boys were off to the looted mound as soon as they finished. They made a beeline to the mound. Heading down their driveway, they came across a brown bird with a white neck, black borders, and brown head. It had long legs and acted like it was injured.

"Let's have some fun with this bird," Roy said.

Ross was shocked that Roy, of all people, would seek to harass an injured animal.

When Roy saw the expression on Ross's face, he laughed.

"It's a Kildeer Ross. It feigns an injury to attract you away from its nest, which must be close. Watch this."

As Roy approached the bird lying down and flopping around, apparently seriously injured, it jumped up, ran a few feet away, and repeated its "I'm so injured" routine while making its unique "Kill-Dee" call.

"You try it, Ross."

Ross approached the seemingly injured bird, and it repeated the action it performed for Roy. Ross laughed and tried it again with the same results.

"Her nest must be back where we started," Roy said.

"How did you learn about them?" Ross asked.

"John told me when we ran across one on Hilltop."

Ross looked back at him and said, "You're so lucky you are old enough to spend all that time with him."

"Yes, I am. Your time will come. Just wait."

They moved around the nesting bird and headed straight across VanRidden pastures and over Clear Creek at the VanRidden bridge. When they reached the looted mound, they quickly scaled the sides and peered down.

Tree stumps were strewn every which way to form caves into the interior. Roy slid down and peered into one of the caves. It zigged and zagged out of his sight. It was obvious that something or things were living there because they had worn and packed the ground down. The surface was hard enough not to leave any tracks. Roy was reluctant to crawl any further back into the cave. Even if it was only a raccoon or opossum living there, they could be nasty if trapped, and this was a very confined area to try to defend yourself. The likelihood of Bootsie getting into a fight in one of the caves was why they hadn't brought her along. If she got the scent of some critter down here and went after it, it could get dangerous for the dog in these haphazard tunnels. He slowly backed out.

"Ross, come down here and check this out."

"Do I have to?"

"Come on, Ross, don't be a scaredy cat."

Ross slowly slid down by Roy. He looked into the small cave.

"Do you see any tracks or bits of fur caught on the roots sticking down everywhere?"

Ross warmed to the subject, closely studied the cave entrance, and crawled into the first zigzag.

"It's all packed down solid. I'm sure rainwater running over it helps to pack it down. But strangely, there is no sign of fur or droppings. This cave is obviously occupied by something."

"That's what I thought, but I wanted your opinion. Let's get out of here and see if John has noticed anything."

They scrambled out of the mound and headed past the rockpile and under the barbed wire fence onto John's pasture. They angled across the empty field to John's bridge across Clear Creek. They stopped to drink the cold water and splashed it on their sweaty faces there. It was close to midday and heating up. The large cumulus clouds broke up the sun's rays, but it would still be hot again. A night out on the mound?

"When are we going to come here and fish?" Ross asked.

He was eyeing some brook trout in the shadow of the overhanging grasses and bushes.

Roy looked at the fish and said, "Let's do it the day after tomorrow. We should have the flying triangle mystery solved by then."

Ross shook his head at the confidence Roy displayed.

They hiked up the washed-out road to Hilltop Farm and found John lubricating his International Harvester combine, getting it ready for use.

"Hello, boys" he greeted them.

"Hi," they both responded.

"Roy, are you still going to drive the truck between the combine and the barn this weekend?"

"Yes, sir."

"Good, VanRidden and I can use the help. That way, I can keep on going with the combine. It will save a lot of time. Now, what can I do for you?"

The boys looked at each other, embarrassed to ask about the flying triangle.

"What's the best way to catch those fish in the creek?" Roy blurted out.

Ross just looked at Roy with his mouth open. That's not what they came up here to ask.

"You need some mealy worms or grubs, a #5 hook, a B.B. split shot sinker, and a one-inch Snap-On bobber. Set the sinker 10 inches from the bait and bobber at three feet. Plop it in such a fish hear it, at least 10 feet up from the fish location, and let it drift slowly past the fish. Repeat if you don't get a bite, adjusting the bobbers and sinker's depths. I've got a couple of rigs if you don't have one. Remember not to take more than two or three fish from a spot so as not to spook the rest."

"Great, we also wonder if you have seen a huge flying triangle thing hover over the looted mound at night?" Roy spouted out.

The boys looked at each other and swallowed hard, almost gulped.

John stood up straight and looked them up and down. He got a fresh chew of Red Man and started walking toward the barn. He sat in the sun on an old bucket turned upside down and leaned against the side of the barn. The boys followed him there and sat on the ground on either side of him. He was quiet and closed his eyes as though getting ready to nap. Roy was afraid he wouldn't answer them, that they may have made him mad.

"There is a big ant hill over here," Ross exclaimed, pointing to it.

John opened his eyes. He spotted the hill and said, "Ah, so there it is."

He loosened a brown stream of tobacco juice at the hill and hit it dead on. Ants ran everywhere in panic and confusion. John and Ross smiled with satisfaction.

What was that thing with ants, driving them crazy? Ross got as much, if not more, enjoyment out of terrorizing the poor creatures as John did. Roy was sure that someday these insects would rise and seek revenge. He wanted nothing to do with that.

"Now, what about that triangle thing," John asked. He looked at the boys with questioning eyes and waited for an answer. Roy stammered a bit, but he got control of his voice. He repeated the story from last night and added what they found this morning at the looted mound.

Ross piped up, "Have you seen this thing? Have you?"

John put a hand on Ross's shoulder and said, "Quiet down, child."

John looked out over the valley, and his eyes became reflective for a moment, and then he returned to the present.

"I've seen lots of strange and unusual activity in the valley. Always from up here, distant from the action. Never up close. That's the way I want to keep it. So, yes, I've seen a strange flying object late at night or early morning. I guess that is expected with the Russians and Chinese building their armies, and we are matching them. You never know if someone is going to make this cold war hot. What with Nike sites close by (An Army Air Defense system of nuclear-tipped missiles) and the testing of highly developed craft, anything can happen," John stated.

The boys shuddered at the thought of the nuclear devices so close at hand. They had already learned the "duck and hide" drills in case of a nuclear attack at school. Everyone, especially the children, was scared and on edge.

The boys asked, "So, you think it is some sort of secret test craft we saw, not some outer spaceship?"

John looked at them for a long time. He shook his head slowly with downcast eyes and said, "I just don't know, but some extraordinary things are happening."

He stretched, got up from the overturned bucket, and started toward the house.

"You boys want to have lunch with me? Homemade summer sausage sandwiches and homemade dill pickles."

The boy's spirits brightened immediately, which brightened John's, and they all headed to the house. They would eat on the back porch, overlooking the west part of the valley, with the looted mound at the center.

The farmhouse was over 100 years old, or at least part of it. Someone had added to it, and people rebuilt parts after a fire. It had a secret staircase that ran from the second floor behind the large kitchen pantry all the way to the cellar. Roy was also sure there were secret passages behind the walls based on the outside and inner dimensions.

There seemed to be extra space there. That would be a great adventure at some later date.

Lunch was great, and they talked about the fish they would catch. John said he would like to come with them if possible. The boys were excited by that possibility. He told them of other schools of trout at different points up and down the creek.

Full of summer sausage sandwiches on rye with onions, butter, and cold milk straight from the cow with a thick layer of cream, the boys contentedly belched and thanked John. They then headed down Hilltop Road home, and John went to take a nap before milking. It had been an excellent morning for the boys, and they looked forward to tonight when they would solve the mystery of the flying triangle.

Bootsie was excited to see them when they got home and chastised them for leaving her behind. She barked and ran around them, even nipping at their pant legs. They finally calmed her down by giving her treats consisting of white Wonder Bread, torn up and squeezed into tiny blocks of processed chemicals and grain. They tossed them to her until Mom saw what they were doing and stopped it. Bootsie was satisfied and quieted down.

They spent the rest of the afternoon planning for the adventure tonight if the triangle returned. They situated themselves on their mound and shared Dad's binoculars. They had managed to call an older friend who was big and strong. He always wanted to go on an adventure with them and assured them that nothing would cause him to be afraid. He will be here after dinner. He had just got his driver's license. Even though he was a few years older than the boys, he emotionally fit in with them instead of kids his age. His name was Jon, and his brother Alan was in Roy's class at school.

The plan they came up with was as follows:

They would wait until the triangle craft left.

Then, armed with flashlights, hunting knives, one good slingshot, and some marbles as projectiles, they would begin.

They would keep silent until they arrived at their destination. They allowed only quiet simple whispers.

Their route was straight down their driveway and across Hilltop Road. They were crossing the barbed wire fence into VanRidden pasture. Then straight across the pasture almost to Van Ridden barn lot. They'd have to be careful not to disturb dogs or the herd. They then would head toward the Looted mound and pass behind it. They would quickly climb up the side of the mound by the rock pile and try to surprise anything in the caverns.

After surprising the things, they would brandish knives and slingshot to fend off any aggression and solve the mystery.

If they ran across aliens, maybe they could travel with them.

End of Plan

The boys shared their story and plan with the family after dinner. Roy was particularly interested in Dad's reaction. Mom was nervous, and Dad was very skeptical about any spacecraft. He had been awakened a couple of times by the droning sound, looked out the window, and noticed light by the old mound, but thought it was the boys out investigating and went back to sleep. He was leaning toward a hi-tech secret craft that the air force was developing. There were articles in some of the magazines he read, about the arms race and possibly of nuclear holocaust. After two world wars and now the Korean Conflict, it appeared that the communist threat was real, and there would be even more arms build-up and world tension. It was not fair. He and Mom have been through two world wars, the depression, the Polio epidemic, and the Korean Conflict, complicated by the ever-increasing cold war. There seemed to be no peace for them and maybe even their children.

He wished them well on tonight's adventure and assured Mom that the worst the boys would experience was a run-in with a skunk. He got up and asked Mom to walk around the property this evening. Things had been calm the last few weeks. It was nice but not to last; it never did.

The boys and Dolly cleaned up after dinner and headed out to prepare for tonight's adventure. Blankets, pillows for sleeping, snacks, and packed backpacks gathered on their mound. Dolly and Bootsie were hanging out with them until Jon arrived, and they got ready for the night's venture. Roy busied himself with preparing a map for the route they would follow tonight. He also had Dad's penlight to use when creeping up on the looted mound.

Jon finally arrived in his mother's car. He was so proud to be driving, he was almost strutting. Dad and Mom came out to say hello and congratulate him on getting his driver's license. Jon blushed and looked down and stammered his thank you. It was almost funny, but the boys knew better than to laugh. Even though Jon was a big boy, he was still like a boy no older than the brothers in many ways. Roy believed their family was more accepting of this than Jon's own.

Dolly and Bootsie went to the house when Mom called for them. The evening quickly fell, and the boys needed to bring Jon up to speed on the plan and route. He studied the looted mound through Dad's binoculars.

"Wow, It's almost like you are standing right there," Jon muttered out loud. He was amazed.

The boys then went over the plan and the map now that Jon was familiar with the target of this evening's undertaking.

"Well, what do you think of the plan, Jon?" Roy asked him.

"It's great, and I'm all for it. Do you think the Triangular Flying Object will fly over tonight?"

"We hope so," the boys responded.

The evening was rapidly giving way to nighttime. It was cloudy and overcast, and Roy wondered if the Triangular Object would show up tonight. He indeed hoped so.

They settled in, discussed what they hoped to accomplish tonight, and played mumbly-peg with their pocketknives. Each boy had a unique technique they challenged each other with. Time passed, and they settled down for the night, and sleep soon followed. The only sounds that serenaded them were crickets and frogs singing to each other, night birds tweeting, and an occasional warble. It was a nocturnal serenade performed every summer night. The boys slept soundly as The Triangle Farm's nightly anthem played on.

Early morning hours came with the droning from the other night, slow and steady as it cast a shadow over the slumbering boys. Roy woke up and smiled as he recognized the sound and the shadow. The cloudy night gave the massive Triangular Flying Object a stark outline against the night sky; Roy woke the others and reminded them to be quiet. They watched the object repeat its action of the other night, making its amazing exit in a blur.

"Oh my," Jon said and didn't look so brave now.

"Are you alright?" Ross asked Jon.

"I don't know; I thought you guys were kidding or stretching a tall tale," Jon said shakily.

"We are not kidding; we have a real mystery to solve. Are you with us, or are you going to drive home?" Roy said with ice in his voice. "We have to get moving."

Roy got up, shouldered his pack, put his flashlight in his pocket, and checked to ensure his hunting knife was in its sheath. He then started down the mound to the driveway.

Ross was up and ready to follow. He looked at Jon, who was sitting there.

"Come on, Jon; we need you."

"OK, I am ready." And he got up and followed.

The three of them quietly walked abreast of each other, looking all around and not saying a word, conscious of any noise they might hear. At the end of their driveway, they crossed Hilltop Road and came to the barbed wire fence of the VanRidden pasture which was vacant tonight. They stopped for a moment and surveyed the area. Except for barnyard lights, all was dark and silent but for the nighttime chorus of insects and frogs with the occasional owl call or fox barking on some hill. These were normal, and as long as they could hear them, they were sure nothing was awry.

Satisfied that all was well, Roy stepped on the second strand of wire, pushing it down, and lifted up on the top strand of wire, making an opening that Ross and Jon could easily bend down and step through. Jon repeated the same for Roy. They were about one-quarter of the way to their goal in the pasture. Now they walked single file with Ross leading. He and Roy knew this area by heart and were confident, even in the dark.

The grass muffled their steps, and they didn't speak, which was difficult for Jon. After seeing the UTO, all he wanted to talk about was that, but they had to be silent until they snuck up on the mound and found out what was causing this. He thought he would burst if he couldn't talk about it soon. That's why Roy was walking with him—to ensure he kept quiet.

They crossed Clear Creek and were getting close to the VanRidden farmhouse and barn; now, they had to be very quiet. Ross halted, and all three of them knelt and huddled.

Roy whispered the next stage of the mission.

"We are going to creep silently, remember, silently, across the next field to the base of the mound."

Roy glared at each of them. The mound was silhouetted against the gray overcast night sky. It was about a quarter of a mile away. Roy put a hand on Jon's shoulder.

 "Hang in there, Jon; you can make it."

Jon shook his head.

"I don't know, it's so dark; I am not ashamed to say I'm scared," Jon said slowly.

"Stay close to me; we're used to being out here at night."

"We like the nighttime," whispered Ross.

"You guys are different."

Both of the brothers silently chuckled

"You bet we are," said Roy. "Come on, let's get going."

They made their way to the back side of the mound and knelt once more.

Ross said, "Do you guys hear that?"

"What," they answered.

"Nothing, it's all quiet."

"Oh shit," Jon murmured and started crouching and shaking.

"Well, that's a little scary," Roy said.

"Yeah, said Ross and stood up and looked around.

"It's probably a fox or coyote we scared up, and everything shut up when it scurried away."

"Yeah," Ross agreed.

Jon was visibly shaking.

"Calm down, Jon; what's wrong with you?" Roy almost snarled at him.

"Roy, stop it," Ross chided him.

"You are right; I'm sorry, Jon."

"It's OK, Roy; it's just the darkness and now the silence.

"OK, let's crawl up the side of the mound and stand up together. Then we'll shine our flashlights all at once and surprise whatever is making all this fuss." Roy declared in a whisper. It lost a lot of its oomph when whispered.

They all started up the sides of the mound. Jon was in the middle. The boys felt that was the best way to keep Jon quiet; he was scared. This mound was much larger than the one in their backyard. Theirs was a simple dome shape. The one they were now scaling was shaped like a loaf of bread. The top had been hollowed out a long time ago by people looking for ancient one's artifacts. There was a big market for artifacts and skeleton parts, particularly skulls. This had left the mound a perfect dumping ground for the tree stumps. The stumps were dumped in willy-nilly, forming caverns that ran to the bottom, zigging and zagging, creating a maze of tunnels and warrens that made a perfect hideout for all sorts of creatures.

They reached the lip of the mound. Roy raised his hand and spoke.

"GO!" Ross said as he jumped up and turned on their flashlights. Jon stayed down, looking at the ground.

They shone their lights all around nothing, and there was nothing but the unruly pile of stumps. Roy looked at Ross, who just shrugged his shoulders.

"What the hell," Roy said. "I don't get it."

Ross shook his head and looked all around the cavity again.

"Jon, you can come out now," Roy sneered.

"Roy, let up on him." Ross chided Roy.

"Not until you tell me what those are," Jon said very shakily.

His flashlight pointed back down the mound.

"What the hell," Roy said for a second time.

Ross echoed, "What the hell?"

Behind them in the dark pasture were four sets of large luminous eyes staring straight at them. The overcast skies provided an excellent backdrop for anything silhouetted against it but was a solid blanket of black when trying to see anything on the ground. All that was visible were the luminous, unmoving eyes that transfixed them with unblinking stares.

"What are they, guys?" Jon whimpered.

"I don't know." Roy stammered, "Let's move to the other side of the mound."

They all shuffled around the lip of the mound to the side closest to their house.

Ross said that maybe they were cows. Jon and Roy agreed, and then all three said no, it wasn't. The eyes were too close together and too low to the ground.

"Should we be afraid?" Ross asked Roy.

"I'm already afraid," Roy answered.

That's all it took. Jon screamed and started down the mound, across the field, and toward home, running as fast as he could.

"Jon don't forget the creek," Ross yelled after him.

Jon disappeared. There was a yell and a splash, more yelling and splashing, and then Jon reappeared and was running again. It was hard to see him. Roy and Ross were starting to laugh.

"Don't forget about the fence Jon," they both yelled as loud as they could.

Shortly they heard Jon scream in pain and fear. They imagined Jon thrashing in the barbed wire. Roy cringed at the thought of those barbs. They were fierce and jagged, as he had come to know.

"Oh my God," said Ross, grabbing Roy's arms.

The seriousness lasted a few seconds, and then the humor took over, and they both laughed even harder when they saw Jon's mother's car careening out of their driveway and down U.S. Highway 16. They finally stopped laughing and remembered the eyes. They turned back to check them out, and they were gone!

"Where are they, Roy?"

"I don't know," Roy stammered.

They surveyed the area all around them. There was nothing to be seen except blackness and not a sound now that Jon's violent exodus was over.

"Roy, I want to get out of here."

"Yeah, me too."

'Where do you think they are?" Ross stammered.

"I don't know, brother. Let's move out slowly and carefully."

They descended the mound's sides. Slowly they started across the field. Roy watched the front, and Ross protected their rear and flanks. When they got to the creek with nothing of note happening, they took a deep breath and looked around.

"I guess we are in the clear," Roy said.

"Then why don't we hear any night noises." Ross worried. He was looking all around with quick, jerky motions.

"Don't go Jon on me," Roy said.

That steadied both of them, and they continued along the creek. When they got to the VanRidden bridge, they crossed over and headed toward their house.

"What was that?" Ross asked.

I don't know; we've seen cows, deer, and foxes, and none looked like that.

They moved quickly, still keeping track of the area all around them. When they crossed the fence, they were happy Jon hadn't torn it down and started down their driveway. The night noises started up again, and both boys stopped and felt the pent-up tension leave them.

"I wonder if we cross the fence again if the night noise will stop again?" Roy pondered.

"I wonder if we'll ever see Jon again," Ross joked, and they both laughed and continued home.

They were at The Glade the next day to recount last night's adventure. They both agreed that they hadn't confirmed anything. They hadn't caught anything unawares in the mound's cavity. They had witnessed the unnerving eyes and complete silence that accompanied them. The eyes had vanished into the night, but the silence continued until they crossed back over the fence to their driveway.

"Roy, this is serious stuff. We witnessed something extraordinary. What in the world could it have been?" Ross almost pleaded to Roy.

Roy was lying on his back alongside the pond playing with Ruby, the hummingbird. Ruby had learned to walk from finger to finger. He chose to ignore Ross's question and focused on Ruby.

"Come on, Roy, pay attention."

To underscore Ross's lament, the giant yellow spider started clacking its fangs, the little rabbit thumped its leg, and Bootsie woofed.

Roy sat up and took a deep sigh.

"OK."

Ross repeated his question.

Roy pondered it for a long moment.

"I have been giving this a lot of thought. I agree that we have experienced something very extraordinary indeed. There seem to be two or three explanations for what we witnessed. One: We saw some sort of secret hi-tech aircraft that is either ours or our enemy's and some creature's eyes. Two: We experienced an extraterrestrial spacecraft and, quite possibly, extraterrestrial beings. Three: We were hallucinating. Do you have anything to add?"

Ross took a deep breath and gazed at the pond intently. He was giving it some serious deep thought. The sound of water tumbling down the rocks as it left the culvert under the tracks was amplified in the silence. The spider even stopped clacking. All else was quiet and still, even the breeze that usually graced The Glade.

"Yes, that pretty much covers all the bases," Ross said.

"Well, which one is it, brother mine?" Roy said with a smirky look. He had his answer.

"After considering all the competing answers, number two is the simplest. So, number two is the answer. Wow, let's go out there again tonight. We don't want Jon along with us. Maybe we can talk to them, ride in the spaceship," Ross said breathlessly.

He was getting over-excited. Even the critters of The Glade were getting worked up. Woofing, clacking, thumping, buzzing, splashing— it was pandemonium.

Roy held up his hands. He was laughing.

"Hold on, gang. Let's all calm down. Ross, take a deep breath."

After a couple of minutes, everything started to quiet down.

"I agree with you, Ross, great deductive thinking. Occam's razor is what Dad called that process, remember? I believe Sherlock Holmes says something similar."

Ross nodded in agreement. He was almost giddy thinking about meeting extraterrestrial beings and riding in a spacecraft.

"I'm afraid they have left," Roy said.

"I'm pretty sure they don't want to be found out, but we'll try again tonight. We don't want to tell anyone, or they'll mess it up," Roy stated.

Ross agreed, and both boys returned to playing with their animal friends and studying a turtle that had just arrived in the pond. They always welcomed newcomers, even if they were only passing through.

That night and the next one, they spent on their mound. They stayed up until dawn began, relieving the night from its grasp on the earth. The triangular flying object did not return. The disappointment was a bitter pill to swallow. The craft and its crew were gone, perhaps because the boys had gotten too close to their lair. They kept the adventure a secret. Eventually, Jon returned and sheepishly apologized for his antics that night. He had severely sprained his ankle when he went headfirst into the creek. The barbed wire scratched him deeply as he fought his way through it. He got blood all over his mom's car and couldn't use it for a while.

Unknown to the boys and their family, in the early 1950s, there was a rash of UFO sightings in Wisconsin, sightings of triangle-shaped objects. The Triangle farm was not the exception.

"Why do so many reports involve strange, triangular-shaped craft—often described as dark in color, virtually noiseless and the size of a football field or larger? What, exactly, are they? And why are so many witnessed hovering or moving slowly and methodically, with no visible contrails?

In the years after the U.S. Air Force coined the term *unidentified flying object* in 1952, reports often referred to UFOs generically as flying saucers. But witnesses then, and since, have described a wide array of shapes: saucers (or two saucers put together), eggs, hats, cigars, boomerangs, lightbulbs—even Tic Tac candies.

Among the most commonly reported shapes were V-shaped, arrowhead-like or triangular. David Marler, UFO researcher and author of Triangular UFOs: An Estimate of the Situation, says he has reviewed more than 17,000 case files involving unidentified triangular craft, sometimes called "black triangles." Whether the sightings represent advanced U.S. spy craft—as some speculate—or something of unknown origin, their purpose remains mysterious. Given their consistent hovering behavior, Marler says, they might be engaged in, 'surveillance of some nature—or scanning. Or analyzing the topography'"

–(Greg Daugherty & Missy Sullivan July 22, 2020)

TALE NUMBER 17

FROM DESPERADO TO DEPUTY

"Imagination is more important than knowledge. For knowledge is limited, whereas imagination embraces the entire world, stimulating progress, giving birth to evolution."
– Albert Einstein.

"There is always a faster gun, and there is always a taller tale,"
– Bill Cheesman

The outlaw, The Ixonia Kid (aka. Ross), laid in wait, between the tracks, for the train he knew would shortly appear. His partner, Blacky (aka. Roy), hid in the bushes beside the tracks. When the train got close to him, The Kid would stand up and make it stop. Blacky would enter the passenger car and begin robbing the passengers. The Kid would make the engineer and brakeman leave the engine with him. Ross, with his captives, would meet Roy at the express car and use the engineer's key to open the vehicle. They would shoot it out with the agent, if necessary, hopefully not. After cleaning out the express safe, they would mount their horses and ride away.

The train was closer now. The Kid could feel the tracks vibrate. He pulled the mask over his nose and signaled Blacky to get ready. That's when it happened, and the plan fell apart.

"Ross!" his mother yelled, almost screaming. "Get down here right now. Get off those tracks. You also, Roy. Both of you get down here!"

A passenger train whizzed by as they approached the house, upsetting Mom.

That's how the adventure ended. Their mom scolded them and promised to tell their father. They spent most of the afternoon in The Glade worrying about what would happen when Dad got home. At the very least, he would probably ground them for several days, maybe even weeks. Even their animal companions of The Glade couldn't cheer them up. The afternoon very slowly went by.

Dinner time was spent quietly, with only polite comments exchanged. Dolly kept looking at the boys and grinning. She knew what was coming. She was glad it wasn't her getting the punishment but happy to see the boys getting their comeuppance.

After dinner, Dad told the boys to meet him in the barn. The boys apprehensively made their way to the barn. Their father was waiting for them.

"Your mother tells me you two were doing something stupid on the tracks today. Is that correct?"

The boys scuffed their feet in the dust and gazed silently downward,

"Come on, boys, speak up now!" Dad said in a raised voice.

Roy cleared his throat, looked Dad in the eye, and said, "Yes."

"What in the world were you doing, Ross, laying on the tracks?"

"We were pretending to be train robbers, and I was going to stop the train so we could rob it," Ross said.

"That was stupid and dangerous. Did you expect to stop a train?" Dad said while rolling his eyes at the mere thought of it.

"I guess that was pretty stupid when you think about it," Roy offered.

"You guess!" Dad yelled at them. "You guess!" What is wrong with you, boys? Are you addled?" Dad shook his head in frustration.

"You morons are grounded from the tracks for one week."

The boys continued to scuff their feet in the dust and look downward.

"You not only did something extremely dangerous, but you also got the roles all wrong. Our family is lawmen, not desperadoes."

"Lawmen?" the boys chimed in together.

"You bet your life. My dad's, your grandfather's, older brother Joe was a deputy marshal in Indian Territory for Judge Isaac Parker, The Hanging Judge."

"The Hanging Judge?" the boys queried. "Why did they call him that?"

"Well, he hanged 160 men and women while he was the District Judge for the Western District of Arkansas, including the Indian Territory. I assume some of them Joe captured and brought in for trial."

Ross asked, "What was Indian Territory?"

"The Indian Territory had become a haven for outlaws, including cattle rustlers, horse thieves, whiskey peddlers, gunfighters on the run, bank robbers, and just plain killers. It was free of white man's court. The only court in the district was the U.S. Court for the Western District of Arkansas, located at Fort Smith, with Judge Isaac Parker and his deputies.

The term Indian Territory is used to signify lands under the control of Native nations, including the "Five Civilized Nations." It included a large chunk of what is now Texas and Oklahoma. The term "Five Civilized Nations" came into use during the mid-nineteenth century to refer to the Cherokee, Choctaw, Chickasaw, Creek, and Seminole nations, who appeared to be assimilating to white man's norms, farming, etc. Hundreds of outlaws lived in the Indian Territory between the end of the Civil War and the late 1930s. Outlaws such as the James Gang, the Dueling Daltons, Cherokee Bill operated out of the Indian Territory.

Joe just disappeared. His fate is unknown, but he is presumed killed by the outlaws he was pursuing and left for the coyotes and vultures."

The boys were wide-eyed and had their mouths open in surprise and anticipation.

"Wow, that is fantastic. Our great uncle was a deputy U.S. Marshall for Hanging Judge Isaac Parker. Wow, again." said Roy.

Ross was all excited to incorporate this into their pretend wild west games.

"Dad, what else can you tell us about our family," Ross asked.

Dad answered, "It is getting late, and these tales are best told by your grandfather Roy Earl in Indiana. We are planning a trip there this summer."

"Awwww," both Ross and Roy complained.

"Trust me, Grandpa Roy Earl is a great storyteller."

Dad turned out the light which had begun attracting many bugs, particularly June Bugs. They were creepy when they landed on you and started crawling around. They headed up to the house to beat the June bugs gathering by the lights, and maybe a treat.

This was one of the few times the boys, Roy in particular, had a pleasant time with Dad on The Triangle.

That night, as they lay in bed, they were animated over how they would use the information about Great Uncle Deputy U.S. Marshal Joe in their play tomorrow. The boy's plans were made to the thudding on their screen window of the June Bugs attracting to their flashlights and bumping into the screen. The scenario they decided on was one where Great Uncle Joe and his partner foiled two desperados trying to rob a stagecoach and terrorize its passengers. The two lawmen could not foil a train robbery because they were grounded from the railroad tracks.

After breakfast, Ross and Roy first went to the encyclopedias. They looked up Judge Isaac Parker and the Indian Territory—the information they found supported what Dad had said the night before. There were pictures of the territory, Judge Isaac Parker and some of his deputies, as well as some Indians. In addition, there were pictures of the corpses of bad men and the gallows. Dolly had started with them, but when they got to the photos of the bodies, she left to play with her dolls and invisible friend. The boys asked her to come outside and join in their play, but Dolly said her invisible friend wanted to stay and play with the dolls.

"My invisible friend tells me that life as a fairy can be pretty dangerous here. There were cars, pesticides, animals, birds, and people to hunt them. She feels safe playing with Dolly and the dolls as long as the snakes and frogs are put away," Dolly told them.

While the boys may not wholly believe in Dolly's invisible friend, they do not disbelieve either. They watched Dolly playing quietly with her dolls. She was sitting in a sunbeam in the living room. Little specks of dust floated about in the sunbeam; one was more significant than the others, and it seemed to hover near Dolly and respond to her talking. The boys watched this for a short period of time and then moved outdoors after making sure Dolly would keep an eye on Bootsie.

"What do you think that floating thing was?" Ross asked Roy.

"This is an extraordinary place with many different myths and legends. We have experienced some of them, and there are so many we haven't even seen or heard of. I'm open to all the myths and legends until proven wrong. I don't think they will be proven wrong so much as clarified and modified or changed as they are revealed."

"Now I'm baffled," Ross said, holding his head.

"Join the crowd. The one thing I've learned since we moved here is that if you are patient and wait faithfully, expecting the answer, it will come. It may not be what you thought it would be, but there will be an answer. I'm still learning. Accepting that you'll never know it all, I think that's part of it; you keep learning."

Ross shook his head and just kept walking.

By the time they reached a spot in John's pasture about halfway to The Glade, alongside the bog, they had forgotten all about floating dust particles and invisible friends. They were ready to mete out justice in the way they imagined their Great Uncle Joe did in the Indian Territory. They had already decided that Ross was going to be Joe, and he had added the nickname "Lightening" because of his blazing swift draw. Roy was going to be Joe's trusted sidekick. Every hero needs a trusty sidekick, even imaginary ones. "Lightening" rode a big black stallion named Fury, and his partner rode a buckskin.

In short order, their vivid imaginations, coupled with the quiet rural surroundings, had them deep in an imaginary world that only young people and exceptional adults have the blessing of being able to conjure up. They were busy laying a trap to catch two outlaws in the act of robbing a stagecoach and terrorizing the passengers. The two lawmen had received a tip on where and when the robbery would be. The deputies settled for a wait after carefully camouflaging their location.

After a short wait, the imagined bad guys appeared and readied to rob the stagecoach and terrorize the passengers. There were two of them. They laid a trap for the coach and hunkered down. The pretend coach appeared, with a driver cracking his whip over the heads of a team of four horses, two abreast and yelling at them to keep up the pace. A shotgun-carrying guard accompanied the driver. A cloud of dust roiled up around the coach as it rolled and rocked across the prairie.

"Giddy-up there, you broken down cayuses," The driver yelled.

The badmen sprung the trap and forced the coach to stop, only to be thwarted by Lightening Joe and his partner. After a brief but violent battle, the deputies prevailed, displaying exceptional skills with guns and knives. The badmen were apprehended. Order was restored. With a tip of their hats to the gentlemen and a wink to the young ladies, the two lawmen with prisoners in tow headed across the rugged landscape to Judge Isaac Parker's court and their next assignment.

The make-believe world in which this adventure took place was perceived as clear and rich in color, smell, and sound as any Western show the boys had seen or comic book read. The boys were the voices of the characters. They shared imagined movements and descriptions of characters' actions with each other, much the same as their sister and her dolls. They went so far as to mimic the sound of the horses. They were two deputies in the act of capturing dangerous men and saving innocent citizens. Sometimes they even received wounds and were not successful. It was all a fantasy world of their creation.

Later that afternoon, they were lying by the pond in The Glade reminiscing about the earlier playing, and Ross asked Roy:

"I wonder what really happened to Joe, Deputy U.S. Marshal of Indian Territory? Did he leave and go somewhere else? Did he die in a gunfight, was he ambushed? How come no one knows? What a terrible end to Joe, killed and left for the vultures; only the killer knows where."

The boys looked at each other and were close to tears—a personal touch to their imaginary world.

"It's a good thing that we have family that loves us and will keep track of us," Roy quietly said.

Ross nodded in agreement.

There are many more adventures of Lightening Joe and his partner that Roy and Ross played out, but that's enough for now, the Old Man thought, and decided to nap.

Digging for Artifacts

TALE NUMBER 18

BAND OF A BROTHER
AND A SISTER

"Where the cheerful children
of unwritten poems,
play all around,
you will find me there."

– Khadija Rupa, Unexpressed Feelings

"Information is not knowledge.
The only source of knowledge is experience.
You need experience to gain wisdom."

– Albert Einstein

Roy sat alone alongside the pond in The Glade. There was light rain falling this late summer afternoon. The aspen branches and leaves provided a canopy that shielded him from the rain. It was such a soft rain that he could not hear it as it slowly quenched the thirst of the land and its minions. It was the kind of day that was still bright and airy; although it was raining. The precipitation freshened the air, making all the smells and colors sweeter and more radiant. The bird's songs seemed more harmonious, and the atmosphere had a golden cast. It was magical in sight, sound, and fragrance. He was glad he was alone so there was nothing to disturb this moment. He savored and breathed deeply, closed his eyes, and laid back on the soft grass. He let himself be carried along in the time, suspended for this moment, totally at peace and one with the time and place. These moments were rare and to be cherished.

A soft buzzing sound intruded into his reverie.

Try as he might, he couldn't get it out of his mind, and he sat up to see what was causing this muffled disturbance. At first, he couldn't see anything, and the sound ceased.

"It must have been a big dragonfly," he mused.

He laid back down and tried to get back into the drifting sensation. He couldn't; the moment was gone. This upset him and started to ruin the magical feeling of The Glade with his contrariness. His spiritual peace was a significant component of Glade's environment. Serenity was not achievable if he was trying to control the moment. He couldn't invoke Glade's mystical ambiance, it was manifested by the lack of self, letting Glade's spirit abide in you, and as a result, you abide in it. Then, you experienced The Glade's beauty, serenity, power, and protection from within. Roy had arrived at the awareness of The Glade's essence over multiple occasions seeking the peace of The Glade. He now acknowledged the intrusion of trying to project himself on The Glade when he attempts to summon it instead of asking it to come and giving up self.

As he prepared to let go of control, the buzzing returned, and he couldn't relax.

"What is doing this?"

He sat back up with a start. He looked around The Glade and saw a tiny object flitting around the flowers, pausing at some and hovering in place. Its wings were a blur. It was too big to be a dragonfly, too small for any bird he had seen here before. As he sat still and watched, it flew right up to his face and seemed to study him. It was a bird. A tiny hummingbird, a beautiful ruby-throated bird, was seriously studying him. On impulse, he slowly lifted his finger to the bird like a perch. The bird darted away, and Roy was disappointed.

The bird returned to the flowers, and Roy prepared to lay back down. He was here to formulate a plan of action, an expedition, to go to the rock pile and looted mound on the far side of Hilltop Farm, where it boarded the VanRidden farm. The mound had been looted long ago, but it still may have contained some artifacts and relics. The rock pile was where John deposited all the rocks that worked their way to the surface; this was glaciated land, along with any relics and artifacts. Roy wanted to sort through those. This was going to be an all-day expedition. They would be required to take a circuitous route to the rock pile and mound. They would need to stay primarily to the roads and lanes because the fields were almost ready to harvest, and the VanRidden had their bull in the pasture with the cows, and bulls became particularly testy when in the company of the cows. It was easy to get him angry. Angry bulls were dangerous regardless of the color of your clothes. His brother and sister were going to accompany him. Ross was a great detail planner, and Dolly was always enthusiastic and would get Mom to pack a great lunch and snacks. Bootsie would also accompany them chiefly because they couldn't stop her. With her banner-like tail, she would lead the quest.

He laid back in the grass and tried to achieve that same serene condition of letting go and drifting, totally at peace with himself and the universe itself. As he did, the hummingbird returned to him and hovered in front of his face again.

"Well, little fellow, have you decided I'm no danger to you, or are you still deciding?"

The bird cocked its tiny head as though pondering his words. The iridescent ruby splotch of color on its throat was like a royal pendant. It is shown brightly in the muted light of The Glade.

"I think I'll call you Ruby, if that suits you."

The bird turned around and flew off a short distance.

"I guess not then. How about Princess? That is a little more elegant."

The bird returned. Roy wasn't sure if the bird understood him and was, in its own way, communicating with him or was being a bird, and he was reading way too much into it. He preferred the communication explanation and went with it.

"Princess, little friend. Let's shake on it."

With that, Roy lifted his finger and the bird landed on it.

"Oh, wow," Roy said quietly so as not to frighten the bird away. "Let me tell you about the grand expedition I am planning."

He proceeded to share his plans and hoped to discover some actual artifacts. The elegant little bird politely listened attentively to his dreams and hopes. When he left The Glade at lunchtime, the Princess remained there, as was the way with most of their companions there. They didn't stray from the safety and the magic of those surroundings.

Over lunch, Roy shared the plans for the expedition with his team. Ross and Dolly were both very excited and happy with their roles. They decided tomorrow would be the "Expedition In Search of Relics Day, E Day."

They all hurried through lunch to get to their tasks. Roy to scout the route and make the screening device to sift the material from the dig. Ross to plan all the items needed and pack the packs. He was also going to research archaeological digs in the library. Roy also asked him to determine what hummingbirds ate. Dolly would work with Mom to prepare a grand feast for their lunch and plenty of snacks. They all jumped into their tasks wholeheartedly.

Roy had made prior arrangements with John to make a screening device. John had a piece of screen that he said would work for their application. When Roy got to the farm, he helped John with some chores, as was the usual routine. He helped John so John would have time to help him. Roy realized this was a Life Principle; tic is always balanced with a tock, the "Tic Tock" of life.

The screening device was fabricated by framing a piece to a quarter of an inch opening screen with a lightweight frame. It was strong but light enough to carry. John showed him how bracing the corners added a lot of sturdiness to the frame without adding much weight. Roy was pleased with it and propped it against the machinery shed to be picked up in the morning on the team's way through. That finished, he helped John with the milking before he was called home for dinner.

The children were anxious that night, looking forward to the adventure tomorrow. They were fidgety at dinner, and Dad got upset about it. He was always upset with them, Roy in particular. Mom would come to their defense, and Mom and Dad would get in a fight. The evening usually ended with Mom and Dad squabbling and the kids getting out of the house until Dad went to work on some project. Roy usually was out back sitting on the mound, which they now called Council Mound, to meditate on something silently. Ross was off in a corner reading, and Dolly quietly played with one of her reptiles and her invisible fairy friend. This was the fairy that had promised to be Dolly's friend if she let her go after capturing her one night a while ago.

While the boys couldn't see this fairy friend of Dolly's, it was undoubtedly genuine to their sister. There were many times when Roy observed Dolly intently engaged with her friend. There was no doubt that there was indeed something there as far as his sister was concerned—something that enjoyed her company and responded to her. Roy had come to believe that it was a shortcoming on his part, not being able to recognize the being. Such was the manner of things on The Triangle Farm, a hint of magic in daily life. It added a sense of adventure to the moment.

Ross, Dolly, and Bootsie wandered up to the mound and sat around him. It was becoming dark, and the evening sounds were beginning. Crickets, frogs, and the chittering of birds settled down into their nests while they proclaimed the end of the day and the beginning of the night. A few bats were flitting about in search of mosquitos and such. The firefly season was over, although the larvae could be seen glowing in the grass and garden.

"Well, I think that we are ready for tomorrow. The packs are loaded, lunch is prepared, complete with snacks, canteens are full, and trowels and shovels are gathered," Ross reported.

Dolly nodded agreement, and Bootsie woofed her ascent.

Somewhere in the woods across the cornfield next to their house, an owl made its mournful inquiry to the coming nighttime, "Whooooooo." Who will be my dinner tonight?

"Here is the map I've made," Roy said as he took it from his back pocket.

They all studied his hand-drawn map.

Roy related the path they would follow.

"First, we'll head down to Hilltop Road and then up to Hilltop Farm. We'll pick up the screen John and I prepared this afternoon. Then we'll go down the back of the Hilltop on the washed-out road and across Clear Creek.

"Why are we going way out of our way?" Dolly asked, "We can go straight across from our driveway."

"The VanRidden have a bull in the pasture with his cows. And you don't want to mess with him, and the crops are almost ripe, and we can't walk through the fields."

"Oh, Ok," Dolly said.

"Once we are down there, across the creek, we can walk through the pasture to the rock pile and looted mound."

"What time do we start?" Ross asked.

"Nine in the morning," Roy said.

"Sounds good; let's go to bed early tonight," Ross suggested.

Everyone agreed, and they headed into the house.

None of them slept well. They were all excited about the upcoming adventure.

They all got up early and ate a good breakfast their mother insisted they eat. She said they were going to need the energy from breakfast.

They left on the adventure well before 9 a.m. And quickly made their way up to Hilltop Farm. After saying "hello" to John, they picked up the screen and began down the washed-out road. They were blessed with a great day for their adventure. The sun was bright, the temperature was warm, and the air was dry. The blue sky was clear of clouds, and there was a crispness to the atmosphere. The kids stopped on the bridge going over Clear Creek. They watched the fast-flowing water that was so clear they could see good size fish swimming against the current, looking for prey. John had told them that some of these were brook trout. The boys talked about trying to catch some of these fish at a later date. They left the bridge and hiked across the pasture, around the rock pile, and to the looted mound. This mound was much larger than their mound. Not only higher, but it was also shaped like a loaf of bread, maybe three times the size of their mound.

They established their base camp in the shade of a tree that had grown between the rock pile and the mound. They climbed up the side of the mound and looked down into the cavity created when the looters dug out the center of the mound. The boys had not been able to find out what precisely had been found in the mound, but apparently, enough loot must have been found to keep looters engaged enough to dig out a cavity about nine feet wide and six feet deep. The sides of the cavity were steep and grown over with grass and weeds.

"Where do we start?" Ross asked.

Roy looked down at the cavity and said, "Let's go to the deepest place. That is probably where the last digging took place."

They all scrambled down the steep sides of the cavity, with Bootsie leading the way.

"Ok, I'll start digging, and Ross, you start breaking up the clumps with the trowel, and then you and Dolly can begin screening the dirt."

Everyone agrees and starts with the task of searching for artifacts. The morning passes by with Roy digging with the shovel, Ross breaking up the clumps and Dolly screening the dirt and sand, hoping to discover a treasure overlooked by past looters. Even Bootsie helped, digging holes, sniffing the dirt, and snuffing at what she uncovered. They worked hard all morning with nothing except beautiful, exciting stones to show for their effort. The pile of screened dirt was impressively large.

"Let's take a break." Ross declared, wiping his brow with the back of his arm.

Everyone set their tools down and sat on the side of the cavity.

"Why didn't we find anything?" Dolly asked.

Roy and Ross looked at each other.

Roy answered, "I guess the looters got everything."

"Yeah, they took this mound apart; too bad," Ross concurred.

"I'm hungry," Dolly said.

"So am I," Roy agreed. "Let's have lunch."

They climbed up the sides of the cavity, carrying their tools. They went to the tree where they had stashed their lunches. It was cooler under the tree, and they settled down to enjoy Dolly and Mom's lunch. It was great. Their favorite sandwiches were three slices of Oscar Myer Bologna, butter schmeared on one slice of bread and yellow mustard on the other. They had a big bag of potato chips to share, an apple and a Hostess Cupcake for dessert, and cherry-flavored Kool-Aid in a big thermos that they strained to carry from home. They devoured the lunch and stretched out in the sun on the grassy side of the looted mound. Bootsie begged for and was given plenty of pieces of lunch.

The boys showered Dolly with kudus for a super job of making lunch. Her face turned red in embarrassment.

"What were you hoping to find in the mound?" Dolly asked the boys, changing the subject.

Ross thought momentarily and replied, "Arrowheads, pottery, beads, and artwork."

"Jewelry, wow!" Dolly exclaimed, "I'd like to have Indian jewelry."

"Don't get too excited dear sister. We would have put it back after we had a chance to study it."

"Why?" Dolly lamented.

"Those items aren't ours. They belong to the people who put them there. We can look at them, but we can't take them. Do you understand?"

"I guess so," Dolly said shakily.

Alright, let's check out the rock pile for artifacts," Roy said.

"Where do all these rocks come from?" Ross asked.

"John says that all this countryside is what is called glaciated." Roy told them.

"We already know that" Ross said.

"Well, the glaciers have been scraping the ground as they grew and picked all sorts of rocks, boulders, and great amounts of earth. When the glaciers started to melt, they dropped all that earth and the rocks. That earth is what makes this countryside, the earth is very deep, and even the mounds and little steep valleys are the results of that glaciation," Roy recited what John told him.

"As the soil freezes and thaws during winter, the water in it expands and contracts. That action causes the embedded rocks to come to the surface, so every year, a fresh crop of rocks will be picked from the fields and brought here. Over the years, this is the pile that has been collected."

"Wow! We are standing on our history right now," Dolly exclaimed.

Roy's ears perked up.

"That's correct; we are standing on our history. It is beneath us, not behind us. This is a fascinating concept."

"I think I'll climb this tree and see what I can see from up there," Ross exclaimed.

He was a great tree climber and didn't want to sit and listen to Roy start developing some strange theory.

"Ross, I don't think that is a very good idea. Why don't you come down?" Roy called up to him, as he was already up fairly high.

"You just can't climb as fast as I can. That's why you want me to come down."

"Yes, you are a much better climber than I am, but that's not why I want you to come down. Look at what you'll fall on if you slip or a branch breaks."

Ross looked down at the ground. It was not nice soft grass but big sharp-edged rocks. He swallowed hard and, slowly, carefully started down.

When he got down, he took a deep breath of relief.

"I forgot to look at the ground I was playing on. As you say, big brother, 'You can't play marbles in a cow pasture, and you can't climb trees in a rock pile.'"

They returned to search the rock pile for any artifact but found nothing. They spent most of the afternoon rummaging through the pile without any success. Bootsie had given up early on and was taking a nap under the tree in the shade.

She's the smartest one here Roy thought as he glanced over at her.

"Do you think John was pulling your leg when he said he put artifacts here?" Ross queried.

"No, I don't," responded Roy. "Remember, he said professional artifact hunters visit these rock piles on the various farms around here. They comb these piles pretty thoroughly."

"Yeah, I guess you're right." Ross agreed sulkily.

"We spent all day for nothing?" Dolly whined.

"Not for nothing. We had a great picnic lunch in the fields beside an ancient civilization site. We also got to explore it and then got a chance to search through this pile of rocks from the ice age. Where else could we do that? In addition, we have a great snack left to eat," Roy recounted to them.

Ross and Dolly brightened up; even Bootsie got into it with the mention of the word "snack."

Dolly cocked her head, thought a moment, and then brightly retorted.

"And we got to do this together."

"Yay," the boys responded.

There was a heightened sense of bonding between them.

Bootsie woofed and jumped up and down, and immediately their spirits lifted. They ate the snack, drank the rest of the Kool-Aid, and packed up. It was a much lighter load heading home without the Kool-Aid and food. That was good because the kids were tuckered after a long day under the hot sun. They crossed the fence, cut across the vacant pasture to the bridge over Clear Creek, and started up the washed-out road up the hill to Hill Top Farm. The hill was steep on this side and exhausted the kids after they reached the top, even after a rest stop halfway up the hill.

John was waiting for them by the windmill.

"Have a good day and find lots of loot?" he queried.

"No," all three kids chimed in

"Like a drink of cold well water?" he asked.

"Well, line up, youngest first, and after your drink, tell me all about it," he said.

After they all had their fill of water, even Bootsie, they settled on the edge of the hill looking out over Triangle Farm.

"Who is going to start?" he asked.

"I will," Dolly piped up excitedly. "We went to the looted mound and dug and dug but found nothing. But if we did, we would have put it back because it wasn't ours. Then we had a super lunch and Kool-Aid. Then we sorted through the rocks, searching for an artifact but found nothing again. Even though we didn't find anything, we had a great day together. That was the best part. We did it together."

John laughed and said, "Well, it sounds like you did indeed find a treasure. The treasure of family, the greatest treasure of all."

The kids looked at each other and then hugged each other. They then hugged John and started down the road to The Triangle. They were arm in arm; Bootsie led the way with her banner-like tail lifted as if leading a parade. Today was a day they would remember.

TALE NUMBER 19

HOBOS OR BUMS – GRAFFITI OR ART

*"As Global Warming raises temperatures, it takes
longer to cool pies on window sills, and I wonder
if this whole thing was caused by hobos."*
– Dana Gould

"Freedom is just another word for nothing left to lose."
– Janis Joplin (The Rose), Me and Bobby McGee

L iving next to a railroad track, the boys were interested in the
writings and pictures on the rail cars. Some trains had cars
almost wholly covered with writings and drawings; some were
practically bare. They took particular note of one unique illustration
of a palm tree with a man sitting under it, with a sombrero pulled
down over his eyes, taking a siesta. Roy wondered who the artist was
and where he was. The artist signed the name "Herbie" under the
drawings, when the freight train was moving slowly enough to read it.

He guessed this was one of the many things he could see but never
know. When the boys went to the encyclopedia and had their father
check out the library, there wasn't much information there.

One sunny afternoon the boys were up on the tracks taking turns
throwing stones at the insulators on the telephone poles. The stones
between the tracks were the perfect size for their young hands. They
were accompanied by Bootsie and their little flop-eared bunny pal.

He studied them with a cocked head and wiggling nose trying to figure out what and why they were doing what they were doing. He eventually gave up and contented himself with looking for sweet grass alongside the tracks. The boys kept moving down the tracks toward The Glade.

They were competing on who could hit the insulator at the farthest point away from it. They kept moving closer to the insulator until one of them hit it. Then they started on the next one down the line. They would throw at it, and if they both missed, move up four crossties and try again. In this manner, they were working their way to The Glade, where they planned to cool their feet in the pond and catch crawfish. They also looked forward to seeing their friends; the damsel fly Queeny and the big yellow and black spider that didn't like Roy and would always click at him by snapping his mandibles.

Suddenly the rabbit stomped his feet and dashed down the embankment. The boys didn't know what was the matter. If the fox was near, the rabbit usually stayed close by them. No train was coming; Ross felt the tracks to be sure. Mom wasn't calling them; everything was fine. Then Bootsie started to bark.

"Hello," the stranger called to them from down the tracks where he sat in the grass above The Glade.

"Good morning, boys. Beautiful day isn't it, though? That blue sky is as blue as the Gulf of Mexico off of Panama City. The clouds are as white as the sand on the beaches. It is just a great day to be alive. Don't you agree?"

He paused and then said, "What's your dog's name? Good looking animal."

"Oh! Pardon me; I haven't even introduced myself. How rude of me."

The boys stared at him, big-eyed and open-mouthed. Bootsie was even transfixed by this mysterious man who seemed just to appear. He was tall and slim. He wore faded and worn jeans that were in good repair. His shirt was checkered, and, like the jeans, worn but in good repair. His boots were ankle high and worn but also in good repair.

He had a full white beard, trimmed nicely, and weather-worn brown skin with bright green eyes that appeared to sparkle when he smiled. His hat was a khaki slouch hat, that was, you guessed it, worn but in good repair. Overall, he was worn but in good repair. His voice was deep and lyrical. Standing there above The Glade, Roy sensed something entrancing about this stranger.

The man looked at Roy and then at The Glade. He slightly nodded his head toward Roy and had a quizzical grin on his face. *What the heck was that all about,* thought Roy?

"I am Herbie. You, perhaps, have seen my signature drawing on the box cars rolling past your house? A palm tree with a little guy taking a nap under it."

Both boys nodded open-mouthed and big-eyed.

"Did you happen to notice my signature under the drawing?"

The boys nodded their heads yes. They were too transfixed to speak. Even Bootsie was mesmerized by this strange, beguiling man in front of them.

"Stranger-Danger, I understand and completely agree. Your parents instill good qualities in you boys, even the dog. That is good. I also am a good friend of the farmer on the hill, John Franger." He pointed to the farm. "That is where I am heading to at present. Care to tag along?"

Suddenly Herbie was past them and walking down the tracks toward the Hilltop Road crossing. How he got past them was unknown. They must have been looking at Hilltop Farm he was pointing at and didn't see him walk past them.

"You'll have to step out if you want to walk with me," Herbie said, not even turning around. His voice was just there in front of them.

The boys hurried to catch up to Herbie. He had a smooth, lengthy stride that was longer than the boys.

He spoke not one word but concentrated on walking to the farm on the hill. The boys and Bootsie tagged along behind him.

As they entered the barnyard, John came around the corner from the milk house side of the barn.

"Why, hello, Herbie!" John exclaimed. "I have been expecting you. I have a ton of jobs waiting for you." John hurried toward Herbie.

"My dear friend John, how good it is to see you again," Herbie responded.

They hugged as a demonstration of their affection for each other. Hugging was a new experience for the boys.

"I see you have met the boys. The boys and Bootsie are adopted Hilltop Farm family."

"Well, we have not formerly met. The boys have been stand-offish until you, John, vetted me," said Herbie.

John waved the boys over.

"I want you to meet Herbie. He is a dear friend and has been visiting the farm for 25 years. He is to be trusted."

The boys stepped up to Herbie, introduced themselves, and shook hands with the hobo. Bootsie even offered a paw to shake.

"Where is Stumpy?" Herbie asked.

"He is around here somewhere," John responded and called the dog's name loudly several times.

They could hear the dog bark, and Bootsie took off to the back of the machinery sheds. Shortly they both came from the back of the sheds. Stumpy hobbling as fast as his stumps of legs would allow. Every time Roy saw him, he was amazed at the courage and life this little dog possessed, full of vigor after losing the lower section of his legs to a hay mower.

"There he is!" exclaimed John. "He was laying in the sun on the back up the hill. The afternoon sun is strong on the hillside."

Stumpy ran right up to Herbie and rolled over for a belly rub which he got. Everyone, even Bootsie, shifted away from the little prone dog as he farted. Herbie was aware of the horrible flatulence that belly rubs stimulated. These gaseous emissions were so foul that they were almost visible.

Herbie chuckled and petted the little dog as soon as the air cleared. This didn't take long on top of the hill.

The ringing of the triangle dinner bell that Mom used to call the boys made them all perk up.

"We have to go home now, but we would love to hear about hoboing," Roy said.

"I would love to tell you all about it," Herbie responded. "Maybe tomorrow after dinner?"

"Great," both boys said and took off running down the road.

Over dinner, they shared the meeting of Herbie the Hobo. Their parents were concerned about the safety of being alone with a hobo. Their father identified hobos as bums or tramps not to be trusted.

The boys responded that John said Herbie could be trusted and was a good friend of 25 years.

"Why don't we invite him to dinner tomorrow? We can meet him and get to know him," Mom suggested.

"Great, I'll set it up. Tomorrow is Saturday, so I don't have to go to work and possibly get hung up there. Dinner can be on time," Dad said.

The boys looked at each other and smiled.

Later that evening, the boys were at the mound, their favorite hangout by the house, playing mumbly-peg. Dolly came to tell them that the hobo and John were coming to dinner tomorrow.

"Boy, that's even better," Roy said after thanking Dolly. "John knows Herbie and is his friend and ours. That's just perfect."

"Yep, sure is," Ross added.

"Yep, sure is," Dolly chimed in.

Both boys looked at her and shrugged. She sat down and asked what they were doing. This was always a bad sign.

"We are playing mumbly-peg," they answered.

"Can I play?"

The boys looked at each other, and Ross nodded ok.

"Do you have a pocket knife?" Roy said, figuring this would deter her.

She immediately produced a little red Swiss Army knife with her name on it from her apron pocket. Every farm girl wore an apron, just like her mom.

The boys were taken aback; not only did she have a knife, but it was top shelf as far as pocket knives went.

"Where did you get that?" Ross asked.

"Dad got it for me a while ago. He said every farm girl should have a pocketknife. Pretty, isn't it?"

"Pocket knives aren't pretty," Roy mocked. "They are cool or neat. That one is both."

Do you know how to play mumbly-peg? Ross asked.

"Yes," she said confidently. "Of course, I do."

"Don't tell me, Dad?" Roy said sarcastically and scowled.

"Yes," Dolly said in a matter-a-fact manner.

"Ok, let's begin," Roy said smugly.

"I'll start," Dolly said.

The boys were astonished as she proceeded to complete the first five motions masterfully, (1) flipping from the palm, (2) flipping from the back of the hand, (3) flipping by a twist of the fist, (4) throwing by holding the blade tip between the thumb and forefinger, (5) flipping from between the teeth, before missing one.

"Where did you learn to do that so well," Roy exclaimed.

"Yeah," Ross spouted.

"Daddy practiced with me," Dolly proudly stated.

The boys looked at each other. They first were angry, then felt left out. Whatever, they shrugged their shoulders and got after her benchmark on #5, flipping between teeth. They both failed. Dolly laughed and clapped her hands.

"You cannot tell anybody about this," they both said.

"Why?" Dolly asked.

"Because you can't," Roy said.

Dolly agreed, and they proceeded to practice their mumbly peg together.

Roy was looking forward to tomorrow night at dinner with Herbie and John. He didn't even mind mowing the lawn in preparation for getting the place in shape for visitors. He even got after Ross to do a better job edging along the sidewalk.

Behind the barn, they raked up extra grass and fallen apples to put in the mulch pile Dad was starting. They took the good apples and gave them to Mom for a pie she would bake for dessert. Dad was busy working in the berry patch and orchard. They both were starting to look good and while there would not be any harvest this season, things looked good for next year.

It started to rain in the midafternoon, so the boys moved to the front porch and started to play Monopoly with Dolly. Being the youngest of the three and a girl besides, she was usually a winner. She possessed an uncanny ability to know what the dice would turn up to be, when to buy a house or hotel for a property, and when to buy or not to buy a property. She said her invisible friend helped her.

Dad worked in the barn, fixing things, and Mom worked on dinner. The aromas coming from the kitchen were wonderful. It was going to be a memorable evening.

Dinner time was approaching, and it was still lightly raining. The temperature cooled, and the smell of fresh mowed lawn and baked apple pie was in the air. It was exquisite.

The evening was upon them. The boys played checkers in the living room, and Dolly was kibitzing. Dad was reading one of his university extension journals, and Mom was finishing dinner. The dining room table was set. Dad wore clean clothes, and Mom wore a pretty dress and make-up. The kids were made to clean themselves up,

John and Herbie finally arrived. Everyone crowded in the foyer. Dad finally told the kids to take Bootsie into the living room, so the adults had room to get acquainted.

John had brought a bottle of wine for dinner, and Herbie had brought Mom some flowers and even kissed her hand. That made her blush and hide her face. Roy had never seen that before and was intrigued that his mother could behave like a regular woman.

Everyone sat down for dinner after the adults had introduced themselves. The children were on one side of the table and John and Herbie on the other. Dad and Mom were on the ends. Roy was surprised when Dad led them all in a brief grace before starting to eat. He seldom did that unless it was Christmas or Easter. The table was a cornucopia of wonderfully prepared food. Mom had roasted a couple of chickens with roasted carrots, turnips, and corn. There was a large dish full of creamy mashed potatoes and a gravy boat full of thick gravy made from roasted chicken drippings. Then there was a plentiful number of fresh biscuits and butter. There was milk for the children and wine for the adults.

Herbie complimented Mom on the outstanding meal and Dad on the farm's appearance. He was particularly impressed with the improved condition of the orchard since he had last seen it. The parents thanked Herbie for the compliments.

Herbie then addressed Dad and said he had heard that Dad was a metallurgical engineer. Dad confirmed he was and seemed surprised that Herbie appeared familiar with the vocation.

"Are you knowledgeable about metallurgy, Herbie?"

"Somewhat," replied Herbie. "I spend a lot of time in libraries during my travels. They are wonderful places to get out of the weather and relax and are free." I have a lot of time to keep current and study various subjects of interest, such as metallurgy, because the trains and railways are mostly metal of one sort or another. Also, geology because of all the varied countryside I visit. Then dairy farming, agriculture, mechanics, and woodworking...I could go on and on. I have the time, and it's all free. Then there are my friends, like John, here, who I visit and help while there. I get to apply things I have read about. It's a great life, and it's all free."

Roy could see his dad's eyes going dreamy and getting a faraway look.

Dad said softly, "That sounds like a great way to live."

Herbie cast his eyes downward and said, "Not all the time. There are the railroad detectives, or "bulls" as we call them; they will work you over if they catch you. Then there are the long stretches where you get caught out of doors in the weather which is tough. The hardest part is convincing people you're not one of the bums or tramps that roam around causing trouble or stealing. That is the worst."

When Herbie looked up, his green eyes were sparkling again, and he smiled at the people gathered around the table.

Roy took a deep breath and blurted out. "Herbie, please tell us about Hobos."

Dad agreed; everyone at the table nodded and leaned forward expectantly.

"Ok," Herbie said. "There have been Hobos as long as there have been railways. After the Civil War, boys going home or not ready to go home used the railways to travel. The Great Depression saw thousands upon thousands of teenagers leave their homes and decide to roam the country in search of a better life by jumping on boxcars and riding around America. That's when I started."

"How old were you, Herbie?' Dad asked.

'I was 16," Herbie answered. "I became lost in the travels and the lure of the freedom I felt on the rails. Many kids did, and now we are the Hobos. The freight trains crisscrossing the country emanated their appeal as a symbol of unbridled freedom. Later generations used them as sites for urban art, such as me. "Hobo" comes from the words 'homeless boy', which applies to all the kids or young soldiers riding the rails. Hobos, instead of tramps or bums, look for work and then hear the siren song of the rails and move on. I have been visiting John for over 25 years. Wouldn't you agree, John?"

"That's right," John said. "He is one of the best mechanics and woodworkers around. Some of the other farmers steal him away. He is excellent for short jobs or projects. It's too bad I can't talk him into staying." John looked fondly at Herbie, who smiled and looked away.

"It's the song of the rails, and I like winters down south. Work the shrimp boats out of Matagorda Bay, Texas, to Pensacola, Florida. Depending on the fishing. I have some good friends down there, and I may take time to stop by bayou country in Louisiana. Love the Cajun gumbo," Herbie said, shaking his head and licking his lips.

"I could use your help with my little tractor. It is not running right, and I can't figure out what is wrong with it," Dad said.

"That little Farmall Cub?" Herbie asked. "Know her well."

Dad nodded yes.

"Sure, maybe two days from now. Got a couple of things to do for brother John first."

"I will pay you for the help."

"No, sir, but another meal like this would do just fine."

"Well, If I have to do the cooking, I can use something done to my washing machine."

"I can do that for a dessert with the meal."

Mom and Dad both nodded ok, and everyone laughed.

"Speaking of dessert, if you children would help clear away the dishes, I have warm, fresh-baked apple pie with vanilla ice cream for dessert. Everyone cheered, and the table was cleared in a flash.

After dessert, the men went to the porch to smoke a cigar and visit, and Mom and the kids cleared and washed the dishes. It was a special evening, and Roy would never forget it.

The next day Herbie was busy all day doing jobs for John. In fact, he was engaged for the next two days. Then he came down to work on the Cub and the washing machine. The children hoped he had time for them; they followed him around as if they could help. They generally made a nuisance of themselves, but Herbie just smiled at them. At lunchtime, they had time to visit with him.

Mom had prepared a delicious chicken salad and served it on homemade crusty bread. Then there was lemon pound cake and fresh Russian iced tea. Mom really liked Herbie. She ate with them on the rear deck. It was a cloudy day, but the sun was shining for them.

Herbie regaled them with stories of his travels, great places he visited, close calls with the bulls, near accidents, tough times caught in the weather, and no place to sleep. Then there were the special friends all over the country. Obviously, he loved the freedom of his lifestyle but made it clear it wasn't for everyone, and it was hazardous at times. They spent the whole afternoon transported around the country on Herbie's tales. Finally, their mother said she needed to start dinner, and Herbie needed to look at the washing machine if he wanted dessert. That got him on his feet.

Dolly said she had a collection of reptiles. Herbie was excited and said he would visit them as soon as he finished with the washing machine. Roy could hear Herbie and Mom visiting while he worked, and she cooked. There was no afternoon radio today. It seemed right and made him feel good. This is as a family should be. Roy went outside to the work Dad wanted him to do in his hybrid strawberry patch behind the barn. Ross and Dolly, along with Bootsie, were out back, with the encyclopedia, on the mound, reading about the mound people, looking over the valley, and picturing how it might have looked back then. Today was a day, as they all should be, productive and loving. Roy could hear John's tractor on the back side of the Hilltop Farm. Herbie brought a certain calmness and harmony to the day.

Herbie finished the washing machine and was rewarded with a slice of apple pie. True to his word, he went to find Dolly and visit the reptile collection.

Ross came and helped Roy. Bootsie stayed with Dolly. When Roy and Ross finished with the strawberry patch, they decided to go to The Glade. When they went to tell Mom where they were going, they saw Herbie and Dolly engaged in rapt, animated conversation.

"Enjoy The Glade boys," Herbie called after them.

"How does he know where we are going?" Ross asked Roy.

Roy looked over his shoulder, and Herbie gave him that quizzical grin and nodded like he had when they first met him. Roy was unsure what that was supposed to mean. He would figure it out.

Herbie and Dolly spent the rest of the afternoon together. She told him how she caught the snakes, frogs, and now turtles and cared for them, how the boys and Dad helped her find out what each needed in habitat and food. He was glad she regularly rotated them back to the wild. She said she had an invisible friend, a fairy she had caught and released after it pleaded to be released. Herbie said he knew, and her friend wasn't invisible to him. He knew her name, and Dolly was surprised when he said it. It said his name to her in turn. They were old friends; he had visited her many times on his travels to visit John. Herbie told her never to stop believing in the magic of this world. It's hard to do, but if one learns the secret of silence, the magic is always there. The snakes and other animals were very comfortable in his hands and would relax or even seek him out if set down, just as they did Dolly.

When the boys returned from The Glade, they all got a snack and some Kool-Aid and went back to the mound. Herbie told them of the history of the mound builders as he knew it, and it was almost like they were there, transported back in time. The sounds of the world around them faded. They could see the villages, hear the sounds, and smell the cooking fires. It was a captivating experience without the noise of their world. That ended only when Herbie stopped and stood up and stretched. After a moment, they all stood up and stretched, even Bootsie did. The spell was broken for them, and the noise of the world entered back into their lives.

"The silence that made it possible to view the ancients is a practice that allows the tales to come alive; it gets much harder as you grow older, much more noise in your life," Herbie said.

"I have the freedom to take time to practice silence; not everyone has this kind of freedom. People value stuff more than silence and experiencing the magical, spiritual nature of the world which we have been given."

Herbie told them many more tales of the "Time Before," as he called it, and they were incredibly vivid when narrated in The Glade and its quiet environment. It was strange how all the friends in The Glade seemed to know Herbie and accept him as one of them. He also spent much time with Dad reviewing the hybrid strawberry patch and how the orchard was progressing. They discussed metallurgy and mechanics as only two dedicated people can. He was interested in the health of the bog. He told Dad that the bog was the anchor for the farm and surrounding area. If it wasn't healthy, the surrounding area would follow suit. Herbie was disturbed that Dad was going to sell some of the peat. He told Dad to have it removed from the center of the bog and no deeper than three feet. That would create a lovely pond attracting wildlife, and the depth was above the heart of the bog. Surprisingly Dad listened to Herbie and did not challenge him. The way Herbie spoke, and the lyrical nature of his voice enamored those who heard.

Then one day, Herbie was gone. John said that was the way it was with Herbie. One day he showed up, and then after a while, he was gone. It's like the early morning mist; it's there, and then it's not.

"You learn to enjoy him when he is here and fondly remembering him while he is gone. It's fun thinking about where and what he is doing."

Roy would spend much time finding silence and picturing Herbie and his adventures. He would also start to develop this discipline, silence, and use it in other areas as his world evolved. In the silence, Roy found peace, spiritual strength, and vision.

This "tool" would be a primary strength when faced with challenges and dangers. There would be plenty of those in Roy's life.

Screechy

Tumblers

Joy

Weimarner Dog

Californian Rabbits

Java Temple Birds

TALE NUMBER 20

SIMPLY A MENAGERIE

*"Man is the most intelligent of
the animals—and the silliest."*
– Diogenes

*"It is much easier to show compassion to animals.
They are never wicked."*
– Haile Selassie

"God looks after children, animals, and idiots."
– Lou Holtz

Many different animals were part of the Triangle Farm. Some by happenstance, some intentional. They all contributed to the fabric of life on the farm and helped the boys appreciate what they had gained on the move to Ixonia.

What follows are short tales strung together under the broad heading "Simply a Menagerie." They appear in the order the Old Man recalls them and not chronologically. They are not all the possible tales but a select few.

Screechy the Screech Owl: It was one of those mornings that Roy called a "crystal morning." It was a cold winter day with a clear sky of a deep azure blue; that was so deep in color that if you looked at it long enough, you felt like you would fall into it. In startling contrast was the pure white snow with ice crystals gleaming in the sunlight.

Every surface *shone with an almost unbearable brightness like sun-struck glass. Every crystal glowed and quivered with intense morning light.*

It was hoarfrost which forms when moisture in the air skips the water droplet stage and appears directly as ice crystals on an object. The scene was breathtaking, and Roy was thankful every morning like this that they had moved here from the city. The bushes, trees, and snow-covered fields radiated the morning's brilliance.

The boys were on their way to the end of Hilltop Road to catch the school bus. As they neared the railroad tracks, Roy felt he was being watched. He asked Ross if he felt the same way. They paused and looked around, and Ross was the one who spotted it.

"There, look there," Ross exclaimed. He pointed to a snowbank alongside the road.

Roy looked but couldn't see what he was pointing at and told him so. Ross kept pointing at whatever he saw and cautiously approached it. Roy followed him and then saw it. Half covered by the snow was a small owl. Its head followed us as we approached it, but Roy could tell that the small owl couldn't see them. It was blind. The boys would learn the bird was "snow blinded" by the glaring sunlight reflected off the snow.

"Ross let's take it home and keep it as a pet," Roy said excitingly.

The idea didn't enthrall Ross. While the owl was small, about six inches long, it had a fierce look about it. It was a raptor, and its beak and claws reflected that.

"How are we going to do that?" Ross asked.

"I'll wrap it in my scarf so it can't claw or bite us," Roy stated self-assuredly."

"That sounds just like a pet the family will enjoy, as long as we keep it wrapped up, so it doesn't hurt anyone," Ross chided.

Roy laughed and very cautiously draped his scarf over the little owl. The bird immediately tried to fly away, so Roy had to pounce on it. While subduing it, Roy gained a small gash from the beak and a few deep scratches from the talons. He ended up lying in the snowbank with the owl in his arms, pinning the hostile miniature raptor to the ground with a scarf and bloody hand. It was a standoff. Roy didn't have control, and the owl couldn't get away.

"I call it the small, blind bird," Ross laughed.

Roy glared at his brother. The owl attempted to escape and ripped a couple of tears in Roy's parka. He managed to quiet it. Ross laughed even harder.

"Ross, I need your help now! If he gets away, he'll surely hurt himself or fall prey to a fox, raccoon, or hawk. He is blind; if he flies away, he'll crash into something and injure himself."

Ross said he'd help but could not stop chuckling over Roy's situation.

"You got a tiger by the tail."

Between the two of them, they managed to quell the bird. They had it completely wrapped up using their scarves, like a mummy. The covering of its eyes quieted it down.

As they walked back home, they heard the school bus go on by. They knew Mom was going to be upset with them.

I'll take the blame for this," Roy said. He was carrying the owl.

"Of course, you will. You are to blame for this whole thing. We're bringing a wild and dangerous beast into our house," Ross mocked. "It isn't my fault, no way."

They walked the rest of the way in silence. They took off their boots and walked into the kitchen. Mom was there reading a story to Dolly.

"What in the world are you doing here? Did you miss the bus?" Mom asked with a frown on her face.

Then she saw the blood on Roy's hands and his torn parka.

"Oh my gosh, what happened? How did you get hurt?!" she exclaimed.

"We found an injured owl and brought it home to heal. Roy got hurt capturing it," Ross replied.

"I'm not hurt very bad," Roy chimed in.

"Let me see," Dolly shouted and ran to see the wounds. "Eww, gross," she said.

Mom checked out the wounds and confirmed they were minor and could be attended to later. First things are first.

"Why didn't you leave it and go to school as you should?"

"It is snow blind and was easy prey or would injure itself if it tried to fly. It was very close to the tracks, and a train could startle it, and it could fly into it," Roy answered.

"Hmm," Mom considered this and said, "Let me see this owl." *It probably is a meadowlark or something, not an actual owl,* she thought to herself.

Roy carefully started to unwrap the bird. He tried to show its head, so he didn't have to contend with its talons. He uncovered the head, revealing the little raptor's fierce gaze. It obviously couldn't see as it turned its head back and forth, unable to make out its surroundings; it became increasingly agitated as it struggled to free itself from the scarves and Roy's grip. When it started to try to get to Roy's hands with its sharp, hook beak, Roy covered its eyes, and the owl settled down again.

Bootsie wanted to check this strange creature out and kept trying to smell it.

"Wow, it is an owl, alright. Perhaps a young one. It is so small for an owl," Mom said. "We need to find a place to keep it while we decide what to do with it and doctor your wounds."

She told Bootsie to stop interfering in a firm voice that made the dog hide in the living room.

"We want to keep it," the boys chimed in.

"This is a wild animal and not meant to live indoors with people, Mom declared. "First, let's settle it until it can see again. Your dad will have the final word on this," Mom said with a tone of finality that meant there would be no more discussion on the matter.

"Ross, you go into the basement and get one of the empty moving boxes. That should work for the time being. Dolly, run and get some of the old towels that are in the back of the linen closet."

When the box and towels were gathered, Mom put them into the box for a nest and slowly unwrapped the owl, trying to keep its eyes covered. When this was done, the bird was gradually put into the nest of towels with its eyes still covered with Roy's scarf and quickly released and the box's top closed. This created a dark environment for the creature. They could hear it moving around to get the scarf off its eyes then it settled down,

"Take it down to the cellar so it is quiet and dark until your father gets home from work. Be gentle with it. Then, we'll decide what to do with it. In the meantime, why don't you research the creature to determine what it is? I'll contact the school and let them know where you boys are."

Roy carried the box down into the cellar with his brother and sister tagged along. It was a significant decision for the location of the box. Each one had a place where it would be the darkest and quietest. Mom finally came down, sent them upstairs, and covered the box with old blankets.

"Now, you kids, leave it alone. Don't worry it to death."

Mom then tended to Roy's wounds using soap, water, and mercurochrome. It stung like all get out, but Roy gritted his teeth and was quiet. A loose bandage, and he was ready to go.

Roy, Ross, and Dolly entered the living room and looked up the owl information. Mom began the challenge of getting a turn on the party line. With seven other users, it could be daunting. Some of the seven were older women who used it like a private line with extended verbal visits with each other. She finally got a line after several attempts. She called the school and explained the boy's absence.

The children discovered three main species of owls that inhabit Wisconsin, the Great Horned Owls, Eastern-screech Owls, and Barred Owls. They further learned that the owl they had captured was an Eastern-screech owl. Screech Owls are highly nocturnal and rarely seen hunting and feeding. They feed on insects, crayfish, earthworms, and all classes of vertebrates, including songbirds, reptiles, fish, amphibians, and small mammals such as shrews and moles. Its length is 8.5 inches, and its wingspan is 21 inches. Its whinnying and trilling songs are familiar, but its vocalizations include rasps, barks, hoots, chuckles, and screeches. The boys had heard it on some of their night forays. The snow blindness will heal independently in a few days, according to the encyclopedia.

They busied themselves with doing the required homework and trying to read ahead. The day passed quickly between the schoolwork, listening to the cold air return registers for the owl, and Dolly taking advantage of them being home and wanting to play games or dolls. It was soon dinnertime, and the boys anxiously waited for Dad to get home to tell him about the owl.

He was early for a change, and the children ran to meet him at the door. They gushed to him about the owl and that they wanted to keep it as a pet, and its name was Screechy. Bootsie joined the clamoring with barks and dances. Dad couldn't make any sense of all the kids shouting and Bootsie barking.

"Quiet!" Dad said in a loud voice that quieted everyone.

"Ross, you go first. What happened?"

Ross related the story of capturing and rescuing the snow-blind owl from potential harm. The other kids nodded their agreement, and Mom leaned in from the kitchen and nodded her agreement.

"It's in the basement now?"

The kids nodded and said yes. Mom said they left it alone all day, keeping it quiet and dark.

"I'll go down after dinner and check it out. It is a wild animal and not a house pet."

The dinner was full of owl talk and how neat the bird was. This was followed by the adults repeating that it was a wild creature unsuitable for a house pet. After dinner, Dad, followed by all the family, went down to the cellar to check out the owl. He slowly opened the box and studied the owl using a small flashlight. It screeched defiantly and turned its head back and forth, obviously blind.

"This poor creature is blind indeed. You were right in bringing it in. This is a good setup to let it heal." It needs to be fed, given some water, and left to heal," Dad said.

"What do we feed them?" Mom asked.

"Well, it is a carnivore. Do you have some ground beef?"

"Yes," Mom said.

"Ok, let's go upstairs and leave the owl alone so it can quiet down.

To everyone's surprise, the owl devoured the beef. In a couple of days, it regained sight and allowed itself to be picked up and handled. It was named Screechy and liked to have its belly stroked. Mom was always after the kids to clean up the poop.

The owl spent days on an unused towel rack in the kitchen, dozing most of the time. It seemed to enjoy watching the kids play games and their toys. The mirrors had to be covered because it would fly around the house, downstairs, and upstairs at night. If it saw its reflection in a mirror, it would attack and crash into it. It was enjoyed for a few weeks, and then Dad said it had to be released. That evening they placed Screechy on the rail on the back deck. The owl sat there for some time, looking all around, but it did not leave. Dad set a bowl with some ground beef in it on the rail. The owl hopped over and ate it.

"That is not good. It must go back to the forest," Dad said.

The children sat on the deck watching the owl who looked at them and then swiveled its head and looked all around. There was a screech from out in the forest when they thought it might be a lost cause (they hoped it was, they loved the little raptor). Screechy answered, and the other owl answered back. That was all it took, and it was up and away, disappearing in the gathering dark.

You could hear the owls most nights, and there was a particular attachment to the sound. The boys had listened to the owl many times on their night forays, not knowing what it was before Screechy.

The Joy of Joy: Dad acquired a horse for the farm. People were always giving him animals because he had a farm. One of the things was a young chestnut mare. She was small but well-built. She had a cream mane and tail, a white blaze on her face, and white stockings on all four feet. She was the most beautiful thing the boys had seen. She was halter broke, but that was it. The rest was up to them. John came down from Hilltop Farm to assist in getting her settled. By looking at her teeth, John confirmed she was young, maybe three years old. That also meant that her vertebrae were still maturing, so she should not be ridden until next year. The boys were disappointed, but John said they would need that time to break her to saddle. He said he would show them how after she settled into her new home.

Dad had made a stall for her in the barn. She would use that at night but be in the field during the day. Rather than build a fenced area, he would use a stake and picket line set he bought. We would stake Joy at various places during the day and let her graze. The set swiveled so she wouldn't get tangled. Bootsie introduced herself to Joy, and they hit it off after touching noses. They would play by chasing each other or they'd just hang out.

Joy was a very friendly horse with a mischievous streak. The first few nights, she was lonely. She had been with other horses at her former home. She whined and made sounds like she was crying. The boys and Bootsie spent the first several nights with her in the barn. This developed a bond. They were all part of her herd from then on. Whenever the boys were home, she had to be with them. If she wasn't, she'd create a fuss until she was. As time passed, she would reluctantly spend nights alone. When let out in the morning, she would make it clear she didn't like being alone at night and was difficult to handle at first.

Saddle training took quite a while. Several steps were involved, none including riding a bucking horse until it was subdued. John would have them lead Joy up to Hilltop Farm for the sessions. The first several sessions had them rubbing her with their hands, so she was used to their touch. One important lesson was that they were never to get angry with her and reward her successes; she particularly liked carrots. They trained her to follow their commands with respect that they were the bosses. They learned how to lean their shoulders into her ribs just behind her shoulders. That is how another horse would do it. She was already halter broken, so they began to saddle break her. This started with just a saddle blanket on her and walking her around. Once she accepted this and did not try to remove the blanket, a saddle came. This took a while. She didn't like this at all. Eventually, she accepted the saddle. The final step was to get on the saddle. John held her halter tight while the boys got in the saddle and sat for a while. It didn't take her long to accept this, and shortly they were riding her with John holding her and leading her around the farmyard.

This adventures of riding Joy around the countryside began, sometimes with neighbor kids. Her trickster mind came out when she got bored. Some of these tricks included trying to scrape you off on a tree or fence post, getting the bit in her teeth, racing toward a fence, and suddenly stopping and watching the rider sail over her head. She would roll on the ground and mess up the saddle when left alone and saddled. She and Bootsie loved chasing chickens in the yard. When Mom hung clothes out to dry, Joy would break off the clothes pins by biting them, so the clothes fell on the ground. One day she followed the kids into the house. Getting her out of the house and down the porch steps was very difficult. There were many more things she would do. She was a natural pet, and the kids spent more time hanging out with her than riding her.

When Roy started driving, he and Ross were gone a lot, and Joy was left alone. Dad finally found a home for her with some other young kids. She accepted her new home and loved the kids who loved her and kept her company. Dad didn't tell them about her trickster spirit. The Old Man smiled as he envisioned them discovering Joy's sense of humor.

Raining Feathers: Dad had the boys help build a coop in the inside eaves of the barn. Dad cut a hole in the side of the barn to create a door to the outside. This was done in preparation to receive some unique birds that a man needed to find a home for.

Dad brought the birds home from work one evening, and the whole family expectantly gathered to see these unique birds. What a letdown. They were just ordinary pigeons. Dad put them in the coop that had the door covered. He said the birds needed a week to "imprint" this location as home. They then could be released and hopefully would return. The boys were to feed the birds daily and clean up the coop.

"Wow," Roy said sarcastically. "We get to take care of pigeons."

The coop was reached by ladder to the loft; when the boys went up, so did Bootsie. Joy made like she wanted up. Luckily, she just whinnied. The pigeon cooed continuously when the boys took care of them. Bootsie went down the ladder also, like it was nothing special.

"I like doing this," Ross said, and Roy reluctantly agreed.

Then on a Saturday morning that was overcast and humid, Dad opened the door. Slowly and cautiously, the pigeons came out and flew into the sky. Once they were all out, they gathered, flying as a flock. Then suddenly, they tucked their wings in and tumbled toward the ground. Everyone, but Dad, gasped.

"What had happened? Why are they all falling?" Everyone said at once.

Then like magic, the pigeons opened their wings and flew back into the sky. They repeated this jaw-dropping routine several more times.

"These are Tumblers," Dad informed them. "Aren't they fun to watch?"

Everyone agreed and was absorbed in the birds dancing in the sky. After several performances, they flew off into the sky like ordinary pigeons.

"How do they know how to tumble like that?" Mom asked.

"They have different shaped heads, and it is in their genes. They also have training. Hopefully, they'll return and breed more birds," Dad responded.

The birds returned to their coop after about an hour. Everyone was delighted.

The birds provided entertainment for several months. Tragedy struck early one fall night. When the boys went to feed the birds, they found the coop door torn open. There were several dead birds and lots of blood and feathers. Some predators had broken in and savaged the flock. The family was distraught. Once there was a count of bird carcasses, it appeared some birds may have escaped. The escaped birds never returned to the coop where they had been brutally attacked. That was the end of any more birds except a few chickens and ducks.

What's a Weimaraner? One evening Dad brought a dog home. This was another animal that the owner wanted to find a new home for. What is better than a farm for a new home? It was a large dog; it was called a Weimaraner. It had a silver-grey coat with long hair and amber colored eyes. It was named Fritz. Dad said the breed was sometimes called the ghost dog because of the color of the coat and eyes as well as its stealthy hunting style.

Bootsie checked him out and decided she didn't like him when he stopped playing. Dad said the dog was skittish because this was all new, and his master wasn't there. That skittishness never left the animal. It always had its tail between its legs. It was a shame because it was a beautiful animal. At the very sight of a gun, it took off running. Eventually, Dad found a family to adopt Fritz.

Urpie the Archeologist: Mom had a friend named Bobbie-Jean. She had a beautiful German Shepherd named after all things Urpie. We ended up with her when Bobbie Jean moved into the city. The dog settled in immediately and became close friends with Bootsie. Urpie became a companion to Bootsie when she joined the boy's adventure and wanderings. She had one bizarre obsession. She would go into the fields, drag large rocks back to the farm, and chew on them. She fiercely protected them until she finished with them.

Her teeth were broken and worn down, but she continued to hunt for and bring big rocks home. It was one of those treasures that turned out to be an ancient artifact. She was a canine archeologist.

Rabbits and Worms: The boys came up with the idea of raising rabbits for income. How they came up with the idea is not remembered. They dismissed the idea of chickens because they kept getting killed in the yard by falling giant Wolf Apples. Dad may have had a hand in it. They came into procession of the American Rabbit Breeders

Association (ARBA) magazine and became members. Armed with all the most recent rabbit breeding information, they selected the various breeds and equipment. They were sponsored by their parents, who would receive the first fruits in return.

What followed was a classic example of jumping to the deep end when only studying the act of swimming. The boys researched the various pens, feeders, and watering devices. They selected what appeared to be the best suited for the project, acquired funds, and ordered them. They also confirmed that the local feed mill would buy the live bunnies from them. They were given access the one half of the shed, and the chickens and ducks shared the other half. As an aside, it is interesting that no ducks got bonked from the falling apples. While all the equipment and supplies were in route, the boys, under Dad's supervision, constructed a two-tier frame for the cages and a sloping ramp under the top tier made of sheet metal that would catch the droppings and urine of the rabbit and direct them downward into the holding area the boys constructed on the floor of the shed.

The material finally arrived after a week and assembling them before the rabbits arrived was a scramble. The boys had selected two breeds. One was a Californian. The breed was touted to reach butcher weight in 10 weeks. They bought two breeding pairs. They have a gestation period of just one month, so they are a real producer. They also purchased a breeding pair of New Zealand Giants that can reach 16 pounds but take longer to reach butcher weight. Things went well with this project; the boys paid back their parents' sponsorship and made a profit. Ross decided to invest in the Angora rabbit for its wool. There was a good market for wool. This backfired for a couple of reasons. The rabbit shed badly. The shed wool coated the bottom of the cage, and all the urine soaked the fur, and droppings stayed on the cage floor. Collecting the wool proved to be burdensome. The Angoras were eliminated.

Then Roy saw an ad in the monthly ARBA magazine that proclaimed you could turn your rabbit manure into cash. You could raise worms in it. This seemed like a perfect solution to the nasty chore of cleaning the manure from underneath the rabbit cages. They immediately bought several hundred nightcrawler eggs/cocoons.

When hatched, the boys could sell them as bait and leave some to keep reproducing. The manure would be kept under control. It was a perfect idea. The eggs arrived and were planted in the manure. They could double their population every 60 days. The boys bought printed bait bags and planned to sell them to local bait shops. They may make more money from the worms than the rabbits. After several days, they checked to see what the harvest may be. The manure kept building up instead of being controlled, and only a handful of worms were collected. Then the boys realized that there was a dirty floor under the manure, and all the worms probably escaped. A hard life lesson, "make sure there is a floor to keep your worms home."

The Java Temple Birds: Mom had just painted a bright red enamel in the kitchen. It was certainly striking. To accent the bright red kitchen, she acquired two Java Temple birds. She wanted them because of their colors and disposition. They have a grey body accentuated by a pink belly and black head, with a white blaze on each side of the face. They have an orange beak. They were beautiful birds. They are the size of a giant sparrow. They have beautiful songs that keep Mom company while in the kitchen. Their cage hung where Screechy used to perch.

Unfortunately, one afternoon Mom was preparing French fried potatoes. She cut the potatoes and soaked them to prevent them from turning brown. She kept them soaked in cold water. When it came time to fry them in the hot oil, she took them from the water and shook off the water that was on them. Regrettably, she didn't get all it off. When the potatoes hit the hot oil, the retained water caused the hot oil to explode, and some of it fell on the stove's burner, and the whole pot of oil became engaged. In short order, the entire kitchen was ablaze!

The enamel kitchen paint caught fire and created a lot of smoke. Mom hurried outside, got the garden hose, and managed to subdue the fire. The blaze primarily affected the surface, and no structural damage was done. The burned paint hung down in blackened strips.

It was a scary, smelly sight. Then she noticed the birdcage. It was covered with strips of black, burned enamel paint. The poor little birds were dead in the bottom of the cage.

The Old Man had many more Menagerie Tales to share at another time, including baby skunks, snapping turtles, show collies, 4H heifers, and more.

TALE NUMBER 21

FARMING FAUX PAS

*"The farmer is the only man in our economy
who buys everything at retail, sells everything at
wholesale, and pays the freight both ways."*
– John F. Kennedy.

*"The farmer has to be an optimist,
or he wouldn't still be a farmer."*
– Will Rogers.

Roy had mastered most of the farming tasks, from milking to planting. It was accomplished under the gentle tutelage of the farmer, John Franger. John's oversight was demonstrating the task and then walking Roy through it. He would finally observe Roy doing the task. John was patient and quick to compliment. Learning under John's instructions was fast and fun. The farmer quickly pointed out the dangers of these tasks and underscored them regarding his infirmities. Roy had become John's trusted right hand and performed farming tasks independently, giving John free time. John had even talked about the possibility of Roy inheriting the farm someday.

Even with this background of training and performing the task, crazy things happened. Roy was a young boy and was inclined to break free of the traces and frolic a bit. Operating a large piece of farming equipment can have potentially disastrous results. These are a few such instances.

Stone Boat Runaway

When turning over the soil in Southeastern Wisconsin, rocks are overturned. These are the gifts of long-ago glaciers. These rocks, ranging from softball size to making a grown man grunt size, had to be removed before final tilling and planting. This was accomplished using a "stone boat" pulled behind a tractor. You would locate the tractor and stone boat in a turned-over field near exposed rocks. Then turn off the tractor, dismount the tractor, and begin gathering rocks. The gathering of the rocks quickly became a mind-numbing, back-breaking chore for a 13-year-old. Using his imagination and intelligence, Roy devised the following process: he set the tractor to its minimum speed in first gear. Then Roy would set it on a straight course and get off the tractor, letting it slowly work across the field while Roy ranged alongside the stone boat, gathering rocks. When the tractor neared the end of the field, he scampered back onto the tractor and turned it around.

This worked well all spring until one cerulean blue cloudless sky morning when Roy became preoccupied with a particularly odd, shaped stone. He thought it might be an ancient artifact and forgot about the tractor heading across the field. When he remembered it and looked up, it was close to the end of the field and the creek that bordered it. He dropped the rock he was studying and dashed for the tractor. Mounting and dismounting a moving tractor hastily or in any manner is dangerous. But for a 13-year-old, there is no such thing as dangerous, and he jumped to the tractor's drawbar and vaulted into the seat while stomping on the brakes simultaneously. The tractor stopped with its nose off the field and its wheels balancing on the creek's edge.

There he sat, engaged in a tug of war between his holding down the brake and the tractor trying to inch forward into the creek. Roy was not big enough to hold the brake pedal down and simultaneously push the clutch pedal down and disengage the transmission. His legs were growing tired and weak, fighting the tractor's trying to inch forward. If he let off the brakes and pushed the clutch in, could he shift from first gear to reverse before the tractor went nose-first into the creek? It was no use yelling for help; he was at the far end of the field and far from help. Putting the tractor into the creek would end his farming career and his opportunity to earn a tidy sum of money this year.

He saw it just before his legs gave out, and he ended up in the creek with the tractor possibly on him—the choke switch, of course. Pulling the choke out would flood the engine and stall it. It was within his reach. He grabbed it, pulled it out, stalled the engine, and stopped it.

Roy regained his breath and settled down. He looked around to ensure no one was watching him, shifted into neutral, and, after a few minutes pause to let the flooded engine clear out, started the engine. Roy was careful not to cause the tractor to be jostled over the edge and into the creek. He cautiously put it into reverse, backed the tractor up, careful not to run over the stone boat, turned it around, and started picking up rocks just as before. This time he ran perpendicularly with no creek at the end of the field. He wouldn't make that mistake again. Always ensure that you won't end up in the creek at the worst.

Sowing His Oats

At harvest time, one of the busiest times is combining the harvesting of oats. The machine used is a combine pulled behind a tractor. The combine is a large machine that performs the direct heading of grain and deposits the stalks (straw) out the back. The straw is later baled and used for bedding. The grain is collected in a hopper on the combine. When the hopper is full, the grain is discharged into a truck that transports it to the farm for storage in the oat bin. This process goes on for several days from farm to farm; all the families helping out. The oats are a valuable commodity to the farmer and are used for feeding the cows all year long, and, in some cases, sold to grain elevator companies.

Roy was given the sweet job of driving the truck between the combine and the farm. He also helped load and unload oats to and from the truck. The truck was a regular pickup with the sides and ends modified to allow for a much larger volume capacity. The truck's tailgate was removed, and a wooden insert was installed. This insert not only increased the capacity of the truck bed, but it also had a small vertical sliding door to discharge oats into the blower. Roy loved this job and was envied by other boys, who were assigned to spreading oats in the oat bin to get the load spread out and evenly. It was a hot, dusty job. The air was full of fine dust, and the nose, eyes, and throat quickly became clogged. They had to work from the side of the bin where they had to hold on with one hand and use a hoe to spread the oats. The oats bin was like quicksand; you'd sink and suffocate without the handholds.

The trick to the process was the timing between the pickup and discharge of the oats between the combine and oat bin. The goal was very minimum downtime on the combine while unloading. Roy suggested that one of the oat bin boys would ride in the truck to pick up the oats from the combine. The boy could start discharging the oats from the combine while it kept going, and the truck cruised alongside. When discharge was completed, the truck and oat bin boy returned to unload oats into the oat bin. The combine never stopped.

This was discussed at lunchtime when everyone was together. The oat bin boys were all for it, of course. It gave them a much-needed break. The farmers were a little cautious, having all that responsibility on the boys, but after much discussion, they decided to give the process a try during the afternoon harvest,

The process went well most of the afternoon. Roy was able to keep up with the combine. There was no extra time, and the boys had to hustle. Near the end of the afternoon harvest, Roy ran behind and hurriedly yelled to his assistant to close the discharge door on the truck. His assistant failed to hear the instructions above the equipment din; they hopped into the truck's cab and dashed down the hill to the combine with the installed discharge door open. The hopper on the combine was almost overflowing. The boys rushed to begin unloading the combine without checking everything. When the truck box was full, Roy began to go back up the hill to the unloading station. He was so intent on driving that he never heard the yelling at him to stop. It turned out that the small unloading door was wide open, and he left a solid trail of oats behind the truck. A substantial amount of the valuable grain was strewn on the ground behind the truck. Roy spent the rest of the afternoon and evening with a shovel and bucket doing his best to collect the oats he haphazardly had sown. He did not drive the truck between the combine and farm the rest of the season. His process to unload the combine, without stopping it, was adopted. (Roy learned not to haul his oats without checking his tail door.)

Geronimo, Bales Away!

One of the most significant harvesting processes is haying. The hay mowing, baling, and storing is done twice a year, depending on seasonal conditions. Hayfields constituted the most extensive acreage in the dairy country and utilized the most men. The hay was mown, allowed to dry in the fields, raked into rows, and then baled. As did most of the local farmers, John baled hay into rectangular bales 16" x 18" x 36", weighing about 60 pounds each. The baling machine was towed behind the tractor and powered by the tractor's PTO (power take-off unit). As the bales left the baling machine, one of two men pulled them onto the attached wagon. He then stacked the bale to the back of the wagon. The other man grabbed the next bale and repeats the action. It takes two men to keep up with the baling machine. They use handheld steel hooks to grab and handle the bales. The bales are stacked in a precise manner to facilitate the unloading process in the barn. When the wagon was full, the baler was stopped, and a fresh wagon replaced the full one, and baling continued. The full wagon was towed up to the barn for unloading. John's barn had an elevation to the hay mow, and the loaded hay wagon needed to be backed up this incline and positioned for unloading. Roy took the hay wagons back and forth to the barn and ran the hay fork during the unloading. The hay fork was large enough to straddle and grasp six to eight bales at a time. Roy was responsible for lowering and orientating forks and jumping on tines to ensure they were fully seated. He then fastened the catch to lock the forks and engaged the lift to raise the load to the top of the barn and travel along the monorail until men stacking bales said to stop. Roy then announced, "Bales Away," and pulled the trip cord, and the bales fell to the mow to be stacked.

Roy thought *surprising the stackers with an unexpected load would be great fun*. He didn't wait for the stackers to say "stop"; he just yelled, "Geronimo, Bales Away." He tripped the forks showering the unexpected stackers with 60-pound bales of hay from the top of the barn. This was not funny and was very dangerous. Luckily no one was injured except for the few bruises Roy received from the disgruntled stackers. Roy wasn't allowed on the hay fork monorail the rest of the season. He was assigned to the hay mow, dodging cascading bales whenever he heard the cry "bales away." Roy learned to think through surprise acts to make sure they didn't injure and instead of surprising them.

It's Not "Die and Seek"

One of the favorite games to play on the farm was "hide and seek." There were so many great areas to hide in. There were also several dangerous, even life-threatening, places that were to be avoided, especially for those not familiar with the innocent appearing dangers.

Roy and Ross were entertaining their cousins Jimmy and Johnny. The cousins were utterly unacquainted with life on a dairy farm, and Roy and Ross were showing them around Hilltop Farm. The farmer, John, gave Roy and Ross the complete run of the farm.

The boys decided to play a game of hide and seek. The cousins would split sides so each team had a member that was familiar with the farm. The afternoon passed quickly, with each team coming up with great hides, but there were two instances of possible life-threatening occurrences.

Jimmy had teamed up with Roy and Johnny with Ross—the oldest paired with the oldest, and the youngest paired with the youngest. The first occurrence happened to Roy and Jimmy. Ross and Johnny were counting down from 100 in the milk house. The milk house was a cool dark oasis during the hot summer days. The milk house was where the milk cans were kept in a tank of very cold water. The tank also kept a supply of root beer soda cold. The rules agreed upon were that they had to stay within the area of the farm buildings. This was a big area with many potential great hiding places, so the "seek" portion of the game could last for a good portion of the time.

Roy and Jimmy headed to the hay mow to hide. Roy climbed into the mow and hid behind some stacked bales. Jimmy vacillated about a hiding place. He tried and gave up on three or four places. This lengthy period of indecision used up the count down from 100. He heard Ross and Johnny coming up the stairs from the milking level of the barn. He panicked and ran full speed around the loose, baled hay stacked on the hay mow floor. Jimmy lost his footing on the polished flooring in front of the trap door used to drop bales in front of the feeding trough on the milking floor. Down he went and slid neatly through the trap door and dropped straight down, landing flat on his back in the feeding trough on the milking floor, where the cows were trying to eat their dinner. He was stunned for a few moments and then shocked by the view of a Holstein dairy cow eye to eye with him. Luckily, he had landed on her dinner, which cushioned his fall, preventing any serious injury; Jimmy shook his head, cleared it, and crawled out of the feeding trough and got to his feet. He then headed upstairs to the hay mow with his brother and cousins.

Everyone was excited to see him; they were getting ready to launch a search for him. His hide was the best so far. It wasn't until later that he explained what had happened.

The second occurrence was when Ross and Johnny were the hiders. This occurred on the hay mow level, also. Ross and Johnny built a cave out of hay bales. There was room for one, and Ross decided to hide there. Ross crawled backward, and Johnny pulled a bale in front of the opening to conceal him completely. Johnny had decided to hide in the back corner of the straw mow. On the way up the ladder, Johnny noted the oat bin. He thought, *what a great place to hide*. A big sign on the bin should have stated in large letters, "Danger!"

Johnny crawled over the barrier and jumped into the oats. He started to sink, and the deeper he sank, the more he tried to return to the opening. It was like being in a pool of quicksand. His nose and mouth kept filling with oats and making breathing difficult. Johnny was getting weaker and weaker. He was sinking further and further.

He was in danger of suffocating. At that time, Roy was checking out the straw mow and heard Johnny's muffled cries. He managed to get Johnny's hand and pulled him to the opening. With Roy's help, Johnny crawled out of the oat bin, struggled to get his breath back to normal, and cleared his nose and throat of oats and oat dust. He strained to clear up his breathing. He was lucky that he wasn't killed in the oat bin. They all learned that before jumping into anything to learn how deep it was.

Four and 20 Sparrows

John bought over 50 small chicks to raise every spring. Some to become replacement laying hens and others to become eventual dinner. These chicks were kept in a brooder house, a small Quonset-shaped wooded building; They had a heater, feeder, and a five-gallon water fountain in the brooder house.

When the brooder house was no longer needed, it was inhabited by dozens of sparrows. The dense population of birds gave Roy and Ross a crazy idea. They stealthily closed the windows, trapping many birds inside. The boys crept into the brooder house, captured over a dozen birds, and put them in the empty five-gallon water fountain. They then carried the water fountain home and brought it into the house. Their mom told them to take that dirty thing out of the house. Roy grabbed the handle on top of the fountain and lifted the lid, releasing the sparrows into the house. Mom was distraught, yelling, pointing, and glaring at the boys. With promises of retribution, she instructed the boys to get the birds out of the house now! Roy and Ross realized how stupid their idea was. They hadn't thought the idea through. Catching the birds in the house was decidedly more challenging than in the confines of the brooder house.

They learned not to release their birds where they had to recapture them.

There are many other faux paus yet to be recalled.

On The Pond

SPLISH-SPLASH, THE POND— SUMMERTIME

"Just because things are not obvious
doesn't mean they are not true."
– The Old Man

"You never knew about people, like you never knew how
deep a pond was because all you saw was the top."

– Terry Pratchett

"A Frog in a little pond can be much
happier than fish in a vast ocean!"
– Mehmet Murat Ildan

During the first summer at Triangle Farm, Dad sold peat moss from the bog at the back of the property. It turns out that spongy, wet, and smelly stuff is valuable in landscaping; who knew? Dad would be at work when they showed up to get the peat moss, so Mom was to show them where to get it. When the day arrived, Roy told Mom he would handle giving the peat moss guy's direction. Dad was already at work, so she couldn't check with him. She thought about it for a while and then agreed to let him do it.

Roy needed to do this because, from day one, he had been haunted by the specter of a pond in the center of the bog. He was convinced that there was one there. When Dad had decided to sell some of the peat, it was like a dream, or more of a nightmare coming true. He had to make sure that the peat removal happened in the right place so the Pond could materialize.

When the crew showed up to collect the peat, Roy guided them to the proper spot. It was difficult for them to get there, and they grumbled about the effort required to meet Roy's demands. They were on Hilltop Farm property, the pasture adjacent to Triangle Farm, so as not to crush the bullrushes and wildlife in the bog. They entered through the gate by the start of the bog. Farmer John had previously okayed use of his property. From that location, the large backhoe could reach the correct area of the bog without actually being in the bog. When the peat moss guys understood, what Roy was trying to accomplish, they were happy to accommodate him. Roy stood on the railroad embankment and signaled the peat moss guys where to dig. It was not very long before the area of 25 feet wide by 40 feet long and three to four feet deep was created. The machine operator scraped the top of the bog first, collecting primarily bullrushes. These he dumped alongside the railroad embankment. Then he had access to the peat.

The bright summer day's air reeked of the smell of rotting organic material as the peat was excavated, the birds that nested in the bog shrieked in anger and flew around in terror. The animals like racoons, rabbits, even a weasel scampered out in panic. Roy had to duck wrathful bird attacks a few times, as did the backhoe operator. Roy did not like the disruption to the wildlife but knew they had minimized it as much as possible,

It all went well, and in short order they were done, and the peat moss guys left with loads of moss in their dump trucks. Roy, Ross, and Dolly observed the hole from up on the embankment.

"It is perfect," Roy claimed.

"Yes," both Ross and Dolly agreed.

Ross pointed out where there was water already seeping into the dugout shape.

"It won't be long," Roy stated.

"Where is the raft," Dolly asked.

"We have to build it," Roy said.

"Build it from what?"

"We got the material in the barn. You want to help?"

"Yes, I do," Dolly exclaimed, clapping her hands together and jumping up and down.

"We'll start tomorrow then," Roy said.

Roy and Ross headed to the Glade after seeing Dolly down off the railroad embankment and back in the yard. She let Bootsie loose. Bootsie had been tied up while the big equipment had been in use, for her protection and for the peat moss guys' as well. Bootsie was very protective of her pack and home ground.

Bootsie made a streak for the boys up on the embankment and was at their side in a flash. She then proceeded to chastise them for tying her up with barks and gruffs (friendly growls).

"Okay, girl. It was for your protection," Ross said as he roughed up her ears.

She settled down and joined the boys on their march to the Glade.

The boys entered The Glade from the top, from the railroad embankment.

The Glade was serene, and the aspen grove provided coolness in its shade. The "quaking" or trembling of its leaves in the breeze acted like a white noise generator. The two eastern hemlock trees bordering The Glade provided the air with a clean, fresh scent. This is just what Roy needed after the hectic time digging the hole in the bog. Ross settled in with Queenie the damselfly on the grassy bank. The giant black and yellow spider was clacking its fangs in Roy's direction and staring at him with all eight eyes. It was still upset about Roy threatening it with a big rock when they first met. Roy tried to ignore it and stretched out on the bank of the Pond, formed as the Hidden Creek exited the culvert pipe which journeyed under the railroad embankment. The gurgling of the water was soothing. The brambles of the railroad embankment were not even disturbed as the little flop-eared rabbit came down and sat next to Bootsie, who was sprawled out, getting her head stroked by Roy as he relaxed.

"There are only a couple of things left to heal on The Triangle," Roy said with eyes closed.

"What are they?" Ross asked.

"We need to fill in the excavated strip in the front of the property."

"How are we going to do that? It's a huge piece of property."

"We wait and see what comes our way. Like The Pond, it just happens. Be patient and see."

"What else?" Ross asked.

"We must listen to the Triangle, and she will show us."

The gurgling of the water tumbling over rocks, the gentle breeze drifting through the Aspens, and the fragrance of the hemlocks made a peaceful setting to contemplate what remained to heal the Triangle Farm. On the first day at the Triangle Farm, they were drawn to wounds made to the property that they were expected to heal. Roy was very sensitive to this and felt a close spiritual kinship to this land and its inhabitants.

After a quiet afternoon playing with their companions and catching crawfish in the Pond, the boys and Bootsie headed home. They walked through John's pasture among the dairy herd, skirting the bog. The bog seemed to have settled down, and Roy hoped that the digging hadn't been too devastating to the life in the bog.

The next morning it was raining. It rained for four days straight. That was perfect. The raft construction was all inside the barn, and the rain filled the Pond with water. Over time, the boys collected two old doors, cork insulation slabs (for flotation), and various hardware. During the next couple of days, the boys and Dolly worked on constructing the raft. In the evening, Dad would check it out and suggest fixing flaws or improving it. The next day the children would incorporate the changes. This routine continued for a few days, kids built, Dad inspected and made changes, and kids built. John even came down from Hilltop Farm and looked it over. He nodded his approval.

Finally, it was done. The raft was built in two pieces. The two pieces would make it easier to move to the Pond. Each of the doors had cork attached to the bottom of it. These doors would each be launched and then joined together while in the Pond, Dad had helped design the method of connecting the doors. Each door had been predrilled with a 2x4 strut on each end and in the middle. Then when in the Pond, the doors were joined using the predrilled struts, so the fit was nice and tight as when first assembled in the barn.

It was a beauty. The doors had been painted white and the struts red. All the children and Bootsie quickly carried it. Dolly named the raft the "Lilypad." Mom made a pennant with Lilypad, and the kids mounted it on a pole attached to the raft. Roy located a couple of poles to provide the power to move around the Pond.

The Lilypad provided endless hours of enjoyment and education over the next few summers before the cork got saturated and lost its flotation ability. The Pond was its own ecosystem. It had its unique aroma, a musky kind of smell. The kids watched all sorts of life, flora, and fauna begin and mature during a season. The Pond was permanent. It always had water in it. Dad said that it might be spring fed.

The plant life was varied. It included algae, duckweed, water lilies, cattails, and lily pads. These would all emerge, bloom, and submerge as their life cycle dictated. And so it was with the animal life. In the Pond were frogs (from eggs to tadpoles to polliwogs and finally frogs). The metamorphosis process was terrific for Roy. He could see the same in people around him. The same type of process took place with the dragon and damsel flies.

Queenie never traveled from the Glade to the Pond. An ethereal presence unique to the Glade attracted and bound creatures there.

There were turtles, crayfish, and small fish living in the Pond. How the fish got there, no one knows. The birds nest there or close by. The raccoons and opossums frequented the Pond. All would travel by as the kids floated lazily on the Lilypad in the Pond. Roy started to formulate his worldview, not from world or metro events, but from daily life as he interacted and witnessed it on the Triangle farm. The new life that arrived with the Pond, the self-healing of the bog as was the earth's way.

There is a joy to be derived from being a part of this ever-changing yet changeless kaleidoscope of life that was so much more than just being an onlooker.

Kari and the Barbed Wire

SLIP'N AND SLIDE'N

*"People don't notice whether it's winter
or summer when they're happy."*
– Anton Chekov

*"To appreciate the beauty of a snowflake,
it is necessary to stand out in the cold."*
– Aristotle

*"It is the life of the crystal, the architect of the flake, the
fire of the frost, the soul of the sunbeam.
This crisp winter air is full of it."*
– John Burroughs

The enjoyment offered by the Pond was not limited to the summertime. During the wintertime, the Pond froze over and offered ice skating. When the snow was cleared off the pond ice, it was rough and bumpy, challenging to skate on. This difficulty was overcome by snaking a water hose out to the Pond and flooding it with a covering of water that will melt and smooth the surface, making it perfect for ice skating when it froze smooth. The boys dragged all sorts of wood and timber to the Pond and kept a friendly fire burning that provided warmth when the skaters got chilled and wanted to warm up. The boys even built a simple windbreak to add comfort and acquired a couple of old quilts to sit on and wrap up in. Dolly and Mom brought out hot coca and the makings for s'mores. The fire kept the cocoa warm and melted the marshmallows.

Mom surprised the children with her ability to ice skate. She could skate backward, do figure eights and other tricks. She was outstanding. Dolly seemed to have inherited the skating gene and was progressing quickly. The boys could go forward rapidly, but when it came to stopping or turning, it was usually a splat on the ice or a plunge into a snowbank. They all laughed good naturally and had a wonderful time.

During the weekend, the boys would spend all day at The Glade and the ice pond. They even tried to spend the night sleeping by the fire. Around midnight Ross, who was shivering and curled up tight against Roy's back, was ready to give up.

"Let's go in, I'm freezing." Ross moaned in a voice chattering from the cold.

Roy was comfortable facing the fire with Ross curled tightly against his back.

"It's not so bad."

"No, not for you. You have the fire and me. I have nothing. Wait for your turn in the back."

Roy's turn came quickly, and he found out how cold it was lying in the back.

"Okay, Ross, you are right. It is frigid. Let us go in," Roy said with chattering teeth.

"I told you so," Ross gloated.

They both hurried to the house and the relative warmth of their bed.

Wintertime on a dairy farm is like the rest of the year, except instead of sowing and harvesting, it is repairing and replacing equipment and facilities. The milking, feeding, and cleaning went on seven days a week, season upon season. The cleaning is increased because the cows spent more time in the barn during the winter. The herd was frequently taken in and out of the barn during the day to facilitate cleaning. Occasionally, one of the bovines will take another's stanchion by mistake. This unintentional "faux pas" can cause a significant disruption in the traffic flow. Like falling dominos, one displacement leads to another, tempers flare, and a cacophony of moos fills the air. There is even jostling and, in some instances, kicking. A cow who has spent years in the same stall is not only in the habit of going to the same stall but also takes a certain amount of ownership in that particular stall. She is not inclined to share it. Younger cows are the ones who usually mistakenly choose the wrong stall, and once they start eating, they are reluctant to move. The cow that properly belongs in that stall is confused and sometimes angry. Very quickly, the complete barn floor dissolves into chaos. Sometimes two cows will wedge themselves into one stall. Neither one is willing to give up the spot and the feed. While the farmer tries to resolve this dilemma, the herd degenerates into a melee. It takes a blend of diplomacy and firmness to settle things down. Stressed cows produce less milk and are more susceptible to illness. In retrospect, it is a humorous scene that the Old Man envisions until he remembers a cow stepping on his foot and refusing to move off it.

The acres of corn standing tall and green and fields of golden oats swaying in the breeze have been harvested, leaving rows of stubble and chaff. This is covered with a shroud of white. A mantel that sparkles and glistens like a gemstone in the sunshine. In the starlight, it winks like pieces of broken glass. The bird and insect serenades of summer are gone, replaced by a peaceful quietness that results from the absence of many creatures and the muffling effect of snow. The hill gives a magnificent view of all the countryside. It also presents a challenge to keeping the access clean. Luckily, the tractors lend themselves to being fitted with plow blades.

Hilltop Farm also offers a super sledding area on the steeper western slope. The slope is clear and falls at least three inches or more per foot for over a 200 feet length. The snow is never disturbed; layer after layer of snowfall accumulates, and a coating of ice builds. It is swift, and one needs to go down in a prone position to clear the barbed wire's bottom row on the fence line at the bottom of the hill. You get a lot of snow in your face but sitting upright gets you barbed wire in the face.

The boys enjoyed this hill and loved sledding at night when they imagined they were all alone and flew down the hill and slid sideways, spraying a shower of snow and ice as the sleds turned sideways when the boys dragged one foot. The downside is the long uphill trudge back to the top of the hill. But the thrill of flying down the moonscape was worth the long haul back up the hill. At the end of the evening, the boys would slide and push their sleds down the other side of the hill to their home.

One weekend Mom's brother and his family came out to visit. Mom's brother's name was Ross, the same as Roy's brother. He was a fun-loving guy who liked living well. He drove a big convertible and seemed to be the quintessence of everything Roy would like to be when he grew up. His wife, Beverly, was model beautiful and had a warm heart and a loving personality — a real snow queen. Roy was infatuated with her and could spend all day gazing at her. This desire continued well into adulthood. She never knew it.

Uncle Ross and Aunt Beverly had two children, a girl named Kari and a boy named Scott. Kari was a beauty like her mother. They were younger than the boys, and the boys were told to watch out for them and take them skating. It didn't take long for them to get bored skating, and they wanted to go sledding. They had heard about the big hill on Hilltop Farm from their dad. Roy and Ross were reluctant to take them up the hill. It was too big and fast for the young ones. Dolly even got into the clamoring to go to the hill. Their Uncle Ross said he would go along and see that everyone would be safe.

They took their sleds to The Hilltop Farm and back to the hill's west side. The hillside twinkled and shimmered in the cold nighttime air as the clouds covered stars and exposed them as they traveled across the sky, creating a moving panorama across the valley, up and over the hill.

Roy's brother Ross went first to demonstrate how it was done. He laid prone on the sled, and Roy pushed him off the ridge. In no time, young Ross was streaking down the hill, and a scream of excitement burst uncontrollably from his lips. The speed that the sled hurdled down the hill was daunting.

"Oh my, that's fast, isn't it," Uncle Ross said quietly and looked down at his little ones with concern.

"My turn, no, my turn," Kari and Scott argued and jostled each other to be the first.

"Calm down," Uncle Ross told them.

Roy hoped his uncle was having second thoughts about allowing his young children to risk sledding headlong down this sharp incline that sparkled and twinkled in the moonlight. He yelled down the slope to his brother, who was starting back up the hill.

"How did it go, brother," he yelled through cupped hands.

"It is smooth and slick," Ross yelled back.

The slope had warmed during the daytime, melted on the surface, and formed into a sheet of ice during the cooling night. This made for what was almost an icy luge run. It could be dangerous if not taken seriously.

"Come on, Daddy, let us go down the hill," Kari pleaded.

"Yes, Pop, let us go down," Scott added.

"I don't know, kids, this is a big hill."

"Why don't you take them down part way and let them go from there?" Roy asked.

Uncle Ross liked this idea, and he and Roy took the sleds about one-third down the slope and held them there so the youngsters could mount them. Scott laid down as he was supposed to, but Kari sat on the sled, facing down the hill.

"She can't do that, Uncle Ross. She needs to lay down like Scott is," Roy said to his uncle.

"She will be okay," Uncle Ross said. "We are a good way down the hill, and she knows about the fence and will stop before getting to it."

Kari nodded in agreement with her dad.

"I don't know about that. I don't think we should do this," Roy cautioned his uncle.

"Who is the adult here? Don't contradict me, young man," Uncle Ross admonished his nephew.

Roy held his uncle's gaze and lifted his hands in surrender.

Young Ross caught up to them and had Dolly lay on his sled. Bootsie was jumping and rolling in the snow.

Uncle Ross said, "On three, let's let them go and see gets down there first." He had Kari's sled, Roy was holding Scott's sled, Ross had hold of Dolly's, and Bootsie was getting excited. On the three count away the three sledders went. Uncle Ross gave Kari a big shove to give her a head start.

The three sledders raced down the slope, gaining speed as they descended. They were yelling and screaming, with Bootsie barking and keeping up with the kids. As they neared the fence, Roy grew uneasy and yelled for the kids to stop their sleds. They didn't listen. He closed his eyes and turned away.

Scott and Dolly were prone, put their heads down, and cleared the barbed fence. Kari was upright and tried to lay back to clear the fence. She was too late and got a nasty gouge on her face close to her lip, and she also ripped her snow coat on the barbs. The cold made the wound bleed profusely. Kari was screaming in pain and terror. Uncle Ross started running full tilt downhill and soon sprawled face first and came sliding and tumbling to rest next to Kari. Dolly and Scott came running to see what the commotion was about. Bootsie kept trying to comfort Kari, who kept pushing the dog away. Uncle Ross got down and looked closely at his daughter.

"This needs stitches. Let's get you to a doctor, sweetheart."

This brought on a new wave of wailing by Kari.

Her father picked her up and began crab-walking back up the hill.

"Let's put her on a sled, and we can pull her. It will be faster," Roy suggested.

"Good idea, Roy."

Kari was deposited on a sled; Roy and Ross grabbed the sled's rope and started quick timing around the base of Hilltop Farm's hill to Triangle Farm's driveway and home. This way is much faster than struggling over the hill. Uncle Ross ran ahead, got his wife, jumped into his car, and started back down the driveway to meet the boys and Dolly. The wound had stopped bleeding, but Kari's face and clothing were covered with blood and streaked with tears. Bev snatched up Kari and Scott and drove away, headed to an emergency room in the closest city, Oconomowoc. Roy and Ross learned that Kari had got a couple of stitches. The biggest obstacle was the shot to offset the danger of tetanus from the old rusty barbed wire fence. There were no hard feelings between the families. Uncle Ross assumed responsibility for the mishap, acknowledging Roy's recommendation not to let the youngsters go down the hill.

He congratulated the boys on holding their ground even in the face of an adult opposing them. Be true to yourself in all things.

Kari remembers the incident to this day and brings up the adventure, for it was an adventure, whenever they get together.

TRIANGLE TALES
THE EARLY YEARS

EPILOGUE

UNIDENTIFIED FLYING OBJECTS, ARCHEOLOGY, HOBOS, AND A MENAGERIE

*"As soon as I saw you, I knew an
adventure was about to happen."*
– Winnie the Pooh

*"When you see someone putting on his Big Boots, you
can be pretty sure that an Adventure is going to happen."*
– A.A. Milnie

"The world is not in your books and maps, it's out there."
– Gandalf

The boys, confident and at ease in The Triangle, had begun their life of adventures. They were close to home initially and relatively safe for the most part. The eclectic group of animals indicated the acceptance of life as it presented itself. While Roy still is central in the tales, he shared space with Ross. This was not the case when he was on his own in adult life.

Extraterrestrials, hobos, a near-death experience, the ancients, and a menagerie combined to start the boy's life of adventure on The Triangle Farm. The supernatural aspects of The Glade provided a sense of serenity when needed. Through all his adventures, Roy had a persistent sense of a benevolent spiritual presence watching over him.

Almost killing his brother and shooting a cow instead began Roy's life of deception, when he didn't tell anyone of it. Ross was a reluctant partner in this. This episode of a weak character by Roy is contrasted by acts of courage, leadership, and integrity in the subsequent tales.

Like most individuals, Roy's actions were driven by self-interest for most of his life. He started to spread his wings and feel an ersatz sense of power and invulnerability. Listening to Herbie gave Roy a proactive vision of a life of freedom, knowledge, and the efficacious power of flirting and dealing with danger. Stumpy, John's small dog, was a constant reminder of overcoming pain and handicap.

The Menagerie and the Pond supplied Roy with a wide variety of life: Learning to let go, build, win, and learn from a loss—to be awed by the world and its denizens. The boys learned of their lawman ancestor. The tensions between Roy and Dad quieted down. Roy toned down his sense of dominance and enjoyed a somewhat normal relationship with Dad. The lifestyle of his Uncle Ross and its accoutrements drew Roy like a moth to a flame.

The Old Man closed his eyes and leaned back against the grand old maple tree. There were many more tales he planned to share at another time. There were more tales of farming faux pas, school days, winter adventures, the great woods war, and more menagerie yet to be told.

TRIANGLE TALES

LIFE PRINCIPLES LEARNED ON TRIANGLE FARM & HILLTOP FARM

A LIFE PRINCIPLE IS A STANDARD OR RULE OF PERSONAL CONDUCT OR WAY OF LIFE.

1. Prime Life Principle:
   - It was what it was (yesterday)
   - It is what it is (present)
   - It will be what it will be (future)

2. Always trust your gut.

3. Always have a sidekick.

4. Never lose; either win or learn.

5. You can't play marbles in a cow pasture.

6. There is always a faster gun.

7. Every bullet hits something.

8. It is always warmer in the sunbeam.

ABOUT THE AUTHOR

Roy Cheesman was born in 1943 in Milwaukee, Wisconsin. His family moved to Ixonia, Wisconsin, in the early 1950s, fleeing the Polio (Poliomyelitis) epidemic. This is where Roy came of age. He attended Ixonia State grade school, graduated from Watertown High School, and completed two years of college at University of Wisconsin-Milwaukee. Roy was a certified welder/fitter and experienced machinist.

In the early 1970s, Roy moved to the Houston, Texas, area to start up a manufacturing company. The company grew and became a force in the market, both nationally and internationally. It developed innovative products recognized as Best Available Technology (BAT) by the EPA for the electric power generating companies. It was bought out by one of its competitors in 1988 and they moved back to the Milwaukee area. Roy was a managing director of one of the parent company's divisions. He retired in 1999 and helped several start-ups and non-profit organizations.

Roy and his wife of 47 years live in Wales, Wisconsin, and spend as much time as possible with their seven grandchildren.

This is Roy's first novel and is a fictionalized biography of his early youth in the Ixonia, Wisconsin, area.